DRAGON SHAMAN
BOOK ONE:
TAMING THE BLOWING WIND

2nd Edition

By

TERESA GARCIA

Formerly Teresa Huddleston-Garcia

THG StarDragon Publishing

CONTENTS

CONTENTS

THE DECISION

Fluttering notes
Float on the wind
Piped from a reed
While fears rescind.

Follow me Ai!
The horizon calls.
In purple distance,
Mountains rise tall.

Come to me Ai!
Burst through
And run past
Skies all blue.

The voice beckons
While shimmering
Forms entrance me
With their glimmering.

I stand at the gate
Where the wind blows
Wondering where
The new river goes.

Still the flute echoes,
Follow me Ai!
Run to me Love,
Before light dies!

Now I must choose.
Do I turn away
And let my light fade,
To keep danger at bay?

Or do I shoulder my fear
Running with long strides
To the beckoning
Where my purpose hides?

The mountains grumble,
The spring entreats
Water leads the way
For bold foot beats.

CHAPTER 1:

REMEMBERING THE BEGINNING
1986 ~ 1998

❖

SHE had gone to bed hours ago. However, just because mother had made her go to bed did not mean that she had necessarily gone to sleep. Mother might have thought that the silence meant that her little bundle of energy was lost in dreams of desert adventures with Hawk and Coyote. This was not so though.

Blue eyes had been open for around two hours after bed-time, watching the Star People spin by in the night sky. A red cotton hand-me-down night gown hung down around her pale and skinny seven year old body while little hands supported a tiny chin as she pouted at the window.

Her father had not been allowed to take her with him to the protest and anti-nuclear power rally, this time because she had been grounded by her mother for skipping school earlier that Arizona spring day.

"It's Coyote's fault, he was the one lurking behind a trash can on the playground waiting for a chance to steal my stuff, including my homework. The teacher wasn't going to believe that Coyote stole my homework. If even Mom won't believe me about him, how does she expect me to show up in class and get made fun of again?"

It had been a long and dusty chase away from the playground after Trickster. Ultimately though, he had out run her, leaving her where old man FourHorses had found her spread out by his well. The school had not been happy. Father had been mildly amused, and Mother was absolutely furious. BlowingWind had always been complaining nearly ever since she could talk that Coyote was either making her do bad things, or framing her for doing bad things.

"It was fun though. I've always liked leaving Town behind. Did he have to get me in trouble for stealing cookies from the jar again too? I swear, sometimes Mom must be blind. He walked right past her covered in cookie crumbs, but I get yelled at for ditching and filching."

A scratching pulled the child's attention down from the moon to the dust outside of the stucco and adobe home. A scraggly and thin yellow coyote sat panting outside of her open window, her now very ragged and dirty red bag at his feet... minus her school books.

"Hey, you ruined my favorite backpack and got Mom mad at me again."

"I'm sorry I got you in trouble again. Why won't you ever come and run with me? You would certainly get in less trouble."

"Father told me that you would get me in trouble no matter what I do, but that I would be safer if I didn't. I'm not like you, you know. I won't come back to life if I die."

"And you won't learn what really matters if you keep hiding safely in Town."

The coyote changed form, shedding his fur in exchange for sun leathered skin that bore wrinkles as deep as the Badlands, though his hair was still as black as the arrowhead point on the Sacred Arrow that her cousin was the Keeper of. His buckskins, although the fine white preferred by the holy beings, were covered with the dirt of a long hunt. Smiling, Old Man Coyote gave her pack back.

"Old Woman Coyote will be angry at you for dirtying your leathers again."

"It won't be the first time." He sighed, a wry smile playing at the corners of his lips.

Coyote was about to leave, when a gust of wind kicked up the dust, causing him to stay.

"Ba'ts'osé, is she still awake?"

The wind settled to reveal the speaker as a large golden hawk who had settled on Coyote's shoulder. Coyote rolled his eyes.

"Yes Hawk, BlowingWind is still awake. Why?"

"You had better stop bothering her and let her get to bed then. Come to Council."

Coyote resumed his animal shape, loping off after the Hawk who had gained the air once again. Shaking her head, BlowingWind went back to bed.

"I hope Hawk doesn't tell Father I'm up past bedtime again. He really will be angry about that."

Laying down in her bed and pulling up the thin blanket, she stifled a yawn.

"He still has my homework hidden somewhere, and I'll bet he ate my lunch. I hope someone runs him over again."

The drone of her mother sewing new clothes out in the living room drifted through the night, another calico dress for a stretching body conjured by a mother's magic. An hour later she still had not found sleep, but a loud knock at the door relieved her boredom. The young and happy voice of her mother carried softly through the home.

"RedFeather, 'tis a pleasant surprise it is to see ye, for sure. Are ye stayin' the night again, *leanbh*? Where's my Soaring'awk now?"

"Uncle was shot Aunt Marie. They want you at the hospital, but there isn't any hope. He's gone."

RedFeather had tried to keep his voice down, not wanting to wake up the little one. BlowingWind had heard though, and heard her mother's anguished cries as the child was forgotten for a moment. BlowingWind got out of bed and went to her mother.

Rivers of red hair spilled down from where a beaded barrette had corralled it while she was working, strands escaping where her curls rebelled. Blue eyes leaked liquid crystals onto high, freckle spattered cheeks, and a tall dark boy handed Marie his red handkerchief.

"Mommy, why are you so sad?"

Marie MountainChild grew silent as she saw her little one standing in her bedroom door, and then drew a breath before diving into carefully crafted words.

"Daddy 'as gone away, and 'e won' be coming back."

"Why Mom? Why won't Daddy come home?"

"Daddy 'as to go somewhere we can't."

"Will we ever see him again?"

Marie looked at the child, and then at RedFeather, who was nodding his head and motioning for her to go.

"You will see your Daddy again." Red Feather bent down to his cousin's height. "He was shot, kind of like when my little brother went hunting the first time when he got too excited, remember? David put that hole in his foot, and you doodled all over his bandages?"

BlowingWind nodded, and RedFeather continued.

"Well, your Dad's at the hospital right now. After the doctors fix him, Kato'ya needs to see him, so he is walking the Star Path. Mommy has some work that she has to do now, but I'll be here to watch you while she is gone."

"Ok. Will you tell me a story Feather?"

"Sure Wind, but then you have to get to bed. You won't receive any dreams from the Ancestors if you're awake."

Marie kissed BlowingWind goodbye before leaving. RedFeather sat down on the blanket covered couch, pulling out the red feather that he always wore, while he waited for the child to situate herself on his lap.

It was a few days later at the funeral that young BlowingWind had begun to understand what the Star Path really was, when she saw Grandmother crying that her son was dead. Not long after her father's death, BlowingWind found herself moving.

"Where are we going Mother?"

"Somewhere new, *leanbh*."

"Mom, why can't you just speak English like other moms?"

"Tis a 'ard 'abit to break for sure now. Would ye rather I spoke like a bloody Brit then?"

"Mom, Ms. Sanchez said it's not okay to call them that."

"Well, then, don' ye be gettin' all uppity there with me. I'm sure that after a few more years 'ere my accent will a slowly change. We're moving to McCloud sure enough now, to answer ye question."

Mother had taken a job in Northern California as a wood worker and carpenter. The house they moved to had been a large two story, an 1800's historical home hidden away in the woods near the old logging town. The mountain forests had suited her well, and she had freely and happily roamed that summer while her mother got everything in order. Eventually, things had settled down enough that they could go camping like they used to.

Watching her daughter perform the prayers that her husband had once done while they set up camp in the high desert that held Medicine Lake had been odd, and it brought the loss back as sharply as if it had been just yesterday. In order to move past it, Marie had paid attention to establishing camp, instead of watching her daughter follow SoaringHawk's footsteps into the forests of spirituality.

When BlowingWind had been singing the old prayers, she had been facing towards the lake. The layers of green reached into the distance beyond the condensed sky that had formed the waters and even further beyond this – like a smiling father – loomed the sacred mountain. Something about the area soothed her wounded soul, and she could almost feel the presence of her father, urging her to look into the lake. And so, after the songs had been finished, she had followed the tugging on her soul.

Twin whirlpools of chocolate and mud had pulled her soul to the lake bottom, creating a longing that the eleven-year-old did not fully comprehend. She felt safe and whole looking into the orbs that were in the water, paying no heed to how guarded they were, nor to the black fur around the pointed face, or the scales running along the lithe body. Neither did she see the great red mane as it waved in the currents where the lake serpent hid beneath the surface. She was in ecstasy that there was someone who could take away her pain for even a moment. In joy, she had called to her mother.

"Mama, look what's in the water. Aren't his eyes beautiful?"

The woman's screams pierced the ears of both the child and the water creature still hiding in the murk and lake plants. They echoed out over the lake, rebounding off of trees and rocks to amplify even more, and flocks of birds abandoned their nests believing it was a warning of danger.

"Whoever ye be, Spirit, leave my baby alone! Ye can't take 'er too!"

BlowingWind watched as the eyes faded, and ripples moved in the water as the creature swam away. Turning, she realized her mother was paler than usual, shivering the way she did when shocked or frightened, like when they had found a rattlesnake contentedly sleeping on their porch not so long ago.

"What's wrong Mother?"

"*Draigan*. Mother was telling me for true, an' she wasn't touched. They be real."

She held her head, rubbing between her eyes, for a moment her gaze pulled from the present into a locked area of her memories. Every muscle bunched and tenses, and hair lifted as BlowingWind watched.

"Mom, are you ok? You're acting kind of weird."

Marie's eye cleared, and once more she was the practical Irishwoman BlowingWind knew.

"Oh, for sure now. T'was but a trick of the light now. Come now, we'll go for a bit of a stroll for some firewood."

"Ok."

Later that same night, a fire crackled only to die down into their makeshift hearth to cook their dinner.

"Alright, story time. What is it tonight Mother?"

"Tonight, I'll be telling a story about long ago, and about a *geas* laid on our family by a *draigan*."

"What's a *geas*?"

"That's a curse, my *leanbh*."

"Oh."

"Maeve was a brave lass, and was among the finest of Brigit's priestesses. There were few warriors better, man or woman, and 'er prowess attracted a *draigan* that knew the magic of shape trickery. As a comely lad, 'e enticed 'er to join with 'im in marriage, and being lonely, she was sorely tempted. There was another lad, a cobbler, in another Clan that also loved 'er, and war was common then."

BlowingWind leaned in closer, and Marie's speech dropped some of the heavy accent, though not all.

"Maeve loved this *draigan*, but 'er service to 'er goddess required that she 'ave permission before taking a 'usband. The well and forge that she was a protector – and keeper – of was attacked before she could do anything about 'er suitor though, and Maeve was one of the priestesses who were captured."

"If she was so good, how was she caught?"

"The story is old, me mother did not remember all of it. Bits 'ave been forgotten over time, they 'ave."

Marie dropped her gaze from her daughter, looking into the fire instead.

"Ultimately, Maeve was dishonored by the cobbler, who somehow was involved in the raid. Drake, the *draigan*, learned of it, and the *draigan* came to stop it, but was too late. She 'ad already been taken, and in a rage 'e had not only killed the cobbler but also cursed any children that the cobbler had ever begotten. Unknown to Drake, Maeve had been more dishonored than 'e 'ad 'eard tell of, and a cursed child came under 'is care due to 'is own wrath. Now, every child of that child loses the first marriage partner to the curse. That is 'ow our family was named, and why the Spirit World is so drawn to you. We 'ave unfinished business with the spirits, an' so ye must be careful with what ye do, and who ye trust."

Understanding her mother a bit more, BlowingWind secretly made an apology to the lake spirit after her mother was asleep.

The next day, she had woken up with a polished obsidian mirror and a swirling snail shell necklace beside her pillow. The child put on the necklace and dropped it beneath her shirt, then hid the mirror. Her mother would surely take these away if she saw them, and the lake spirit obviously had given them to her. There was power in the gifts, and she knew better than to refuse the sacred medicines she had been granted guardianship of.

A year later on another camping trip, this time with friends, she met a boy there of about her own age. Strong and well built for his youth, he had impressed her with how he was able to keep up with her on heart pounding runs through the wilderness. His dark eyes had captivated her, always reminding her of the unnameable and only half-remembered shape of the thing that had been calling to her soul from ever since she could remember. The boy had always been there on every trip after that she had taken, until her mother put a stop to her going to the lake. After a while, he had begun to show up in town to walk with her. This was a discovery that her mother could not and did not reject out of hand.

BlowingWind had never questioned it. It just felt right. When he was around, she felt like she belonged somewhere, as if she had roots of some kind. Obsidian was a fixture in the family before the three even realized what had happened.

Time roared through the wilderness with alternating snow and drought, pulling the dreamer with it. March of the year 1998 arrived, after a winter of record snowfall, and snowboarding practices bogged down by poor visibility and sticky slush that had tested many young men and women taking their first tentative steps into adulthood. Mount Shasta, the patriarch of Northern California, sparkled in the glorious and much prayed for winter sun. Hundreds of high-school students from all over the state milled over Douglas Butte like an army of ants, including BlowingWind.

The day passed her by in a glorious blur, and once more she was the carefree girl she had been, streaking down the race course only to ride the ski lift back up to man her station, in order to make sure the others had actually cleared the gates.

Her final run of the day had also been the very last for the day. The wind rushed around her body and over her helmet as she bulleted down the mountain, and knocked on the gates. It was biting cold, and yet she relished it. To her, the world was a perfect waterfall of sound, the scrape of her edges on ice, and the white ice that she danced over like a surfer riding a great frozen wave. As she skidded finally to a stop at the bottom, she saw him grinning widely next to her mother and wildly ringing two great cow bells, right along with a couple strange looking women from the Big Valley Ski Team, and one from the Yreka Ski Team. Willow, or Angelina as she now preferred to be called, a racer from the Big Valley Team who was also in her senior year, blew an air horn while shouting at her friend.

"You rock!"

"No! No rocks, rocks are bad for our equipment."

BlowingWind suspected that Willow had sweet-talked the mountain spirit into allowing the weather for the championships to be clear and cold. He had been focusing this year on gathering enough water underneath his mountain to restock swiftly falling water tables, but Angelina had been worried about someone getting hurt racing in white out conditions.

As she quickly undid one binding to get out of the clearing area, she eyed him through her goggles. Tall and lean, Obsidian's tanned skin spoke of long days out in the sun while his long black hair poured behind him in a great waterfall. His chocolate eyes sparkled with glee as her time was announced. Before she could even stand her teammates and a few others from different schools in District 2 and 3 had glomped her.

"Dude, you pulled off turn three without catching your edge, sweet!"

"Awesome, MountainChild."

"Hehe, I'm gonna rub the Buddah for luck, ski championships are tomorrow"

"Hey, this suit has no padding guys. Get off, and whoever just grabbed that is going to meet Mr. Slappy."

Mother had laughed and yelled that she would wait in the cafeteria and send up something for her.

"Mom, don't leave me to this pack of hyenas! Obsidian, help! Don't you dare lift me."

"Do I look crazy? They all had tall Mountain Dews. I keep telling you that stuff is dangerous."

"Gee, thanks for your support Obsidian."

When she had finally escaped the writhing mass of fellow adrenaline and caffeine junkies, he had been waiting for her with a steaming mug of hot cocoa, just what she had been planning to go and get from the cafeteria.

"Congratulations, Miss Number One for Female Varsity Giant Slalom in Snowboarding."

"Really? I didn't think I was going that fast. Thank you Obsidian."

He had placed a chaste kiss on her cheek as he put the cocoa in her hands, and she drained 16 ounces of the steaming liquid in one long pull.

"How could you not? You are up there four days a week practicing after all. This is your last year, what are you going to conquer next, Little Warrior?"

She blushed at the compliments and the heat in the young man's gaze.

"I... hadn't decided yet. Universities are lining up for me, but I don't know where to go."

"Maybe you could stay here? I... could help you."

"I suppose I could. What are you really trying to ask me? Hey, are you blushing?"

"There's too many people here. Say you'll be mine, and I will tell you everything later tonight."

"Ok, but you're telling me what this is all about later. No more secrets."

"No, no more secrets after tonight."

The simple shell necklace that she wore around her neck began to heat beneath her clothing, and she began to wonder what she had just agreed to.

He had eaten dinner with them, Marie insisting on taking them out to the Black Bear Diner on their oddly roundabout way back to McCloud. Her excuse had been that she needed groceries, even though their hometown had a grocery store. The teenagers played along though, pretending to have forgotten all about the store. BlowingWind couldn't help but laugh in joy as her mother told her how the others on her team had placed. Eventually though, dinner ended and they had driven home.

"Don't you need a ride home Obsidian? The streets are so icy at this hour, and that road into the main part of town isn't what I would call exactly plowed."

"I'll be fine Mrs. MountainChild, thank you for your concern though. Good night."

Instead of going to where his home really was, he had hidden in the trees until after Marie had gone to bed. BlowingWind was so tired from her day that she had prepared to go to bed as well, when a snow ball exploded next to her window. She stormed to the window, opening it to glare outside.

"Who did that?"

"Did you forget?"

"Oh, sorry Obsidian. I'm just so tired."

"I understand. I'm sorry for disturbing you. I'll trouble you no more." he said, then turned to go.

"Wait! You said you would tell me everything. You aren't a normal human, are you?"

He looked up at her once more after turning around. There was a stronger quality to him now, as if part of him had been in hiding. As she watched, his clothes changed from the modern T-shirt and jeans, morphing instead into a leather suit. His leggings, tunic, moccasins and breech-cloth were a finely done pale color, like the holy beings wore, and resplendent with quill-work. Nothing else changed, yet he held out a hand.

"Do you trust me?"

"Yes. Why wouldn't I?"

"Come down, I have much to tell you, as long as you will listen and believe me."

He watched as she withdrew from the window, and seeing how

much it looked like his heart was being pulled to pieces as she backed away, she gave him a gentle smile to ease the pain. She threw on some warm clothing, and then made her way out of her room, before stretching over the squeaky floorboard in front of her mother's door. Feeling her way down the dark hall to the stairs, she found herself becoming high on yet another adrenaline rush.

"I'm going to need a nap in the car on the way back up the mountain tomorrow morning. What is he?"

Finally, she was down, through the entry room, and out the door, paying no heed to the blue oriental carpet or the fire that was dying in the fireplace. The snow covered the porch in a thick mantle where neither she nor her mother had bothered to shovel, leaving only a path out and down to where he stood waiting, unaffected by the cold. The stars blazed overhead like diamonds set in a rich field of blackened velvet while the pines whispered among themselves in their quiet groaning language that only they spoke. Soft light danced in his hair, giving him an ethereal cast, as if he was only a dream that would vanish when she opened her eyes.

Rushing forward, the young woman surprised him by engaging in a flying tackle, pinning him beneath her in the snow as she gazed eagerly down at him. The woman had no idea of the effect she was having on the spirit below her, with the hunger in her eyes that was waiting to devour the knowledge he would finally divulge.

"You had something to tell me?"

"As soon as you let me regain a more dignified position."

"Sorry."

They sat on their knees side by side, neither looking at the other.

"Do you believe in spirits?"

"Yes. I believe in spirits."

"You have no idea how much easier that makes this. Would you believe me if I said that I was a spirit?"

"After seeing you change your clothes without undressing, what do you think, Obsidian?"

"If I was a spirit, would you still agree to be mine, as I would be yours?"

"Yes. Why are you skirting around this, just spit it out!"

He drew in his breath and looked up at the moon, before gazing into her eyes, blushing brighter the further he got into his speech.

"I, Obsidian, am the current guardian spirit of Medicine Lake, and I am asking you to be my wife and my vessel to convey blessings to this world that has nearly forgotten me. I ask you to live with me and give me children after your studies are over, and I will always provide for you, keeping you safe for all eternity."

"Is that all? Here I thought you were going to tell me that I would be childless if I still accepted, or that I would never be in the Human World again."

"Just like that? No throwing me into the wall screaming about the nerve I have in even thinking of fathering your children?"

"No. We've known each other for years. You've been my date for my Junior Prom, and you'll be my date for my Senior Prom. Why not get married?"

She leaned in to kiss him, but his face turned before she hit her mark, her lips grazing his cheek instead.

"You aren't ready for that, as much as I want to. Besides, if your mom gets restless and looks out her window and caught us doing that, we would both regret it."

"Good point. Mom may slowly be loosing her Irish accent, but she still has the O'Drake temper."

"You're tired. Go to bed Love. But don't grab any Mountain Dew or chocolate on the way. You still have regular Slalom tomorrow, and then after that you have to help with the skiers' gates."

"Party pooper."

"Caffeine addict."

"I'll hold you forever in my heart Obsidian."

"I will love you forever, my BlowingWind."

Late March of that year had still allowed the forest to harbor patches of snow, while the spirit of Mt Shasta had continued to keep his mountain cloaked in that crystallized water. The championships had been over now for about a week and a half. As she and Obsidian had been hiking in the silent chapels of the forest perhaps two miles from her home, one of the ravens had winged overhead. Fascinated by the beat of wings, she had paused to watch it pass in awe. Unknown to her at the time, Obsidian had been watching her child-like joy, drawing up behind her to grasp her hand.

"There are times that I wish I could fly like that. It must be wonderful to ride the wind, to feel it lift you up." She sighed as she closed her eyes, mentally following the flight.

"What if I granted your wish?"

"I'm just a human. If I had been meant to fly, I would have been born a bird."

A short bout of silence fell companionably around the two as the spirit held her wrapped in his arms. The shaman's breathing was contrasted by the lake spirit's lack of breath.

"What if I told you that I can fly, even though I too am no bird?"

"You would have to show me, seeing's believing."

"Really? Then hold on to me and what ever you do dear one, don't let go."

BlowingWind went to shift her weight, finding less resistance on her feet than she expected. Experimentally, she flexed an ankle, only to find nothing.

"Oh God! We're gonna fall!"

He squeezed her hand tighter than he was already holding it, pulling her body closer to his own. Embracing her now, Obsidian held her until her initial terror passed.

"I would never let you fall, don't you trust me yet Love?"

"Yes, I trust you. I don't trust the ground not to smash me if I slip."

"BlowingWind, look down."

"No."

"Aw, come on honey, you know you want to see for yourself."

"No."

"Hey, you're the one that said you wanted to fly. If you don't like it, I'll take you back down."

She cracked her eyes open slowly, processing the spires of pine and cedar reaching for her feet.

"Woah, it's like I'm standing on glass. How are you doing this Obsidian?"

"I can't tell you, to understand it so soon would take the magic away. Without magic, life means nothing. Maybe in a couple years."

"Can we do this more often?"

"Of course. I rather like the feeling of not being alone up here."

The wild forest continued to breathe through her seasons, the spirit and the human just two parts of her greater whole, joining and separating in a dance of love and time, and the struggling dreamer was pulled along with the currents of time. Late winter's snows gave way to the early spring showers of April, then the warmer days of early May as other spirits and animals lived, and died. Gradually, the nature spirits' activities grew to fevered pitch as they desperately fought for their continued survival against invading Man.

Two spirits in particular were most concerned about the drilling only one mile away from the sacred waters of Medicine Lake, dark forms meeting at the geothermal power plant for yet another night of mischief.

"Obsidian! Why are you here tonight? Shouldn't you be in the lake, making sure that all is ready for your young bride? BlowingWind already worries about you enough."

"Saksque, I thought you had been satisfied after you dismantled their heavy machinery and spooked last week's workgroups so badly they quit. Everything's prepared for BlowingWind when we go home tomorrow night, but I have to finish disabling those turbines tonight."

"Idiot, tomorrow night is your wedding night. Take a break. You'll be too tired to do anything with her."

"Exactly. She's going to live with me down below for a month our time before I return her to her mother for a visit. I don't want any interruptions, I've waited years for this, and I'm not letting some capitalist big wig wreck my honeymoon by distracting me with his unholy machines."

"Always the overachiever. Five shells to a trout that the magnetic grid transport system messes up again when Angelina goes to learn from SingingSerpent and drops her right on your lake surface again just when the two of you settle down for a nice tussle."

"Yeah, ok Bigfoot, that's a bet you'll lose. Her school doesn't get out until next month, which gives me two weeks before she visits the mountain spirit again. See what damage you can do up here, I'm going to screw up those turbines of theirs."

The giant of the forests shook his wooly head as he watched his friend dive into the wound that the developers had inflicted on Mother Earth.

Hours went by and the sky was beginning to grey as dawn approached.

"Oh Lover-boy, you might want to come out before this thing powers on for its test. They put it on a timer and I couldn't disarm it, stupid computers. They probably have this mess hooked up to a secret power source this time."

"Coming, I think I got it."

There was a popping and snapping sound echoing back up the shaft, followed by a string of expletives that had been learned from irate fishermen.

"What happened?"

"I slipped."

"You slipped? Giant talons of death, and you still manage to slip?"

"Hey, I'm only five hundred years old, ok? Just because I've reached full size does not mean my talons are completely hardened.

That doesn't happen until my horns begin to come in fully at one thousand."

"Fully? They'll get *bigger*?"

A low humming began to fill the air as generators that had been set up for the test began to come to life, and computers clicking as they began to store data on the plant workings down below.

"Aw crap, they did. Get out of there, moron."

"I'm stuck."

"What?"

"You heard me. I can't move, I'm trapped, I'm stuck. My midsection is wedged in such a way that I can not get out fast enough. How else can I say it?"

"Then get unstuck. You can't leave her like this. That human you charmed built her life around you."

"Tell her I love her, and to be happy."

A final click while the dragon was still struggling to free himself where his mid-section had become wedged and knotted, and the turbines began to spin. His last thought was of BlowingWind, and how bright her smile had been when they had been planning what followed their elopement. Miles away, BlowingWind sat up in bed, glancing where her dream catcher had been only the night before.

"My God, what a nightmare. Maybe I shouldn't have burned it yesterday, should have made a new one first. Either that, or I'm more nervous than I thought. Yeah, that's it. BlowingWind, you're just worried about shadows, and here you are talking to yourself again."

Lying back down, she closed her eyes, forcing herself to rest. Without a transition, she was standing in line with the other graduates of her class, taking congratulations and waiting for Obsidian's embrace.

"Wait a minute, this is pretty familiar. Oh no, not again. Please not again. Come on, wake up. No more dreams."

She was in fast forward, her life blurring before her eyes as she ran out into the night with her bag, shedding her cap and gown like the refuse they had become until she only wore the doeskin dress and moccasins her grandmother had sent her. The streets of the town fell behind and she took to the safety of the forest, speeded on her way by wind spirits who recognized her as the one who had been chosen by the Medicine Lake.

"Obsidian!"

She had passed the night in sliding through the forest, following the call of her heart. Against all reason, thanks to the secret portals between trees that folded space, she made it to the lake by daybreak.

Instead of the purple water dragon that she had found in her waking life that day her world had ended, the lake itself had dried in her dream, and fish lay rotting in the sunrise. The shell at her neck shattered, and so did her dream.

"The worst yet. Why can't I just die too and be done with this nightmare?"

A large lake lay quietly beneath the blue sky, reflecting the glory of the winds in the heavens like an oversized mirror. All around the edges towered great trees while rocks lurked and grasses waved. Fish swam or rested happily in the big blue, while ducks dove below after the lake weeds or minnows. A bald eagle swooped down like some great chief to grab a trout from the natural reservoir, and nature's beauty was at its finest in the morning.

She threw a rock out into the lake, watching the ripples spread and gazing into her mind.

A howling pulled the young woman out of her reveries, demanding her attention now as her hair was whipped around her head, even though there was not much to pull anymore. One of the fish spirits had left her some of his fish and a knife for cleaning them a few days ago. She had eaten a little of the fish, first using the razor sharp stone blade to cut her hair once more, curling forward around her jaw.

Another rock skipped across the water, just like her thoughts skipped across the lake of her mind, skimming the surface and never going far below until there was no more energy left to fight with. The memories pulled her down into a dark oblivion that even He could not have kept her from drowning in. Her soul was shattered and her heart broken, lying on the forest floor to be found by archaeologists thousands of years later to piece back together and wonder at. He was gone, and all she had left to her were ephemeral dreams, a necklace, and her Shaman's mirror.

"What do you want with me? Leave me alone! No more! I failed."

The voice that called to her through the wind froze her heart and yet caused it to burst with joy. It was the one she had been dying to hear, the rich sounds a melody to her ears. He had come for her at last.

"You are still mine. Follow me, *reidou*."

"*Reidou*? What's a *reidou*? Obsidian, where are you?"

"There are earthquakes and mountains here, and forests. Start again."

An image filled her mind. It was an island country that had interested her greatly in school, full of hot springs, volcanoes, fault lines, and other such powerful medicines. On one of the northern islands there was a river restoration project going on, and an engineering school there had earlier courted her.

Most importantly, there was a lot of territory in the islands, all things she had never seen before. There were far too many memories here. Moving away over the salt water, she could make new ones. He had promised to provide and protect, and he would. He would lead her to where he wanted her to be.

"Come."

Smiling for the first time in two weeks, BlowingWind began to head back to civilization.

"I wonder why Japan."

CHAPTER 2:
PULLING OUT ONE'S ROOTS

MILES had fallen behind her feet as she hiked somewhere along the Medicine Lake road, and the sweet morning wind blew her along her way. It was a lovely summer day, with the sun smiling from his blue sky, and the mountain was still managing to wear his white skins, even though they would soon muddy into brown. The countryside was already beginning to go brown, the grasses bending under the breeze and the rabbits hopping in between. No one had been at the Medicine Lake Campground when she had checked, and so she had decided to head back on her own.

"It was better when the lake was still nearby, at least the air was a little moister. Welcome to the High Desert, where you're an idiot if you think the forest will keep you cool."

The crunching of tires on the road behind her drew her away from her personal diatribe, and she held out her thumb. The green Ford truck slowed down, the trailer it was pulling stopping too.

"Young lady, what are you doing way out here all by yourself?"

"Well, I was on a vision quest, but I'm done now and need to get to Mount Shasta... Mr. Sanchez, is that you?"

She looked over the familiar dark, slightly rounded face and the stern salt and pepper mustache. He looked much like any other Hispanic/Native American cross stock. The dark police sunglasses screened his eyes...she'd never known their color. Her guess was brown though, since his daughter's eyes were blue, his wife's blue, but his son's a nice dark brown.

"BlowingWind? You look different without your snowsuit and helmet. Hop in, we're on our way to Mt. Shasta anyway."

"Thanks."

Mr. Sanchez hopped out of the truck and popped the seat forward, looking like a grizzly bear to BlowingWind. Squeezing into the back between Willow and her little brother, she held her pack on her lap and breathed a sigh of relief after she had buckled in and the truck was rolling again.

"I'm so glad you stopped. It would've been a long, hot walk. What are you guys doing so far from Big Valley though?"

Willow shook her head, her long black hair held back in a pony tail as her emerald eyes sparkled in amusement.

"We're in the same grade, remember? My graduation ceremony was just a couple of days ago. Now we're on our last vacation together before I head up to SOU for my geology program. Can you believe we're done?"

"No. So, was there any development in your pet project?"

"Oh sure, the cracks in Valentine widened by two centimeters this winter, and the temperature is another degree higher. That's an increase of seven degrees on average since I started monitoring the cave. What are you going to do?"

"I'm getting ready to go to Japan."

"Cool. Comparative Religions?"

"Engineering and Geology."

"Wow, heavy stuff. You've got my address still, I want a rock from Fuji for my collection."

"Will do. From the crater like all your others, right?"

The rest of the ride passed by in chatting about Willow's ambitions and hearing about the other plans that the few skiers from Big Valley had for themselves. At length though, they had pulled up by her bank, and BlowingWind was waving good bye as the Sanchez family rolled on to their next destination. Turning around after they were gone, the small brown building stood invitingly before her, beckoning her inside with a cheerful sparkle of glass doors.

"Oh my God! Wind, you're ok!"

Having gone through the second door and been spied by the

newest teller, BlowingWind nearly fell in shock at hearing the familiar
voice here of all places. Her best friend from school, and a former
member of the McCloud ski team, she had forgotten that Summerrose
Smythe had taken a job at the bank after graduating last year. Relief
glowed from every pore of the pale woman, her deeply green eyes as
piercing as pine needles. Black hair had been pulled up in a severe
bun, giving the late teen an air of command softened by the pastel
blue hues of her flowing dress.

"Hi Rose. Yeah, I'm fine."

BlowingWind tiredly made her way over to the counter, steeling
herself for the barrage that was sure to come.

"Why did you run off and where were you hiding? You worried
your mother sick!"

"Something happened to my boyfriend. I've been out in the
woods where we first met."

"Wow. Tough luck buddy. He was a really nice guy. Are you
going to be ok?"

"Yeah. I'm going away for a while. I need to clean out my
account."

"Too many memories?"

"Yeah."

"Number?"

"277349180003."

Rose's fingers tapped out a rhythm as she input her friend's
account number.

"We are going to have to issue you a check for $30,000. Here is
your other $5,000 all in cash. Bet you're glad you saved all your
birthday money and sold all those dream catchers through Black
Bear."

"Fine by me, and yes I am."

"Wind? Say goodbye to your mom before you go. Don't just
disappear like you did that summer you were 16 and stupid."

BlowingWind remembered the trip with Willow below the mountain, and into the parallel world that her friend had become part of. Time between the planes did not flow evenly, so what to her had been a week had resulted in a month within Terrah with the Shadows.

"We'll see. Goodbye my friend."

"At least write!"

After BlowingWind had spoken with the head teller and gotten the check for the rest of her money, she silently left the credit union, her thoughts chasing through her head.

"I've already got everything, my passport, birth certificate, driver's license, and the few things I just couldn't live without. What would I say? Bye mom, I've only got the vaguest clue what I'm doing?"

As Summerrose watched her old friend leave, the young woman knew that this was the last time that she would ever see BlowingWind again. It was a while before her break, but when it came, she would be certain to call Mrs. MountainChild to let her know that her daughter was alive.

"Adios mi amiga. May your winds blow fair."

BlowingWind smiled after she was away from her friend.

"Sorrow and regret bind me to Mother, but who am I to ignore a call once given? I'd better pick up some light provisions, and I know just where to go. It could be a long trip to Redding if the spirits aren't with me."

A right turn after she crossed the street brought her around the corner to the best natural foods store in town. Entering the swinging doors, the familiar and comforting smells of coffee beans, sage, and incense warred with the fresh flowers while she drifted back to the nuts and berries.

"BlowingWind!"

A short older woman with long hair gracefully becoming silver, the proprietor reminded the young Shaman of an earthbound angel with the way she seemed to float everywhere in her gauzy dresses. Grey eyes worriedly locked with her own where she was filling her shopping basket with water, nuts, jerky, and dried berries.

"Namaste, Angelique."

"I heard rumors that you ran away little one. What really happened?"

One hand had begun to toy with her necklace as she felt like bursting into tears again. Angelique had always been the kind of person who you could spill your problems out to, no matter how crazy, and she was sorely tempted to do so right now. Angelique was a devout Buddhist, and had a broad range of things that she had studied both metaphysical and mundane. Some rumors even claimed that she was an *onmyouji*, a magic practitioner.

"Did you hear about the mess out at the geothermal plant?"

"From several sources child. Why? What's wrong dear?"

Angelique had already been worried when the news of the secretive young woman's sudden disappearance had reached her, and that worry only increased as the one who had always seemed larger than life began to fold in on herself.

"Do you believe in spirits?"

"Dear child, I am a Buddhist. Of course I believe in spirits."

"He was my boyfriend. But he's gone now, and I need to follow him. He has a plan for my life."

"He?"

BlowingWind tightened her grip on her necklace as she drew herself back together again, whispering a name while her eyes begged the woman to understand.

"Obsidian. I was told he got stuck down there during one of his sabotage attempts, and didn't have time to get out before the turbine test. He was always such a klutz when we went into the lava tubes, he should have known better."

"Are you sure dear? Scientists apparently still haven't been able to identify what or who it was. It could have been anything they found."

By now, they had made it over to the counter, where Angelique was ringing up BlowingWind's purchases in the empty market. Tears threatened to spill out of the young woman's eyes, yet they did not.

"I just know. How much?"

"$30."

BlowingWind paid for her food before giving the older woman a hug over the counter.

"Thank you for listening, for caring as much as you do, and good bye."

Not even bothering with a paper bag, BlowingWind put her items directly from the counter into her knapsack. As she was doing so, Angelique got a glimpse of something dark that had wrapped itself around her soul, resting its heavy head on her shoulder. Shadowy and serpentine, it did not seem to be threatening, but instead like it was trying to comfort the young woman who was embarking on a journey she did not know the ultimate outcome of. As the small form faded out of the door, the older woman sent up silent prayers for the child, and made a note to request special prayers for her from the monks at the local monastery.

"I'll go to the monastery today and ask the monks to pray for you Little One. I always wondered what made you so different from your peers. There are more of us than you think."

Sure that she would have plenty of food for her journey now, BlowingWind walked through the busy streets, bound for the highway on-ramp and a new life. The few minutes she spent walking past the various stores containing sundry items passed by her like an eternity, until she reached the intersection again

"What a doofus I am! The only Japanese I know is 'Ramen.' Well then, I guess I'll be stopping by the travel book shop first. They always have a great selection of books for learning languages."

When the little green man lit up the pedestrian sign, the woman made her way across the street, just another woman in a sea of traveling Buddhist monks, Goths, Punks, and normally dressed people.

She sighed in relief when she finally made her way in to the new bookstore, then looked around at the large array in confusion. The silver haired man at the desk came to her aid.

"Can I help you miss?"

"Yes, sir. I'm looking for some books on learning the Japanese language. I'm going there, and I want to be able to understand what people are saying to me."

"This way miss."

Thankfully, the gentleman in the store just sold her a couple books after helping her find and select them, which took all of two minutes thanks to his superb organization. She wouldn't have been able to pick him out in a crowd, he was so non-descript, however he radiated a warmth that she decided she loved.

"Thanks, if I wasn't moving, I'd tell people to come here."

After she had made her purchase, the woman scurried for the on ramp.

"I still would like to know why Japan. Boy, I hope I get picked up by somebody sane and not some nutjob."

CHAPTER 3:
GREAT SPIRIT WILL PROVIDE

"**W**OW, this is boring, and dusty. Do all these people passing me by think I'm going to mug them or something? Even the guys look at me and keep going. Gees, I must have been here like an hour already."

The telltale rumble of an old engine filed the air, and BlowingWind looked up hopefully as she stuck out her thumb yet again for a lift when a dusty brown pickup pulled over. Stopping only a few feet from where she sat in the summer dust, the passenger door popped open and a young man's voice shyly poured out.

"Do you need a lift?"

The Native American stood up and grabbed her knapsack, slinging it over her shoulder in a practiced motion that told of great outdoor experience. Blushing while meeting the stranger's gaze, she made her reply.

"I need to get to the Redding Airport. Can you help me?"

"As luck would have it, I'm on my way there myself."

BlowingWind couldn't help her jaw dropping.

"Really? I was only expecting to get as far as Redding itself and then have to walk to find another ride."

"Yup, really. Hop in, uh... What's your name, Miss?"

Eagerly scrambling onto the wooly Navajo patterned seat cover, she buckled herself in and shut the door. Looking her savior in the eye, she noticed that they were a strange yellow color, like gold, or what one would find on a mountain lion. He had sun kissed skin possessing a healthy glow and sandy hair exactly the color of the hawk feathers that were plaited into two braids hanging over his shoulders. The more she looked at the man, the more he reminded her of a hawk, right down to the sharp aquiline nose carrying a slight downward tuck at the end.

"BlowingWind MountainChild, sir, but my friends usually call me Wind. And you are?"

"Nice name. I'm Freedom WindSong."

Checking his mirrors and glancing over his shoulder, the man maneuvered his vehicle back into the steady flow of traffic, using his signals when needed and seeming rather hyper alert. He did not calm down until they were actually merged onto Interstate 5 and matching the speed of the others. Freedom had left his window down, which fluttered the feathers on the tiny dream catcher that hung from his rear view mirror, drawing the woman's attention to them curiously.

"Freedom. I like that name. How did you come by that?"

"Father is from the Karuk tribe, and mother is an Ute. The tribal Elder, my grandfather, called my parents one day before they even knew she was carrying me. Grandfather told them that the spirits had just informed him that mother was pregnant. He went further predicting that I was a boy and that I should be named Freedom."

Freedom shrugged.

"Apparently I was supposed to have a hand in helping someone become free. Oddly enough, I was indeed a boy, so they went along with it. How did you get called BlowingWind? It suits you somehow, but it's pretty weird in this world of Mary, Sally, and Britney."

"My dad was a Shaman of the Apache Nation. One night he had a dream, and Hawk had told Father that his daughter would be called the Blowing Wind. So, when I finally came, that's what they called me."

Silence filled the truck for half an hour as they passed through the luscious mountain country, reveling in the caresses of the wind together and exclaiming mentally at the Sacramento River as they passed over it. The whole countryside was alive and vibrant, dancing beneath the summer sun as its hidden spirits went about their secret lives. After a while though, talk resumed.

"So, why are you going to the airport, if I may ask?"

"I guess you could call it a spiritual calling."

"You too, huh? You know, as soon as I saw you sitting there, I said to myself 'Freedom, she's a Shaman in need of some help,' though I have no idea why. So I stopped to see what I could do. Ultimately, I'm on my way to Tahoe. I don't know what I'm going to do there, but two weeks ago I had this awful urge to go. Where are you going?"

"Japan. That's all I know."

"Spirit sure is mysterious."

"Yes. At this rate though, everything's mysterious."

Freedom laughed.

"I hear that. BlowingWind, if you look in the glove box, you will find my wallet. Open it up and take one of my contact cards. When you get where you are going, send me an email. I would like to keep in contact with you."

"But I don't have email."

"No problem. They'll have plenty of Internet cafes over there. Just sign up for a free email when you visit one and drop me a line. My laptop has wireless, and I'll be doing the same until I get set up down there in Tahoe. This way, you'll have someone that you can talk to every now and then."

"Ok. Thanks."

The training Shaman did as she had been asked, chuckling a little at the picture of Freedom and his friends goofing off at Burney Falls, that was the first thing one would see opening the parcel. The rest of the trip was spent in telling each other of hilarious exploits with their friends, and BlowingWind actually felt a lot better laughing as much as she did. Obsidian wouldn't want her to be sad, and although she missed him, she needed to continue on and be strong. She would see him again, she was sure of it.

At last, they had made it to the airport, and Freedom dropped her off at the terminal. She eyed the yellowed paint and outdated architecture.

"At any moment, I swear that a Fuller Brushman's gonna pop out of there... blue suit, brown shoes, and all."

"I'm going to go park, but here you go to spare you a little walking. Good luck, and remember to drop me a line."

"I will. Thanks again Freedom."

She waved a last time and turned to go into the terminal, pausing as a gust of wind enveloped her. Looking around, she noticed that the truck was completely gone, nowhere to be found out in the parking lot. In the near distance she could see a small hawk circling, as if it were watching something or circling for prey. Touching her hair where she felt an unaccustomed weight, she found a small braid into which a hawk's tail feather had been tied with twine.

"Strange, the wind's been doing that a lot lately. Was he a spirit? Had to have been, how else would this feather get here? I'll have to try and be more observant from now on for the differences. I could have been spirited off into their world really easily."

Shaking her head in confusion, BlowingWind resumed going inside. Goose bumps instantly formed on her arms in the air conditioning, a shock to her system that was used to the outdoors. The terminal was large and open, encased with glass, giving the facility an empty feeling despite the rows of gray seats for weary travelers waiting for their flights. An expensive cinnamon roll and coffee shop could be seen, and across the way waited the ticket counter. It was for the polished efficiency of the attendant that she headed, forcing tentative steps across mint green linoleum tile.

"Hello, my name is Robin. May I help you Miss?"

Slightly rounded, her black and red uniform further drove in the resemblance to the bird that was her namesake. Short red hair fell in a perfectly arranged bob to her chin, and laughter seemed to sparkle from her dark eyes.

"When is the next flight to Japan?"

"One moment while I check for you Miss."

The attendant clicked in a few commands on her keyboard, chatting about various inane things that BlowingWind found herself not hearing while the commands were processed. At last, the computer screen brought up what they were waiting for.

"The next flight for Japan leaves in an hour on United. There will be a two-hour layover in LAX, and then your flight will arrive at Tokyo International. The flight after that leaves..."

"The first one is perfect. How much?"

"$900."

"Sold Robin."

"And when will you want to come back?"

"One way is fine."

"Very well Miss, your information please?"

As if in another dream, she gave the necessary information, showing her identification to confirm her identity. As the money changed hands, she watched herself smile and chatter about dreams she never knew had lived in her heart.

Her thoughts echoed in her head. "Who is this woman taking over my body? Am I really going to do this? What should I do first when I get there? I'll climb Mt. Fuji definitely, but what happens the rest of the time before school?"

Tickets in hand, the wait went by quickly as she snacked from her traveling provisions. After a short eternity her flight was called and the young woman boarded her plane. The safety instructions passed her by unheard as disbelief closed in all around her, paralyzing her. As the jet engines roared to life, she was reminded of the roars of a great dragon preparing to fling itself into the air. They began to taxi forward, and her eyes turned to gaze out of the window, watching the ground pass them by to fall away.

The numbness gave way to relief eventually, and she pulled out one of her books to begin studying the language she would soon need. Unknown to the young Shaman, the spirits of the winds were relaying information about her departure ahead of her. The spirits of her new home needed to be alerted of her approach.

Tongues of orange and red danced across a lake of magma to kiss and lick the iron red walls with subterranean light born of the river of magma far below, inside the chasm. Obsidian deposits reflected the light further here and there to direct the beams down otherwise darkened hallways teeming with moving shadows. Here, where the earth liquefied in the internal fires, was the realm of dragons and other spirits aligned with the powers of earth, fire and the nurturing darkness before birth.

Emerging from the river of fire where he had been held prisoner by his father and liege lord for five long years, a strapping man who seemed to be in his early twenties could be seen trying to smooth down his hair. Formal Japanese kimono in blazing red and yellow waved around him in the heat, as the personified tongue preened. Rich and dark like earthen secrets, his agitation swept the short spikes into a frenzied mess. Eyes dark and rich as chocolate gazed hopefully up at the edge of the crevasse where he knew his father gazed down at him.

"Is it time yet *Otou-sama*? May I be released?"

"Not yet Ryu, you have just a few more days of your confinement left. Be at least a little patient, be a good example for your servants. You know I don't like it any more than you do. Next time, don't meddle with their affairs so closely as to loose yourself. Humans are not suitable for such as you."

The voice was deep and gruff, roughened from an effort to hide how much he actually sympathized with his son.

"Yes father. I'll not seduce another weak human."

Heaving a bored sigh, the spirit of the magma tongue rolled his eyes before diving back into his liquid heat. Leaving behind the form that he would use above ground, he assumed his birth form to slide through, and attempt to find something to occupy himself with. Black scales shed the heated rock like water as his blood colored whiskers and mane waved gently with his currents, the former image of the Japanese male seeming to be just a mirage brought about by the infernal heat.

"I'll just find a stronger one next time, a beautiful maiden who has not yet killed her magic or belief. It will be sweet indeed to have such a treasure of my own and to be away from my Otousan's weekly lectures."

Ryu had the extreme 'good fortune' to be a son of Take Fujiyama, who was the Konohanasakuya-hime's highest vassal, and Fujiyama-san was the next in line for control should she meet an untimely end in the occasional spirit wars that reordered Heaven and Earth. She herself had not been the original head spirit of the workings of the ancient volcano, having taken over at the retirement of the older *Ainu* fire goddess Fuji who had once been responsible for the eruptions that both destroyed and replenished the lands below the summit.

In other words, Ryu had quite a bit to live up to thanks to his noble father's post.

"Thank Heaven that my professorship contract had expired before he dragged me back here. That really would have been a mess for me to clean up. What's so bad about teaching Humans a little bit of history? I'd rather them not repeat their silly mistakes. Or even any of ours."

Ryu continued to swim lazily as his mind drifted over thoughts of his father.

It wasn't that his father was truly against humans. After all, he processed most of the offerings gifted to the goddess that their clan gave allegiance to, and took care of a great deal of the ever dreaded paperwork that came with such high ranking managerial positions. The problem was that Fujiyama conceived of most humans as weak, spineless, greedy, smelly, rude, over-populous and idiotic. Even worse in Fujiyama's view was the impermanence of their forms, a human would only live a hundred years or so at the lengthiest bodily longevity, and their women could not bear many children as they harbored the growing beings inside.

Fujiyama also thought that humans stank, quite literally. As his mind crossed over that, Ryu snorted.

"Only the bad humans smell like rotten meat. She smelled very nice, like a summer meadow. Roughly half of the world population is female. The only time I wouldn't set eyes on a female would be if I joined a unisex monastery. So I like to date human women now and again. Big deal, we used to breed with them."

He came to a wall of solidified granite, turning in the slow current.

"How did he find out about her anyway? I swear, I said my father was a hoary old dragon caught in convention once, using it as a metaphor, and the next day I'm here. It's not fair." Ryu continued in his mutterings to himself.

As he swam through his elemental subconscious, an unaccustomed breeze managed to find its way down from the surface through the secret passages the spirits used. Rising back up to check the disturbance, the young magma dragon lifted above his own surface, and the wind caressed him with feathered wings. The scent of the fresh air was warm and spicy like cinnamon, and laced with pine, temporarily overriding the thick fumes of sulfur.

A hawk's feather fell out of the incorporeal being, floating on updrafts as it slowly worked itself down to him.

"She's coming, prepare yourself."

Why it was brought here, the magma lord had no idea. He could only puzzle over the odd pulls as the wind dropped a hawk feather into the fiery river to flame away.

With the entrance of the feather into his being, the magma lord felt a sharp needle pierce his heart, connecting him to something and causing a sleeping heart to ache.

"That was odd. I wonder what the wind spirit meant to say. Prepare myself for what? I hope it's not another random inspection."

Ryu was not the only one that the news had been relayed to though, and from where the spirit watched from his place at the entrance of the medical wing of their division, a very similar dragon smiled to himself.

"Watch over my *Reidou*, sire. She is going to be quite the handful if past serves out the same."

CHAPTER 4:
PUPPETS AND STRINGS

THE hawk stopped his circling as the jet plane roared into the sky with all the eagerness of a mountain lion lunging for his prey. In the high winds produced, the spirit phased into the Wind Realm in a flash, and if any humans had been watching his majestic flight they would have assumed he had only been a mirage produced by the heat shimmering from the cement and tarmac. Releasing his news to his brothers and sisters to have it sped nearly instantaneously to a land far across the Great Salt Water, he assumed once more his illusory human shape before the leader of the Hawk People.

Perched on the top of a high and craggy mountain was a similar looking spirit, although obviously much older judging by the fine lines finally beginning to make scores around the eyes and mouth of the personage. Buckskins of the palest variety garbed him perfectly, and the quill-work resembled the currents of wind dyed in blue and bleached white. Leaning on a ledge below his naked feet was a Brother Shield with a single Hawk painted on.

Other wind spirits for North America and sundry Winged People went about their business in the surrounding sky or holding learning circles in the forests far below. Eagles mingled in with the Hawk People in some places, exchanging news and services, or even just chatting peacefully together. In all, the main camp was a busy place, and the children of his people took advantage of the bustle for their adventures.

"I have done as you asked, Hawk. The child of your pet human SoaringHawk has been assisted."

"I am pleased Freedom. SoaringHawk was very special to me when he was alive, and it eases my mind to know that she is finally following her destiny."

"What is so special about the human, Great Father of our People?"

"I may not say yet, only she can decide. Based on her father's performance as a Shaman though, I believe that we can expect great things from young BlowingWind when she comes into her own prime. Now, I believe that you need to attend to your new home? There is a young woman there who will need your teaching."

"Yes, sir."

Hawk watched as his young relative swirled back into the winds to soar to his new home.

"With any luck, more people will begin to see the world as sacred once more. It is strange to think how it is up to the humans themselves to teach each other to use the Medicines once entrusted to them so long ago."

Hawk looked down at the rest of his people who were unaware of the loss of one more of their number.

"If the White Skins had never arrived, what would the current time be like for Turtle Island? Some of the Old Folk still listen and follow our teachings as well as a few of the other colors, but even the mixing of the races of humans had done little to bring about peace in this chaotic world."

He followed the path of his friend's daughter as she winged her way across the skies in the belly of her metal bird.

"SoaringHawk, will you rest when you see your daughter in safe hands? When she is at peace, will you finally leave the earth and set foot on the StarPath?"

A dark eyed Asian male – seemingly in his prime – sat behind his low teak desk, resplendent in golden robes that shone with their own light. A large and imposing nose easily lent a rather intimidating air to the deity. Hair currently as dark as midnight was held captive in a topknot, and his otherwise fine features betrayed his nobility if one could not gather it from his garb.

Tall in height and of otherwise average build, the Heavenly Grandchild never the less had an air of authority that made him seem twenty times more imposing than anyone else ever could. The staff that he usually carried when he went about his patrols leaned unobtrusively in the corner of his serene office, waiting for its master. Curiously his hand reached for the envelope that had just materialized on his desk.

"That is odd. It is from Kazekami-san. He never sits down long enough to write anything, much less attend to his paperwork."

"What does he have to say, my grandchild?"

Grinning as he carefully opened it, Sarutahiko surveyed the form of his grandmother. She too appeared to be in her prime at this time, shining with light from both her body and golden robes. Like his own, her hair was also of the darkest midnight, streaming down freely behind her like a veil far past her buttocks.

Kneeling demurely on a cushion, Amaterasu sipped contentedly at a cup of tea as she visited with her grandson... one of many. He was very busy as the leader of all the Earthly *Kami* and likewise she always had much to do as the leader of the Heavenly *Kami*. So it was that they treasured these moments where they got to visit with each other.

It had not always been thus though. In fact, at their first meeting both Amaterasu and Ninigi, the grandson that she had chosen to rule over the land for that time span, had both been very frightened by his looming presence at the entrance to the human world. Eventually Ninigi had come to take his position as the leader of the *Kunitsu Kami* after Sarutahiko had relayed his intentions as guide through Uzume.

After Ninigi's passing into the Land of Death though, Sarutahiko had taken both Konohanasakuya-hime and her sister under his wing and assumed responsibility for this August position. By this time, Uzume had become his wife, and though she was not what one could call pleased at the arrangement the three women had worked matters out among themselves.

"Maybe he is finally asking for an assistant to do his paperwork so that he can devote himself to the field work entirely. It would certainly make it much easier to read his reports."

"That I doubt very much, although I do agree it would be easier to read his reports."

Sarutahiko's smile dropped from his face as his eyes scanned the hastily penned *kanji* from the lord of the Divine Winds, left to lay on the desk like a forgotten rice cake as the meaning began to sink in.

"Apparently, an *onmyouji* of some sort from the Americas is being sent here. Her guardian has been killed, and there is no one suitable for her temperament on either continent. She is one MountainChild BlowingWind, one of the mixed race people. Grandmother, is this name not shared by a woman chosen by the Grand Council of World Gods as a gateway?"

"Yes, I do believe so. I remember hearing Coyote, Hawk, and Raven babbling on about her at the last meeting. She was to be conjoined with a lake dragon if my memory serves me."

"Grandmother, is it not against policy to so easily accept someone of her position into our lands? Especially as the intention had already been announced?"

"Yes, but what else can we do if she is already on her way? My worry is over whether she is strong enough to keep from being claimed by one of the darkened *Kami*. The world already has enough *onmyouji* that misuse their spiritual powers. I will leave the matter in your hands."

BlowingWind had already gotten through all of the exercises in her first book, and was now on her second book. To her relief, it also contained sections on normal Japanese life. It didn't have much, mainly focusing on getting through an intermediate level conversation, but at least it was something.

"This is stupid. What if the offer doesn't stand anymore and I can't get a job?"

The aggravated wind currents tossed about the jet, intent on jostling the passengers, and BlowingWind began to panic. As a first time flier, she had been ignoring the thoughts of dying a fiery death as the jet crashed into the ground, which had happily been rumbling around the back of her head like thunder from an approaching storm front. Children and other new fliers of all ages joined in her frenzied screaming as mothers tried to hush their offspring, and young men patted the hands of their girlfriends soothingly.

"Oh God! I don't want to die! Not like this!"

"Wheeeee!"

The shrill whoop from somebody next to her pulled BlowingWind out of her nosedive into the pits of despair in complete confusion.

"Of all the things to say when the plane is going to fall out of the sky like a rock, somebody has the audacity to enjoy their last few moments of their human existence? Of all the nerve!"

Muttering to herself as she looked to her left at the aisle seat, the Shaman found a young man who looked like he was probably from the military at one point. Blue eyes sparkled in glee and his teeth gleamed in the sunlight streaming through the windows. Sporting a reddish buzz cut and outfitted in a meticulously cared for T-shirt and jeans, he had his hands in the air like it was a roller coaster.

"Some fun, huh, kiddos! Wheeee! Don't you all want to be pilots when you grow up?"

His enjoyment started to rub off on the kids, who eventually began laughing as the ride smoothed back out. When the children on the plane were quiet again, the man's eyes pierced straight through her.

"There now, that wasn't so bad. Was it? There are children on board. We weren't going to die kiddo, but if we were, why make them panic?"

She hung her head.

Unbidden, vague memories of Obsidian cluttered her mind. She missed his warm arms, and how he would nuzzle her ear with his nose when she felt down. BlowingWind missed his bad jokes, even the ones that she didn't fully understand because of their own cultural barriers they had crossed. Just once more she wanted to feel his lips graze her cheek or his teeth nipping her ear playfully.

Dwelling on what she had lost would do no good at this time though, and she hastily shoved her thoughts into another dark corner of her mind. Her seat partner had not unpinned her yet from his incredulous glare. His eyes stung like spears in a gaze that only someone from the military could manage.

"I'm sorry. There was no excuse for my lack of courage. Your point is taken."

"Don't worry too much about it, it happens. So, I take it this is your first time on a plane."

"Yeah, it is."

Silence fell between the two for a moment while she returned to studying. The realization that there was not anything holding them up still scared her, and her knuckles turned white as she gripped her book. The man watched her from the corner of his eyes as the plane continued on and tears began to form silently, to roll down and hit the language primer that she was reading.

The silence stretched out as the woman's eyes went blank, going over things that obviously had nothing to do with what she had been reading. With the grief and loss etched onto her face at that time, the man had to wonder what had happened to such a young woman to give her that look of bitterness. The tears continued to fall, dampening the paper, and he pulled a blue and white bandana from one pocket to sop up the mess and then pressed it into her hand.

"Whatever it is Miss, you have to move past it. I've lost lots of very good buddies in my line of work, and even though they are gone I soldier on. You seem like you were a strong woman at one time. I saw it in your eyes while you were reading earlier. Soldier on girl."

"This is your pilot speaking. Please return everything to its upright position and stow your gear. We will begin our descent to LAX shortly. Thanks for flying United."

The pair stowed their gear away, and as the plane began to descend the young man grinned at the woman next to him.

"Now, we are only landing. Don't scream this time. My ears can't take it."

BlowingWind couldn't help but laugh from behind her drying tears.

"I'll try not to, but I've got another whole flight ahead of me after a couple hours."

"Really? Where are you going?"

She dabbed at her eyes.

"Japan."

"What a coincidence. So am I. Do you have a two hour lay-over, then a flight to Tokyo?"

"Yes. How did you know?"

"Because that is what they gave me. Usually I get flown directly to the Air Force base, but this time I've got a stop first. My wife is having our first baby soon, and I managed to talk our transport department into routing me through her home area. It's my fourth tour of duty there now. Would you like me to help you with your Japanese?"

"Would you? It would really help."

"Sure. Verbal practice is the best way to learn any language. Besides, it will hopefully keep you from freaking out too much. It's going to be a long flight. Do you like coffee?"

"Love it."

"So do I, but I can't have it for now. How about I buy you a big one and myself a bottle of water and pretend it's coffee. I'll watch you drink it, we start out with simple conversation like the weather, food, and family, and then get progressively harder."

"O... k... But I don't know your name."

"I'm sorry, Shawn Bowers."

"BlowingWind MountainChild."

Here, he gave her a critical eye while laughing.

"What an unusual name. Going by your clothes though I thought it was something like that though. I thought it was 'Burns in the Sun' actually. I take it either your parents were New Agey people or one was American Indian."

"I do burn in the sun, it sucks. Mom is Irish, Dad was Apache."

"Ready to start practicing?"

The wheels hit the ground with a bump, and BlowingWind barely managed to stifle a squeak. She hadn't realized they had nearly finished landing until that jarring wake up call. Looking out the window, she saw the glassy buildings reaching out shining arms for the sky while the tarmac slowed down, rolling by.

The sky was a dingy blue, tired under the weight of the pollutants pulling her weary head down. It had been bad for BlowingWind the times that she went to Redding with her mother, but here the need for space and greenery was even worse.

"Yeah, uh, hai. Where's all the trees?"

"**W**here are you?"

As Ryu swam in his magma, his urge to just get out had grown even worse. Something screamed in his head to go somewhere, to find something. The problem was where did it want him to go?

The frantic tugs continued on his heart and bowels. His whole being was experiencing emotions that were not his own – ranging from mind blowing grief to intense excitement. He had the oddest urge to reach out and wrap his arms around this felt presence, but when it became nearly tangible to his spiritual sight it would vanish again.

"Whatever you are, you're definitely female. Quit teasing me already! I swear, when I get out of here, I'm going to catch every wind spirit until I find out who cast this blasted spell on me. Then I think I'll squish it, or bottle it, or something."

Blue eyes watched the lord paddle around the river of fire again as the owner's slightly pointed ears twitched a little at every foul word uttered from time to time.

"The master is working himself up quite well on his own, and when the time comes, guess what lucky dragon gets to be the one calming him down."

The eyes' thoughts were disordered though by a flute-like voice from behind.

"Ob, dear? You need to take your medicine before your scent becomes too apparent. Remember the last time that you forgot and all the sectors were in an uproar over a human invasion."

A slender and pale hand pressed a purple vial into the lurking healer's hand, as another wrapped around a black and red clad waist. Her unique scent wrapped around him soothingly as she pressed her body lovingly to his back.

"You are right Mayu, as always. Besides, if he smelled my relation to the child you have prophesied coming, it could certainly throw the whole time-line out of alignment. It's still disgusting though."

"The potion, or the thought of Ryu chasing your mother?"

"Both."

Ob gulped the mixture down quickly under the matching eyes of his mate.

"She won't be easy for him to entice. You should pity him when your memories of her are fresh."

Having finished the last of the glowing goo from the vile vial, Ob pulled a hideous grimace.

"I'm sick of pretending to be something and someone I'm not. I really hope that snake was telling us the truth of who I am, who I will be. If only I..."

"It is in the past. We have to live the present Ob. We still have some time before our services are needed again. Come with me."

As his treasured mate purred into his ear, Ob relented his hold on his tortured thoughts. Turning after her warmth left him, Ob followed after the slender form that retreated into shadows. He savored the last of the light bouncing off of the copper hair and green kimono their resident priestess dragon wore, as the darkness of the medical wing enshrouded her and their path to their den.

"The wounded soul blown by the wind and shattered by the lake is for the magma destined. Crossing the sea, she answers a call. A channel is drawn away from Death's cold thrall. Yet here is the danger that she must accept, the missing piece by a stranger is kept. Ryu, fight her despair. Love through her fear. To Heal her Heart and Soul, obstinately hold her dear."

The words of the dragon woman floated unheard past her mate, the woman's prophetic advice meant only for the irate spirit still chafing at his captivity and testing his father's bonds. As the words of his old friend lilted into his ear, the troubled dragon stilled.

"Mayu only is gripped by the words of Those Beyond Time when something important is befalling the clan. Why do I hear her words now though, when she is supposedly in Isolation as her Fertile Time nears?

His eyes grew heavy and his blood sluggish, despite the super-heated rock he was in. Grumbling to himself again, Ryu allowed himself to float upon the surface as his orbs slid shut in light repose. The gamut of emotion was a thing he had become unused to, and sleep would help to regenerate his wasted energy.

CHAPTER 5:
BROKEN HEART, BROKEN SOUL

PEOPLE milled about in the shops, and two fairly normal seeming Americans sat talking while they sipped their drinks at the tables outside of the airport coffee shop.

"You mean to tell me the bathroom's a glorified closet?"

"That's about it Wind."

"Ugh, in that case, I'm going now. There is no way I'm going to use a closet masquerading as a toilet."

"Ok, we'll practice more when you get back."

"Oh joy, I know I am terrible. You don't have to be so nice about it."

BlowingWind had enjoyed drinking her coffee and chattering on with her current escort surprisingly well in Japanese, given the fact that she had only just begun to learn the language today.

"Ugh, it's gonna be a long flight to Tokyo. Time to go hide for a little bit. Sure I had friends due to boarding, but we're all just a group of loners. This plane stuff sucks. What happens tomorrow?"

She continued muttering to herself as she navigated the people filled hallways, trying desperately to keep both her personal space and her dignity. Finally, she ducked out of the throng and into the peace of an empty room.

"Obsidian would want me to move on and be happy, but this still feels like a betrayal."

Pushing open the inner door to the Porcelain Hall, she noticed that the room was blissfully free of other women. Twenty stalls stood in boring rank and file as their doors gaped open waiting to devour all of a woman's filth and flush it away. The walls of the room were of a white porcelain tile, and a single path of forest green trekked around the mid-level. The floor was a standard white tile as well, as cold and empty looking as the floor of a morgue, as it lurked under the accumulated film inherent in the very nature of the function it served.

Choosing the nearest stall, the woman sank down and attempted to relieve herself of all that had been accumulated. Tears ran silently down her face as she pondered the nature of existence yet one more time, wearing salty tracks where their brethren had run before.

"How could I have forgotten the curse, even for a moment? Now I pay for that mistake for the rest of my life. The spirits were right to distance themselves from us and become the things of fairy tales to us. Our love was doomed from the start."

She pulled out her mirror, gazing into the inky depths.

"Where are you now Obsidian? When humans die and leave their fleshly bodies behind, numerous things can happen. Some move on to other planes of being, either paradisaical or hellish depending on the personal beliefs and how the person had been. Some of those eventually return to live other lives and some others do not. Some go directly back to the Source of All that Is, their part of the Dance of Creation done. Some humans move right into another life, the soul retaining memories and lessons learned while a whole new ego was shaped for the next life. Where did you go?"

The surface of the black glass swirled as she searched for a glimmer of him anywhere.

"Very few would have conscious memories of their previous lives. When I die, where will I go? You spirits don't die so much as you enter a type of suspended animation. Even if you are reborn somewhere, who knows how long your childhood will last or even if you would still possess the same feelings for me?"

The mirror showed her a fuzzy picture of the two of them when they had discussed the afterlife while walking between her beloved pine trees.

"What about concurrent incarnations? He had said that I wasn't open enough to understand yet and that it made his own head hurt to think about it."

The image in the mirror cleared as the figures from the past settled lightly into a favorite perch in one of the swaggering pines forming the forest at the foot of Mt. Shasta. In her mind, she could hear the discussion.

"Play another song for me. Your guitar and voice is such a welcome distraction from the tedium of waiting for the others to catch up."

"Willow doesn't get up here very often to hike with us. You should wait for her."

"Serpent will make sure she and the others don't get lost. I would rather not share you."

"Sometimes, I don't even know who you are Obsidian."

"Even in the course of one's earthly life, there are many lifetimes within one incarnation."

The image in the mirror faded to black, and she wrapped it once more before putting it away. Wiping away the tears and half-formed thoughts, BlowingWind stood once more and re-shouldered her pack.

"I must move ever onward, leaving what is done behind. Only the earth and sky go on forever."

Resolutely she emerged from the stall, pausing at the sink to wash her hands and face before drying them using the air dryer. Pushing forward, the door opened for her, a gateway unnoticed between two very different worlds. As she was exiting the physical space of the restroom, a dark form solidified before her, pressing her back into the empty room as the door between the two realms locked.

Picking herself up from where she fell from the unexpected attack, BlowingWind again noticed that the room was empty. Looks could be deceiving though, as she had learned before, and as the hairs on the back of her neck stood the shell of her necklace warmed in a familiar warning fashion.

Although it was visually empty, a being still filled the room. The looming sense of malice and disquiet affected the very air, chilling her to the bone and pinning her with a great weight. The sinister presence caused her hackles to rise even further, and if she had actually been blessed with fur her size would have increased exponentially.

"You are no ordinary being. Name yourself."

Her voice echoed off of porcelain tile and polished mirrors, empty, yet commanding and now slightly mocking in intonation and inflection.

"You are no ordinary being. Name yourself."

"I asked you first spirit. Father taught me far better than that."

A flicker at the corner of her eye alerted her to movement. A dark shape was beginning to meld into the wall, seeking to avoid her gaze. Her turquoise eyes locked the Shadow into place.

"Let me go!"

The panicked spirit finally used its own voice in its demand. Empty and hollow, the tone spoke of years of bitterness and regrets that bound this being to the material realm.

Desperation led the being to his next attempt upon her sanctity. No spirit had his or her protective and guiding claim upon the young woman, leaving her open save for her own rather developed defenses. However, everyone had his or her own weakness, and he had watched as she had wallowed in her own pain and self pity.

Leaping from his wall haunt, he wrapped around her spirit, taking advantage of the loneliness that palpably oozed from her being. She was strong, but the fresh wounds on her soul promised sweet weakness and the possibility of a fresh young host.

"How dare you touch me! Obsidian!"

The savor of her suppressed pain called to him and every other being with ears to hear an unprotected channel into the world of physical form. The music that their souls gave off was unmistakable, the heavenly notes lilting off of the living soul as it spun inside the physical shell that clothed it.

BlowingWind was shocked that a low-level spirit would dare to wrap around her own spirit. In her whole life, none other had attempted to embrace her soul so intimately except for Obsidian, and that had taken him years to attempt. He had always done it at the lowest points in her life since their meeting, and always his arms had somehow healed the gashes in her heart.

If she allowed it, she would no longer be alone in her own body, a possessed person hosting an unknown spirit.

"We are both so lonely. If you let me join with you, neither of us will be lonely anymore."

The thing continued to whisper to the bewildered woman. Her loneliness grew as the memories swept from the chest in her mind where they were kept as treasures. BlowingWind remembered how Obsidian's hand had felt in her own as they walked or ran together. His eyes twinkled with unshed tears at the look on her face when dealing with grief every year on the anniversary of her father's death.

The smell of water and pine that filled her nose when she would bury her face in his neck after loosing one of her many goldfish easily came back. Memory after memory ran before her vision, and her heart bled with loneliness. Ragged breaths tore from her chest as she fell to her knees in tears, unseeing of her surroundings.

"Where are you Obsidian?"

The memories began to move into the dreams she had shared with Obsidian. They were simple things, such as teaching their children to swim or what a spirit gathering would have been like for her to attend. Fantasies of what their children would have looked like danced before her vision.

She thought that she had already mourned what would never be for them, but apparently it had not been enough. The blood of Kato'ya the rainbow rattlesnake, known also as Quetzalcoatl to the Aztec, no matter how diluted it was by the generations among humans, would not mingle with that of Obsidian to produce another powerful medicine guardian for the Apache Snake Clan she was part of.

"Just another task I have failed at."

At this time, the shade had wrapped completely around the kneeling woman. The darkness was nearly palpable around her as she fell further below the weight of her own sorrow. Her own power bequeathed to her by her spirit ancestor was forgotten and abandoned as she lived the false life inside her own mind while her focus turned even further from the danger she was in. Her memories and dreams were like a drug, stupefying her spirit into stillness and utter vulnerability.

"I'll hold you forever in my heart Obsidian."

BlowingWind's usual parting words to Obsidian as she last watched his skin clad form melt into the forest drove a stake through her heart. She never knew his true shape, whether he was a snake like the ancestor of her clan, or a fish, a beaver, or even a coyote. The dragon shape that she had seen could have been just as illusory as the shape he had chosen for her to be at ease with as he courted her. All the mysteries he had been planning to show her in their own divine wedding that would ignite a new clan would be forever lost, and never again would she find a true place in either world.

Or so she thought.

"I will love you forever, my BlowingWind."

The parting words that he always gave her echoed back in reply within the memory she was currently trapped in. As the tall pine trees swayed in the hushing wind to mask their heartfelt whispers, and the disguising mist rose around him while he took his true shape and disappeared, the last of her childhood fell around her as petals from a wild mountain rose going to seed.

It was at this moment that the last of her shields shattered, and she was completely open to the being seeking to possess her, as open as the day she was born and lost in dreams. The light in her eyes was gone as they stared into an eternity he could not see. Her desperately grasped innocence shone before him like a beacon as the delicate turquoise bead that was her soul rose from it's shell in a wish to follow an unseen vision.

"What luck! How lucky I am to have found a woman so weakened by her own grief."

Carefully he drew closer to her being. Long ago he had already encircled her with his amorphous clouds so that she would be lost in memory. Now all that was left was to enter her body, pouring in like dirty mop water.

"We will be one forever, and you will forget this ever happened."

The first tendrils of his being touched her flesh and began to penetrate her skin.

Something inside of her snapped awake at the intrusion of his touch, some survival instinct disengaging from her soporific dreams. Her Shadow, that part of her being that she did not fully accept, was wary of this new energy seeking entrance within her house of flesh and bone. Her very blood began to rebel, and formerly paralyzed limbs rose in her defense as repressed emotions and an urge for self-defense boiled to her surface like an erupting volcano.

"Don't touch me!"

No holy light emitted from her slight form, nor did anything else happen of an otherworldly nature, as she was still a child of man and much of her spirit ancestor's DNA remained inactivated. Instead, the unrepressed RagingTornado merely got off of her knees. Rising to her feet like the Shadow-side of her name given to her long ago by the spirits, blue fires were burning in her eyes as wind whipped up storms to ravage the earth through the Channel.

Reaching out for the being she had just knocked away, RagingTornado scoffed at the gentler parts of her soul that were still lost in their shared pain like babes in the woods. BlowingWind had expressed her light side for long enough, and was not able to help right now.

"Now is the time for Chaos and Destruction to find release and be employed in their protective and creative nature. BlowingWind's spirit was broken by sorrow and grief, and it is up to each of us four that composed her spirit to do whatever we can to defend and heal her." RagingTornado's voice was a harsh whisper as she spoke to the spirit.

Unnoticed by the dominant aspect and shadow aspects, Wisdom and Love flew off to a place they knew would be safe, following the Red String of Fate that bound them to another spirit in a distant land. The souls of Gentleness and Roughness were left alone within the mortal body.

"That was a dirty trick, making me relive that, Dark One. I am not that weak."

Shadow became flesh beneath the shaman's touch, and a young man materialized from the swirling blackness. Gold shone beneath the fluorescent lights while bottomless blue orbs sparked back in indignation like white capped lakes.

"Really, are your most treasured memories that bad? You're just like her then. She left me because our precious memories caused her pain."

"I don't know what you are talking about Lost One. However, I am not going to let you cheapen my memories of him. I deny you my being."

"What are you going to do about it?"

"Is that a challenge? You picked the wrong time to mess with me. Go away."

As always, her obsidian mirror was near the top of her pack, and skilled hands were blurs as they pulled it out. She was no direct link to the Otherworld like some were, but with the proper tools she could push others fully one way or the other. Hers was the gift of Life and Death, a Healer as well as storyteller.

"Be gone!"

The former guardian of BlowingWind's spirit was no longer accessible to her, but the mirror responded to its misplaced mistress anyway. The shadowy depths reflected the black nothingness of the Infinite Possibility that was beyond the Veil of Living Existence, fascinating the malicious shade as soon as his madman's eyes fell on the spiritual implement.

With a flash of the light hidden somewhere in that creative darkness, he was gone. All access to the mortal plane was now cut off for him, and he was left to find his way home on his own.

The rest of BlowingWind that was still present within her body began to wake up. As the dominant aspect of the woman began to regain her power from where it had been dropped, her Shadow stepped back within her mind.

"This has to stop somehow. Love leaves me too open. No more romance for me." BlowingWind thought to herself.

Unknown to BlowingWind, RagingTornado had also decided the same thing. With the light and dark aspects of her spirit in agreement, a formidable wall formed around her heart. Brambles grew between the trees in the interior forest, and wild animals took shape to wander about, hungry and willing to devour any being who dared to intrude so far into her being.

Somewhere in the depths of her mind, a pale woman surveyed her work with icy, glacial eyes. The fringes of her black dyed buckskins played in a waterfall's misty breeze. A thin and weary hand tucked an earthy red-brown lock back behind an ear, as the hair was still unused to its current length. The waterfall that was the source of her being was now well protected from invasion. The birches, aspens and pines had been forced to re-grow from where the fires of grief had reduced them to ashes. It was the passageway not only to her heart, but also beyond that to where her spirit originated.

Any man that wanted her love would have a difficult time finding his way through the wilderness of her own fears. Friends she would have, but never again would she be as wounded as she had been by the loss of a prospective husband.

A knock sounded on the door of the locked bathroom, and a concerned voice called in to her.

"Uh, BlowingWind, are you okay? We need to get to our gate before they start boarding."

"I'll be right there."

Carefully, she put the obsidian mirror back in her pack, wrapping it back up in a length of leather tanned by one of the Modoc Native Americans that she had been friends with back home. She had little of her beloved lake spirit left to her, and she did not want to damage this special item.

The soft leather shrouded the shewstone and protected it, and BlowingWind wondered what had possessed her lake spirit to ask her that fateful question when she knew he had to have heard her mother's story that day at his lake so very long ago. Angry tears trickled out of one eye, which she swiped away in irritation.

"I just had something to take care of."

Her newest friend and traveling companion was taken aback at the power of the dry grief welling from behind her eyes as he saw her emerge from the room. She had slipped even further into the darkness chasing after her soul. In his line of work, he had seen it happen to countless others. As quickly as he saw it, the *tsunami* passed. The young woman threw up a cheerful façade, grabbing his hand and beginning on a dash for their gate.

"Come on! You've got to get to your wife! She's due any day remember."

False laughter rang out, fooling everyone but herself and the soldier she had befriended.

❧

A writhing mass of red, black, and green coiled within and above the nest the pair had constructed of precious metals and jewels. The volcano dragon halfling and the forest dragon that was his mate had melded the objects together long ago, beginning just after their mating ceremony. That day so long ago had resulted in a small clutch of eggs, but they had never hatched.

So it was that they were trying to breed again.

Somewhere between the status of *Kami* and *Youkai*, the healers were unbound by the restriction of only breeding when natural features and energies needed guardians. However, they were still bound by their own biological clocks; hence the long and arduous wait; hence also their rather arduous mating.

Mayu extracted her impeccable fangs from the scaled midnight neck of her mate, licking her lips where some of his blood remained. Ob purred in appreciation as her green scales reflected the torchlight and her leathery wings stroked his sides.

Take Ob finally managed to extract himself from his mate's embraces, even though he was a little worse for wear after having done so. Having bred in their dragon forms, it was a very rough process on the male, often resulting in more than a few missing scales. He was lucky this time, and she had been surprisingly gentle with him this time.

Soon, she would be laying their eggs and beginning the long brooding process. Mayu was probably capable of carrying their pups within her in a mammalian fashion, but as Ob was only a *Kami* through his father's blood, it was important that those *Kunitsu Kami* around him did not realize that he was not purebred like they were. It had been a long time since a half-human had been recognized within their ranks.

"It is time. Go."

"Yes Mayu."

Ob thanked the *Amatsu Kami* that he had remembered to take his potion to disguise his scent. The one time that he had forgotten to take it and had begun to smell human the whole mountain had been in an uproar looking for an intruder. What a mess it had been, and he had nearly been caught as what he really was.

It was a dangerous predicament that he had grown up in, and it would have been even worse if they had realized why he had been found orphaned. Exactly how could he have explained the fact that at that time his parents had not met yet, while a hatchling still without the power of speech?

"Lord Healer Ob, where are you going?"

The deep voice of one of the gate guardians broke into the young dragon's thoughts, dissipating slowly awakening memories. Truthfully, he didn't know where he was going. By all rights he should be guarding his bride and their nest, but here below Fujisan there were no dangers to guard her from. No one had penetrated the Take Clan fortress for centuries without an invitation, and Nobunaga had long since ceased his oppression of *Youkai*, *Kami* and Priest alike, dead for a long time.

All Ob knew was that he had to get to the surface and into the woods. He didn't know why, but something was calling for his help. Perhaps he would gather some herbs in the forest while he was searching for what was issuing the call for him in the human world. It was simpler to remain in the spirit vibratory range and easier to be unobserved by passing hikers or climbers, but the urge told him to drop his vibration for a while. Still, he would need to assume his human shape and be very careful in the human realm.

"I will be sojourning in the Sacred Forests for a while, Chin."

"Very well then, Ob-sama, please be careful as the climbers have become more numerous from the last time that you have been above."

Ob left the armored forms of his clansmen and childhood playmates behind, passing more guards every few *Li* as he navigated the upward wending passages carefully. It had not been often that he had gone to the forests, but he and Ryu had gone so often in their distant youth that it was a simple matter to find the exit.

Finally, gentle breezes kissed his face and stirred his black and red silks around his form. Darkness gave way to twilight and then the light of the full moon as he emerged from the fern encrusted mouth of the secret cavernous world below and within Fujisan.

Ob looked around the forest clearing, and admired the lichen-covered boulders of the ancient high seat, and the moss mantled cypress and pine trees. Not too distant from where he stood, the source of a stream delivered its water into the care of the stream spirit.

The water sang to itself a newly filtered tune as it was set on its course. Usually, the stream and spring were more observant when any member of the Take Clan actually emerged from the volcano, but it looked like they were mired in red tape at this time.

"Yuck, it must be terrible to be bonded to a place. I remember too much work."

A young woman's voice resounded in his mind and conjured a thin face that he could almost place, and then the memory was gone.

"Where are you Obsidian? I don't want to be alone."

A troubled frown marred the Asian's face.

"My life was far easier when I did not remember my past. Mayu has been my mate nearly since I can remember, but I still feel guilty."

"Why have you abandoned me?"

The voice had not been in his head after all, and while the pair of Honshu Clan water dragons argued over their watershed reports, the healer began to dash through the woods towards the heartrending wails. The trees and boulders flashed by with his supernatural speed as the young spirit nearly flew along the ground. Animals watched curiously as the non-bonded *Kami* passed them by, and yet he found himself drawing no nearer.

Ahead of him, a slight and glowing form darted through the forests in its own headlong dash, and its sobs sounded distinctly feminine. No smell was left behind, and Ob found himself wondering just what kind of spirit he was chasing.

It ran as fast as the wind, and yet could not have been a wind *Kami*, as it possessed what had to be a solid form as the branches were pressed aside for its passage. Finally, the form collapsed on the ground motionless and exhausted.

Ob drew near to the being, turning it over carefully to see the face of the creature capable of running as fast as a dragon. The body was solid, and yet possessed of translucence that marked it as a soul.

The face was strikingly familiar, one that had haunted his dreams ever since his childhood a thousand years ago when a powerful tree *Kami* had brought him from a hazy past to his proper family. The features were angular and foreign, and yet there were many similarities to his hidden human features within her pink light. Rounded ears marked her as a human soul, yet her spirit was obviously broken, as this soul was only one color, one layer of the human spirit.

"Oh my."

He set about doing what he could to make the soul more comfortable, shocked at seeing the woman in this state. The soul was wounded; great gashes had been ripped into her being as if she had fought a hard battle against something. Cleaning and bandaging them from a kit that he always kept hidden in his pockets, he was startled when a silvery being bearing the exact same features and wounds came crashing through the underbrush.

Her voice was cool and stern as the winds that swept the summit of the mountain where the various *Kami* lived as she addressed the disguised dragon.

"Step away from us and declare your identity spirit. Then you will tell us how it is we find ourselves so far away from our other two souls."

Slowly Ob put down his kit so that the conscious soul was able to see what he was doing, and then retreated a few paces to put her more at ease. Lifting his face to study the new soul that had disturbed his work, he was dismayed at the extent of the injuries.

"Where is your mortal body? It will die if you are gone too long and you have sustained such injuries."

The woman gasped as she saw the face of the spirit attending to her Love soul's wounds, instantly recognizing the face of the one she had been looking for. Yet, in this astral existence that she was in, she saw clearly something that had escaped her when she had known his other incarnation. A red string led from his heart to somewhere deep within the earth and two cords of black and green wound tightly with it in the strong rope of a soul bond. The being that she had come to find was bound to another already.

"Obsidian."

"Hello, my *Reidou*. It seems that we have much to discuss, and much of it you will not remember until the time is right."

"I am too late, aren't I?"

"Yes and no."

The silver soul collapsed on a nearby boulder, the deep blue of her eyes darkening as the *tsunami* of the past swept her away for a moment.

"If I had known what would have happened, I would have stayed with my own kind instead of searching for a bride among humans."

"No, everything happens for a reason. There has to be some reason why our threads have been woven into the Tapestry of Creation in the manner they had been. Everyone's thread has a part to play in the greater whole."

He watched her the way she watched him, and was dimly aware of how his thoughts played in the back of his mind. This particular life he was living now would most likely be his last in this realm, and it was to be used to correct his mistakes. BlowingWind was his beloved Mayu's descendant from her human incarnation, which made her family.

She was also something even more important to him, and although he had only been newly born the last time he had seen her as Ob, she was still the woman responsible for his living body. He was not sure how it was, but the old tree spirit who was his mate's father had been adamant that he was a child who had traveled through time to serve his mother.

"You died, and I came to find you, hoping that when and if I did find you that you would feel the same way about me as you once did."

"I do, but it was never meant to be. Our paths are different, but there is someone to help you revitalize the blood of humanity if the two of you can brave our family curse. On another continent the solution is also beginning to play out, if it makes you feel any better."

"Love must not know about this. It would destroy her."

"Ah, so the pink one is *Ai*. You would be *Shin* then, Wisdom."

"I ask again Obsidian. Why are we here?"

"Always so direct. Please listen without interrupting."

"Fine."

Ob drew in a deep breath in an attempt to order his thoughts, and carefully began to relate in English what Wisdom would need to know in order to guide the other three aspects of herself in the right direction. He could not tell her everything, as the future was not carved in stone. Still, he could tell her a little, and hopefully his sire would be able to help BlowingWind find her lost souls and heal her broken heart.

He also hoped that she did not figure out what his prehistoric term for her meant.

CHAPTER 6:
CROSSING INTO THE UNKNOWN

BLOWINGWIND had dropped her friend's hand sometime during their dash to the gate, and slipped quickly through the spaces between people and baggage.

Shawn forced his breathing to remain normal, as he also did his best to run through the crowds that threatened to make him late, but his friend's smaller form made it easier for her. As they wove through the crowds to their gate, he could see her composure solidify, until at last they were at their gate.

The pair skidded to a halt, BlowingWind narrowly missing tripping over a child's ball that rolled into her path.

"Where the heck did you learn to run like that? You should join the military."

Wind listened as Shawn gasped his question to her. Shaking her head, she made her reply.

"Nah. I couldn't stomach taking orders or killing someone. I had a lot of self-training, and plenty of extra-credit for gym. Let's get in line."

The pair looked at the already long line extending from the check in desk, and then groaned. Those forming Group One were already starting to come together in anticipation of the flight. Taking advantage of the wait, Wind checked out her surroundings.

"Wow. Good thing we checked in before getting those drinks."

"Yeah, we'd better get in line with the rest of our boarding group."

As could be expected for a major metropolitan airport, the gate was thronging with people. Dark and light, tall and short, young and old, all of these dualities and more mixed together to create a living palette to paint the lifeless canvas with a daily and ever-changing masterpiece. The cushioned blue metal chairs alternately sheltered tired bodies and released them once more into the hectic dance that took place even when people were just waiting. Some of the people filled her with dread. A few leered at her, licking their lips. Most paid no attention to her though, caught up in their own little dramas.

"Creepy."

By now, the first boarding group at a neighboring gate had just finished, and the second group was being called. She wondered if she should just stay standing or if sitting down would ultimately be the wiser choice. Shawn's voice broke her thoughts.

"Have you ever seen an official international jet?"

"No."

"Then you should. We've got a bit of time before they call our group, why don't we look out the window and see our bird?"

"Ok, but I don't see how you can still be comfortable around so many people. It's so noisy."

As she caught sight of the plane, the sheer enormity of the jet nearly took her breath away. Gleaming metal baked in the sun, and with the logo for Japan Airlines boldly rising from the tailfin like the rising sun it was, it lurked just outside the bay as the crew worked on pre-flight preparations. The ramp-way was extended and joined to the door near the front of the beast to allow the thronging hoards onto the mechanical bird.

"Thank you for choosing Japan Airlines for your travel needs. Group One is now boarding Japan Airlines Company Flight 75 bound for Tokyo Japan. Group One is now boarding."

The bored voice of the flight attendant echoed over the speakers. Looking at the desk, BlowingWind saw the Asian man pushing the button that changed the green LED bulletin to display which group was now boarding for any hearing impaired fliers. His female partner stood by the ramp in her smart red uniform checking the passes of those who had already begun to board from their group.

She shuffled forward in line, praying that the creepy men would just leave her alone. Wind wanted nothing to do with their oily appearance, stringy hair, or suspicious leer. She had never had to deal with guys looking at her in that manner and it made her feel dirty. It had been one thing beating up one of her male classmates for molesting Summerrose in a dark corner at their perennially postponed prom. It was a totally different ballgame when someone else was making eyes at her.

Shawn noticed what she kept glancing at. If the truth were to be told he did not like how the men looked either. They could easily be hijackers, walking bombs, rapists, or anything else. On the other hand, they could also just be travel weary fliers hoping to get a smile. With the look in their eyes he doubted it though. It was the same kind of look he gave his wife at times.

Unfortunately, BlowingWind wasn't helping matters by watching them and giving off the helpless victim vibe.

"Don't look in their eyes, and quit looking at them like that. It's what they want. Just look straight ahead and mind your business."

"Ok."

BlowingWind stamped down her urge to inspect the carpet. Instead, she looked at the terminal display behind the check in desk, noting how many flights were lined up after her own. It amazed her that any place could be so busy. So many cities and countries were connected to the LAX, and she found herself wondering what places like Denver, Sacramento, and New York were like. Continuously inching her way up in the parade that consisted of the line, she was blindsided by a comparison to what it must be like to carry a silken dragon at the Chinese New Year.

She smiled to herself as she thought about her favorite type of beast. In the Land of the Rising Sun, she would no doubt find many images of the fantastic beasts to fuel her imagination, and perhaps she would be inspired to write songs again.

"With the kind of luck I've been having, something interesting is bound to happen. This is it though. I'm leaving the country."

As the thought rebounded through her mind, BlowingWind felt guilt at leaving without even saying goodbye to her mother. What kind of daughter was she to just abandon her like that, not even

telling her how much she meant to her for one last time? She almost
wanted to call it off and go home, but to do so would be to live
forever mired in the memories of the area and her beloved boyfriend.
What was done had been done though, and even though a large part
of her wanted to wallow in the past still, she had to move on in her
life. Perhaps she could forget the pain in the process of setting up in a
new place. Maybe she would work up the courage to call once she
was settled.

"We had better get moving if we don't want to be last."

BlowingWind drifted after her friend, superficially responding to
his summons, disturbed at the lack of emotion other than guilt that
she felt in leaving everything that she had known behind. The
BlowingWind who had run laughing through the forest with
Obsidian had died the night that she found out about his death. She
had been buried when his friend Saksque had found her wandering
by the lake and told her his last words of love for her.

Her body continued onward, mechanically doing what it was
supposed to. As she passed the bin where the flight bags were, the
stewardess handed the woman one. BlowingWind took it with a
distracted "*Domo Arigato*," and walked up the ramp. However well
she seemed to be functioning in the outer world though, her thoughts
had gone back to when she heard the news from Saksque himself.
The cold and sorrowing air could be felt on her skin once more as she
replayed the scene in her head.

She had been at their special place, sitting on a cold rock and
dangling bare feet into frigid early morning waters. The lake had
been still, no welcoming presence stroking the soles of her tired feet
or trying to steal the soft moccasins temporarily abandoned at the
shoreline. As she had gazed into the waters, the imposing and hairy
forest spirit had lumbered towards her from his precious trees to
gently rest a large hand on her shoulder.

"He really loved you above even his lake you know. Obsidian
would want you to find happiness." The weight of his hand lingered
momentarily despite the distance.

Now she felt an emotion, and it was one that she did not want.
She was angry that Obsidian had been taken from her because of his
involvement with the geothermal power plant. She also felt anger at

him for not coming out of the tunnel sooner, and for getting caught in the turbines. Most of all, she felt angry at herself for affecting him so much that he had gone to such lengths to make the day of their union perfect. She was even mad at Saksque for not having been able to save his friend.

In her mind, she sought to strike a bargain with the Creator. She knew she was not quite ready to let go of Obsidian in much the same way that the great ancestral snake spirit of her Apache Clan Kato'ya had not been ready to release his beloved human Kaliñya to the Star Path so many uncountable cycles ago.

"Oh, please let me find him. I'll do whatever you want me to do God, just reunite us."

Unknown to the young woman, her Creator was watching and listening. She had made the vow that *They* were waiting for, and was in agreement with *His* Plan. Now, he could reach forth *His* hand and write a bit more of her story.

Although she had not spoken a word out loud as to her thoughts, the change in her breathing must have alerted Shawn that she was being sucked back into the tides of grief. He took it upon himself to make sure that she was in her seat, glad that they had been placed together. Luckily, the three men who had been making her nervous had not boarded the plane, and he desperately hoped that they were waiting for a different flight.

"Here, let me get that for you."

"Huh?"

She had been quickly pulled out of her morose thoughts when Shawn addressed her, marooned in a sea of reality to look around in confusion. BlowingWind had no memory of having gotten onto the plane. She could dimly remember walking the ramp, but not actually boarding the plane. Shawn had his hand out for her knapsack, which she relinquished grudgingly. It seemed to be becoming her security object because of the precious mirror that it contained. Making a face at herself for developing a dependency on an object for security and for having spaced out, she spoke again.

"Oh. Sure. Thanks."

"You know 'Wind, I've told you pretty much all about me, but you haven't told me much about you."

"I'm not very interesting."

"So? Neither am I. We just killed two hours talking about my family."

"Fine. But I hate talking about myself. I guess it's fair though."

Time could work against her, but it could work for her as well. As the next group began to board, she began to weave him a story. A blond man in the seat across the aisle turned his head to listen, but she was too immersed in thought to notice him.

BlowingWind talked through lift off, slipping in between Japanese and English when she was not sure of how to say something in Japanese. When this happened, Shawn would correct her gently, listening to what she told him, and peering in between the unwritten lines for the parts that she was withholding.

"Well, that's a pretty crappy reason to move to Japan. And you didn't even tell *su madre, 'adios?'*"

The unexpected baritone made both of the conversants jump in their seats, their heads swiveling quickly to match gazes with the blue eyes of their tanned and golden haired eavesdropper. BlowingWind narrowed her eyes, already disliking him.

"I suppose you have a better reason to go to Japan?"

"Of course. After a bit of exploration, I'm going to Hokkaido to help with a river restoration project. If things go well for me, I might make the move permanent, or not. It all rests on the heart of a pretty maid."

"I hope you and your girlfriend enjoy yourselves then."

"Oh, she's not my girlfriend... yet. As soon as she meets me though it will be magic."

"Lovely."

BlowingWind refrained from gagging and returned to her storytelling, much quieter so that hopefully they would not be heard. The man took no notice.

"I am Señior Queso."

"Yes, you are. Thank you."

Shawn rolled his eyes. BlowingWind smirked.

They continued talking after she had told what she was going to tell about her life, even through the meal that was provided. At last though, BlowingWind fell asleep, slipping away from the stress and strain for a few precious hours of sleep.

Wisdom rubbed her head, her silvery hand ghosting over her brow. The flow of time was not really something that she had thought much of before, as she had not had to think very deeply about it. This was the first time that her personal drama had been involved in such a grand dance.

"So, basically, you want me to move on in my life so that you can be born to help break my curse, so that I can be happy with some guy you won't even tell me about, and so that you can be born and we can be together again? Do you know how confusing that sounds? This has got to be a hallucination brought on by some kind of head trauma."

"Yes. I am confused too."

Dragons were highly skilled with language, speaking all tongues of the world easily. After all, it was the dragons themselves who had given the humans the gifts of speech and writing. He was lucky in that, as he had not been exposed to English very often, having reached maturity before the English even came to the country. If he were completely human he would never be able to understand the English speaking soul that he had been with, which he had been conversing with, given his pitiful experience. Unfortunately since he was also half-human it took him a little longer to phrase things in her native language than it would have if he were wholly dragon.

Shin sighed.

Ob had taken off the black outer jacket of his kimono, leaving him clad with his black *hakama* and the red *kimono* that he wore beneath his *haori*. The *haori* he had folded into a packet to provide a pillow for the still unconscious Ai.

Although she had received the same wounds that Shin had, it seemed that they affected her worse than her cerebral counterpart. The soul would need a nearby host to hold her and heal her. Ai would not have the constitution to make the travel back to her body unassisted. She would need to be invited home.

"I'm sure this will work."

Wisdom shook her head again, angry at not being able to fathom such a seemingly simple and yet surely impossible happening.

"I don't buy it. If you haven't even been born yet, then you shouldn't even be here. Time travel just isn't available without moving at the speed of light. Even then, it requires movement and makes time relative. At least that's what I understood in math."

"Shin, there is much that you do not know yet. You are still young, I am hundreds of years old, and I was hundreds of years old when my mate's father brought me here to my clan. Time travel does exist."

"Doesn't telling me about it create a paradox then? I think Albert Einstein wrote something about killing one's own grandfather if time travel was possible. I don't know for sure, it was a really boring conversation between the class eggheads and the math teacher."

"But it would also create a paradox if I didn't tell you."

"And now I have to find the rest of myself again and get RagingTornado and BlowingWind to work together before the two of them get so addled with emotions that they can't function."

"Only if you want to heal."

Wisdom crossed her arms where she sat on a rock, partially irritated to be addressed by a non-English version of her name.

"What happens if I don't?"

"I cease to exist. Why? Don't you want to heal?"

"I meant what happens if I fail. Any number of things could happen. I might not like the guy. BlowingWind and RagingTornado could ignore my whispers. I could get so caught up in my studies, and then work, that I totally miss dating at all. I might even not have that offer still at the University, and end up having to go home, or starve, or something. Most importantly though I still maintain that the future isn't fixed."

"You're right, the future isn't fixed. You have a great deal of choice."

"Are all spirits as cryptic as you?"

"Not all. I suggest that you get going though."

With a withering glare Shin, or Wisdom as she called herself, contracted into an orb. Spinning angrily, she zoomed off into the night, searching for her body and following the invisible cord that would bind her to it until her death.

Ob was left alone with Ai now. He could not carry her back to the stronghold in her current form. She was still bound to her body and carried the smell of human on her due to her low vibration.

"Well Ai, it looks like it's just you and I. I'm going to have to encase you in something, but I do have a place where you can rest and heal safely. You will like him."

Ob produced from one of the many folds in his robes a rice ball that he had recently made. The cooled bundle of rice was slightly sticky, and as white as the moon currently overhead somewhere above the canopy of branches. Having a greater need for food than his counterparts, he always kept a little something or other to snack on with him. The smell of the *onigiri* would hide her own smell, and the ball itself would serve as the perfect vehicle to where he was planning to place her. The healer spirit began to chant his spell beneath his breath, his voice echoing in the stillness between the syllables.

"Kiwamete kitanaki mo tamari nakere ba kitanaki to wa araji uchi to no tamagaki kiyoku kiyoshi to maosu."

Love, or Ai as Ob referred to her, contracted into a small orb of pink energy. In a sleepy voice, somewhere between voluntary oblivion, and a desire to feel no more pain, the soul reflected back and inward the spell in her own language as she reacted to the gently forming directive energy. Ai did not understand the words consciously, but the shaman translated the feelings behind them.

"Even for the things which are the most impure, even if things I have left undone and in disarray, respectfully I ask that the spirits hear and grant me complete purification and clarity, both inside and out."

Three times Ob chanted in Japanese, and three times Ai replied in her own language. At the end of the spell, Ob took the sleeping soul of the love that BlowingWind's spirit was capable of and guided her into the rice ball.

As carefully as the *Kami* who was responsible for being sure each soul was seated into an infant's body, he checked his work to be sure that all was in order. After being satisfied that it was, he wrapped this special offering in a silken square that he produced from yet another pocket in order to be able to tell it apart from others he had with him.

This special rice ball should only be eaten by one particular *Kami*, and he knew just who to give it to in order to facilitate this very special healing. True, it would be a bit of a role reversal, but it should be easy for this particular *Kami* to put the soul where she ultimately belonged.

At least, Ob hoped so.

Jikokusecchuuki stood in the sparse room where Sarutahiko had summoned him. The time *Kami*'s short brown hair and dark eyes were a product of these times he found himself in, yet he still wore the brown and green kimono he had adopted ages ago to match the tree that he had become.

"You wished to see me, oh noble leader of all the Earthly *Kami*?"

"Jikokusecchuuki-san, you are known as wise. Kazekami-san has brought to me most disturbing news. There is a *Miko* riding his back to our country even now, who hails from the American Lands. I need your help in this matter."

The old time spirit could feel his respiration quicken, but he caused himself to remain still. It would not do to reveal his hand too soon, especially if this was not the young *Miko* that he was expecting. He had learned over the long course of his existence that time was not as linear as most thought it to be, more like the cocoon of a silkworm wrapped upon itself. By sending out his roots and studying the way the threads of time and destiny wove together he had made predictions that had come to pass, and had foreseen many things happen that were unavoidable.

If this was the child that he was thinking of, then whatever happened would be what needed to be, and it was always possible that he had misread the tapestry of time. She was the only one who could write the story that would unfold; it was not for him to tell.

"What would you have me do, Lord?"

"She intends to stay in our country permanently, and Amaterasu-o-mi-Kami-sama is worried about one of the unbalanced among our number claiming her for a priestess and gaining power."

"What does the Shining One from the Heavens wish done, my Lord?"

"The Lady wishes to know what lies in the *Miko's* future, and how best that we may turn her to our wishes."

"My Lord, we can do nothing. We must watch to see, for this section of time is still being woven. One can not tell a story before learning it."

"I see. You may go then time teller."

Jikokusecchuuki bowed low before exiting the audience chamber of Tsubaki Jingu. Going out into the courtyard, he spied the energy of Ame-o-Uzume watching some of the shrine dancers, unseen from one of the porches.

Gone was the time when the greater *Kami* allowed themselves to be seen by their worshippers, hiding away in unexpected places, although some of the lesser *Kami* still lived among them. At the same time though, the *Kami* were gradually losing the energy that they needed. With the decreasing belief in their powers, many of the lesser *Kami* were dying out.

Walking unseen past the dancers and the scattered ones who came to the shrine to make their requests, the time teller went back to pondering something that had puzzled him for centuries now. Just where had the dragon that had eventually become his daughter's mate come from? Why had he been abandoned by his own Clan, and how was it that the hatchling had even found his way into the small clutch of new tree dragons that had contained his daughter Mayu?

As he continued his walk through the capital towards where his own residence was, he paused to glance at a clock in a shop window.

"For the first time in my life, I do not know what the future contains for many of us. Our Lord should have asked my little Mayu. It is she who serves as priestess to Time."

The molten rock surrounding him glowed with its own light, heated further by his impatience. Sulking at the bottom of his elemental self, the mobile consciousness coveted the freedom to explore once more. Yet, he also wanted rest.

For a while now a sad voice had woven through his unconscious mind, whispering his loneliness to himself. Although he was surrounded by many unbound spirits who sought shelter within Lady Fuji, he had very few that he could share his troubling dreams with.

"I wish I could talk to Ob, but he has so much to do that I don't see him often anymore. He and Mayu are always brewing some strange potion, or busy performing healing services for the various other *Kami*. My siblings, even of my own clutch, aren't any more help. Whether bonded or not, they could at least send word. Not once have they visited me these five years, it should be easy to slip past the guards."

The magma dragon stretched and continued muttering to himself, one half listening to the other half complain.

"I'm sick of being in trouble. I never asked for material existence, maybe I could have been happy with no other body than just this magma and this realm. I at least wouldn't be aware of this terrible boredom. Then again, it's not like I really had a choice, since father and mother had decided they wanted to brood over another clutch of eggs!"

The other half of his mind nodded in agreement, continuing the stretching and striving.

"Time to get some exercise Take."

"You're right Ryu. If I keep sitting down here pouting, I'll just get more bored."

"Exactly."

"I think I'll play some lava ball!"

Ryu gave up on sulking at the bottom, slithering and slinking upward through the viscous goo. It was going to make a mess for the servants to clean up, but at this time he didn't really care. He just wanted out.

"May Sarutahiko and Amaterasu provide me with a suitable challenge to dissipate some of this energy once I am released."

CHAPTER 7:
BOILING POINT

TEN hours after her flight had left behind the American soil, BlowingWind was rudely awoken from her fitful rest.

"Please fasten your seatbelts and return your seats and trays to their upright and locked positions. We are experiencing minor turbulence. Currently, we have just entered Japanese air space."

"Are we going to die? Can I panic now?"

Turning her head to her left where she fully expected her panic insurance to be, she was disappointed to find that Shawn was actually sleeping through the disturbance. Shaking the man vigorously did nothing to rouse him from his dreams of who only knew what, nor did her shouts in his ear do anything. As the hand luggage in the above racks slid around the compartments noisily, BlowingWind could only think of all of the movies that she had seen about plane crashes.

She began to wonder what kind of death would be preferable. Would it be the fiery death, burnt alive until oblivion claimed her mind, that was the kindest? Was the choicest death having her neck snapped by the impact into the sea? Would it be better to drown in the cold and salty Pacific instead? She certainly could not take the idea of dying of starvation in a life raft, or eating a decomposing corpse.

"Shawn?"

BlowingWind shook her travel companion again, hoping to rouse him. They had not reclined their seats when they fell asleep, and they had kept their seatbelts on. Still, he continued to sleep.

"And you're in the military. If I had a bugle, I'd be blaring revelry in your ear. I bet that would wake you up."

Still the young man continued to sleep, exhausted from the long shifts that he had been pulling before his transfer back to Japan.

"Perfect. Some travel insurance you are. Must you sleep now?"

It wasn't that she was afraid of flying. It was the crashing that bothered her. Flight was something that she had enjoyed once upon a time. Obsidian had taken her.

BlowingWind wished that he was there to hold her hand now, but he probably never would again. It was a hopeless dream she was pursuing. Still, her hand reached for the simple lake snail shell around her neck. Dismally, her thoughts of the happy past left her behind. The words that had given her the unexpected invitation onto the back of the wind rang through her head.

"Don't let go."

The shell bit into her hand, drawing her blood. The sting brought her back to herself. In his own way, perhaps Obsidian could still calm her, despite the fact that he was no more.

"I have to let go. I am not this weak."

That determined thought soothed her in an odd way, yet it also felt like she was dying just a little more inside and betraying something important.

"I don't want to move on though, not just yet. Am I falling into depression like that girl who shot herself in Fall River last year, after her boyfriend dumped her? Do I need mental help?"

BlowingWind rested her forehead on the cold glass separating her from the wild storm tossing her plane around. Gazing into the shifting clouds, she could almost fancy that it was trying to keep her from her destination and her new life. It was like a guardian or gatekeeper in her imagination, and unless it lost interest then surely it would send them all to their deaths.

"Yeah right, it's minor turbulence by my mirror and Father's pipe. I know I saw a gremlin out on that wing, I'm about to blow chunks, and find myself afraid to die. What would Obsidian and my ancestors think? Surely they would think me weak. No, when I die, it will be when I say."

The ride smoothed back out as the jet hit a stable patch. She was very thankful for the airsick bag that had been tucked into the pouch in front of her, and filled it with the roast beef that had been her in-flight meal. As she finished, the voice of the captain spilled out of the speakers.

"We are beginning our initial approach and descent to Tokyo International Airport. Thank you for maintaining your seats and trays in the upright position."

The relieved voice of the captain had been a welcome distraction for the shaman, and dropping below the cloud-line was a thrill. The city played peek-a-boo with her as the jet assumed a holding pattern while it waited for landing clearance, followed a half an hour later by a shy emergence as she approached the ground. The bump and bounce as the tires kissed the tarmac awoke Shawn from his sleep.

"Ah, home sweet home. I see you managed not to panic."

All BlowingWind could muster as a reply was a glare. After the initial wave of irritation, she managed to find a better reply that was more in keeping with her Irish heritage.

"Oh sure, we only hit a bad patch of turbulence about 250 miles or so ago, flew through a bad storm, and listened to the luggage do the Electric Slide in the overhead bins. If I had brought my guitar, I would have to replace every single string."

"Really? Why didn't you wake me up?"

"I tried. You sleep like a log. Has anybody ever blared revelry in your ear?"

Ob returned to the secret entrance cave into the sacred mountain, pausing here and there to gather herbs, berries, and roots for their medicinal or magical values. The ancient forest willingly yielded his secrets to the healer that was employed for the spirits and *Kami* dwelling within, and upon, the mountain. His trained eye had learned long ago where to find the answers to his needs, and Ob was glad that this area of the forest was still undeveloped by man. True, the occasional *Yamabushi* did manage to find it, but the *Tengu* that still called the mountain forest their home often managed to lead the old priests astray.

Still, the humans had encroached further into the forests with their bulldozers for housing developments. He had heard of spirits losing their clear streams for the humans to have houses or stores, or meadow masters finding themselves master over apartment buildings that eventually contained the guardian spirits for the indwelling families. Those spirits that could not assimilate into the new web of energy either died, or had to wander until they found a new home.

Ob paused in the lovely clearing, looking around at the pristine wilderness.

His eyes fell on the small trickle spring feeding the stream that danced away down the mountainside. The two spirits must have worked out their problem, for they had released their semi-corporeal forms, once more becoming the amorphous indwelling presences of bonded *Kami* living within the natural features.

"How many people understand the intricacies of this place any more?"

He shook off the gloom that threatened to engulf him each time that he worried about the preservation of the area where he found the bulk of his medicines. It did no good to dwell on it though, as death was also natural. Even the greatest *Kami* would one day fall under the power of the ultimate transformation, making way for something new, just as Izanami-no-Mikoto had.

Ob entered the cave, descending from twilight into inky blackness darker than a stormy midnight. The floor of the ancient lava tube frowned up at him forbiddingly, just as it had for thousands of years for not only his predecessor, but many others who made the medical and healing division what it was.

After 300 yards of midnight pitch, a red lantern was revealed, glowing serenely forth for the workers of the mountain's innards. Ten yards later, another red silk lantern magically lit the eternal night. In the shadows beneath, Ob heard the guardians shift their nebulous presences in acknowledgment of his passing. Eight red lanterns total he passed by and then eight yellow. Here, the guards were less shadowy, and more formed, as the forbidding passage before had kept intruders out for centuries. Finally, brash torches blazed from the walls, and fully formed guardians greeted the Head Healer.

"Welcome home Lord Healer. Has your mission been a success?"

"Yes guard. I do believe that it has been so."

"That is wonderful, my Lord. I am sure that you will work many miracles on behalf of our masters." He bowed.

Ob moved on, many similar exchanges happening between him and the respectful guards. Finally, the orange glow and rampant heat of his master reached out to warm him. Ob felt a flutter of excitement when basking in the safe and familiar energy.

"He is quite active today. I wonder what's wrong now."

Running through the last few yards to the central chamber of the division, Ob saw fireballs streaking up from the pit. Now it was clear why the energy had been roiling.

"Just peachy. What a way to have an excuse for a visit. How old is he now?"

Ryu had snapped and was going to make everyone else just as miserable as he had been for the last five long human years. The fully-grown dragon was throwing himself a nice juvenile temper tantrum, complete with magma balls.

Dodging a deadly glob of lava that had been hurled by the laughing maniac dancing on the tongue surface, Ob dug out a reed pipe from the pouch tucked into his obi belt. Weaving to the edge of the crevasse, he had only one thought as he prepared to fire.

"I really need a raise."

At the edge, Ob grinned. Ryu had assumed his human guise in an outrageous act of defiance. Whirling on the surface, Ryu was scooping up handfuls of the molten rock and flinging it as far as he could. The great lord looked like a complete lunatic, and it wasn't long before he bent over and presented Ob with an irresistible target while scooping up more ammunition.

Raising the reed to his lips, Ob blew.

"Ow! Now there are wasps down here harassing me?"

Ob smirked at his handiwork, admiring the black feathered dart sticking out of the magma lord's posterior. He waited for the medicine to take effect, having used it on Ryu enough to know just when it would take effect.

"Three, two, one, and down he goes."

Ryu knelt down, staring at his elemental surface while holding his head. Suddenly, he was feeling quite relaxed, if more than a little dizzy.

"Can I come down now, or are you going to continue making a mess for me to get blamed for?"

"Ob, what are you doing up there? *Otou-sama* said I was not to have any visitors."

"Oh, it is just a routine intervention, your Father won't mind. Sometimes, my job can get me into interesting places. Are you hungry?"

Ryu's eyes widened as he pulled out the small but powerful dart. "This makes ten. If I didn't know better, Ob, I would say that this was your favorite method of delivery. I'm starving. Just what do you put in these things anyway?"

Carefully schooling his voice to be more remeniscent of a sage than an amused youngster, he replied. "It's an ancient Japanese Healer's trade secret Ryu-sama. Catch!"

Ob pulled out the special *onigiri*, tossing the precious package down to the confused dragon-man. Eagerly Ryu unwrapped the black package, and then scowled down at the pearl of rice grains.

"Kind of a meager offering, isn't it?"

"Oh, don't worry. It will fill you up more than you would imagine."

Carefully sniffing the ball, he spoke.

"I'm not biting. You put more medicine in it, didn't you?"

"What's wrong sire, don't you trust me?"

"No. A doctor who shoots his patients with unknown drugs I do not trust. I especially don't trust this little medicine filled *onigiri* since I know how bad you are at cooking, and with how many pranks that you have pulled on me since our youth."

Ob couldn't help the cheeky grin. He was on thin ice and he knew it, but he had also inherited a small love of trouble.

"Come on Ryu-sama, my cooking doesn't destroy the kitchen anymore, just the pots."

Doubtful, Ryu took a small bite, followed by another. Thoughtfully, he nibbled on the ball, trying to place the exotic flavor. Eventually, the mouthful was gone, and the flavor was finally identified. It was not one that he was overly fond of, as he was not a fan of spices, and yet it held a certain attraction. Confused, he muttered to himself.

"You're still a bad cook. Why would rice taste like cinnamon?"

Ob smiled as he watched the *Kami* devour the rest of the rice ball.

"I have no idea Ryu-sama."

CHAPTER 8:
CUSTOMS

"**W**E have landed at Tokyo International Airport. Thank you for choosing Japan Airlines for your international travel needs. Please to remain seated until we have taxied to a full and complete stop." The stewardess repeated herself in Japanese as well, but it went unnoticed to the ears of one young woman who was eagerly peering out the window.

A few minutes later, the 747 had stopped, and the ramp-way had been extended out to the door. A bit later, the lights for the seatbelt were turned out, and after retrieving her bag from the overhead bin she gratefully poured herself out of the plane.

"Land! Sweet land! I love you ground!"

Shawn couldn't help but laugh. By looking at her, one would think that perhaps she had just emerged from a minor car wreck, with her hair standing on end and a desperate gleam in her eyes. Either that, or that the woman was just plain crazy.

"Technically, BlowingWind, we are still on the ramp-way. Then we will be in the terminal. You can't spout that cheesy line until you are actually on land."

The ramp was soon left behind, and BlowingWind found herself passing through customs once again. She had gone through the U.S. customs on her way out of her country, but she had not really paid much attention to all of the X-rays and security checks as they had been focused on preventing the export of illegal substances. Now that she was going through the incoming customs checks of another country, things were rather different. It was more than a little odd having people looking through her few belongings and checking her papers to make certain that she was who she was claiming to be.

The smiling Japanese woman looked through her papers, then

looked again more carefully. The smile turned into a slight frown of concentration, and then an expression of worry.

"MountainChild-san, I am afraid that you will have to come with me for an examination."

"Is there a problem ma'am?"

"I am sorry, but I can not seem to find your statement for reason of entry."

"I came here for schooling. I was planning to see the country while waiting for the next school year to start and use that time to learn Japanese enough to facilitate my schooling."

"I can not find any proof of your acceptance to any of our fine universities. Not to worry though, this happens all of the time. We will just go and see my supervisor, and he will put in a call to your university to confirm your acceptance and reason of entry."

"Oh, okay then."

Shawn had noticed BlowingWind's problem. He was ready to move on, and his escort was probably waiting rather anxiously for him. No doubt his father-in-law was the one waiting. It was always his lovely Haruko's father who picked him up from the airport when coming home.

Customs could take a long time for those with missing paper work. Who knew exactly how long it would be before she was released?

"BlowingWind, here."

He pulled his notebook and black ballpoint out of his back pocket, quickly jotting down his contact information. Ripping out the tiny leaflet, he pushed it into her hand.

"Give me a jingle when you get done if I'm not here. You have to meet Haruko, so you are staying with us. You can pay rent if you want, before you start protesting. She'll help you get acculturated and find a place to stay until the school year starts up again."

BlowingWind looked at her friend, truly grateful for the help that he had given. With any luck, she would get to stay in the country. There was so much she wanted to see. She wanted to visit each shrine, to experience the tea ceremony, and to get past her soul-weakening attachment to her past.

"Thanks, I will."

Shawn smiled, and then picked up his bag one more time. He was finished with customs, and it was time for him to go and collect the rest of his luggage where his gifts were safely stowed. It was time to go, and he was sure that she would be fine.

As he walked down the corridor with the other passengers, BlowingWind wondered when or if she would ever see him again.

"This way Miss, please."

BlowingWind followed the aging customs official through a door emblazoned with strange red characters, noting the strands of silver that flashed now and again in the otherwise umber brown hair of the woman in front. The official's black uniform set her apart from the other airport workers that she had seen so far, and the American could only assume it really was to set the different groups apart.

The further down the corridors she was led, the more ominous and imposing the vibrations were to her. Out where the main groups of the travelers were screened the atmosphere had been cheery, the white walls relieved by stripes of color, and the halls had bustled with activity. Here, through the door that had no doubt been marked for "authorized use only," the hallways were stark and white, lifeless as any morgue. Even though the air circulated freely the walls gave no impression of space. The smallness of her current location reminded her yet again of her fear of enclosures.

At the end of one hallway, another door stood before her. The official knocked three times on the door, and a voice issued from within.

"Enter."

The door was opened, and BlowingWind was ushered inside to where the supervisor was waiting at his desk. While Shawn had hurriedly given her his contact information, the official had made a quick call to alert the man of her situation.

"So, this is the student who forgot her acceptance papers. Have a seat please."

Although his order had been disguised as a request, there was no room for argument. His dark eyes were like twin holes of oblivion threatening to swallow her very being.

"Papers please."

BlowingWind handed in her passport and other documentation, bravely trying to hide the fact that this particular person had turned her insides to Jell-O. The dark business suit that he wore made her think of FBI agents from some political film, or perhaps some gangster. No, he was even worse than that really, more like the creepy American Government teacher she had way back in her freshman year of high school. As he looked at her immunization records, it appeared that he was disappointed.

"Well, it seems that your immunizations are all in order MountainChild-san, as you are not required to have any for entry. However, you have no paper of permission to land and no Visa. The proper procedure would have been to obtain these things before boarding your plane. Which university have you supposedly been accepted into?"

"Hokkaido University, sir. I was planning to attend the Fukuhaku campus."

"A forgetful American will be attending one of our universities, really! With all of the competition between our students, I do not see why they would allow a backward American, who probably can barely speak enough Japanese to survive in a restaurant, to take a spot from one of our more deserving students. Never-the-less, I will call and confirm your status." His tone was stern as a father's, then gentled when directed to her guide. "Yura, please watch our guest while I confirm."

"Yes supervisor."

BlowingWind had not formally accepted the spot yet, and had not brought her letter of acceptance with her. It had been filed with all of the other acceptance letters she had received that year, safe in a folder in her mother's filing cabinet. All she could do now was to pray that she would be allowed to stay in the country. With every fiber of her being, BlowingWind released her wish, and awaited her fate.

Red and white hairs hung limply disheveled around a thin, and aristocratically, haggard face that had recently gained a few more worry wrinkles etched into the glacial mask of sorrow. Frozen lakes gazed sadly at a picture reverently held in one pale and thin hand, while the other hand mechanically lifted a mug of steaming coffee to sorrowing lips. Woodenly, Marie gulped the scalding liquid, not even noticing the pain.

So many years ago, the smiling young man in the photo had been cruelly wrested away by a curse that she had never really believed in, as imaginary a thing as the little green dragon that she had once believed in. Now, the little girl in his arms had been dealt the same hand if the ever-truthful Summerrose could be believed. The child had called on her lunch break earlier in the day to tell about seeing BlowingWind.

Marie wished that she could go back and change the past, perhaps to stop whatever accident had befallen the gentle boy who had been her daughter's dearest friend, or to prevent the pair from having fallen in love. Such wishes were in vain though. She was no time traveler, and certainly no witch or priestess of the Old Ways, as had been the women of her clan for generations into the mists of the past. That had fallen to her elder sister.

Marie could remember the many further years ago when she too had fled from her home, and her own mother. Mother had insisted that she be married to the young man that she approved of. It was a tradition in her extensive family, that all marriages were arranged by the mother, who would be better able to choose matches for her children based on the head, and the future, rather than the heart. It did no good to marry for love when it could not be guaranteed how long the first husband would live. It had to be assured that any children would be well cared for, so that they in turn could tend Brigit's Well.

According to the local legends that supposedly had been handed down since even before Saint Patrick had landed on the shores of Ireland, the old stone well at the top of Draganpáirc was where the triple goddess known as Brigit made her home. At one time, her forge had been nearby, but she supposedly took it back down the well after her beloved children were systematically stamped out. Only a few had survived, and hidden under the guise of Catholicism they had sought sanctuary, eventually breeding up to an entire community. Mother had been the Keeper of the Well, and had told stories about encounters with Her, the Gentry, and the Dragons who still called the area home.

Marie had never encountered the Goddess, or any of the Wee Folk, and had seen no evidence of dragons, to her memory. She had thought her entire family crazy. Not seeing any point in retaining a silly superstition and not wishing to be tied for life to a man that she felt nothing for, she fled the country the day before her wedding. Marie wanted to marry for love, and had argued many a time with her mother about it. As a consequence after running away, she had not seen her Mother, sister, or half-brother since. Was the separation and alienation among family members also part of her curse?

Marie had not believed in curses, fairies, or magic until the day that a lake dragon had nearly bewitched her daughter. That day when she saw the dragon she no longer thought of her own family as crazy. The headache that had washed over her had been immense, and to this day she could not shake the sense of something shifting and stirring, partially unlocking within her mind. That very night by the campfire eleven years ago she told the old legend, warning of the dangers of dragons.

"Soaring Hawk, where did I go wrong? What would you do, and where would she go? Please God, watch over my baby."

The temperature in the room dropped suddenly, and the wind picked up sharply outside, howling around the house. She could almost hear a voice in the wind, it always seemed to sound like a person to her. It even managed to penetrate inside, swirling around the slim figure to further place her appearance in disarray. For a moment, Marie imagined that she could feel her dead husband's presence around her.

"Odd, I thought I managed to fix all of the drafts."

She was filled with an urge to look through her daughter's college acceptances. Walking to where she kept the filing cabinet, she remembered how proud she had been when they had all come in, excited that her daughter was eligible for so many fine schools. BlowingWind was very intelligent and much better at math than she gave herself credit for. Most of the colleges had wanted her for their snowboarding teams though, not for her academics. In fact, all of her offered scholarships had been for snowboarding. Ultimately, her baby girl had decided to attend Southern Oregon University for its scholastic and athletic programs as well as its commutability.

Her footfalls echoed dully through the house. The door creaked. Outside, only the normal sounds of the woods broke the silence. The house itself listened and breathed.

BlowingWind had said that she wanted to be close to her, but Marie knew better. The handsome Obsidian had more to do with her decision to stay local than the girl would admit.

Marie opened up the black cabinet, carefully bringing out the folder where she had kept each letter. After a moment of reading through them, the wind died back down, leaving her alone once more while she lingered at looking over the space the letter that had pleased her the most should have been. She put the folder back with a sigh. It had excited her daughter also, as it was one that she had not even thought of applying for. Her school's guidance counselor had filed on her behalf, acting on BlowingWind's interest in the foreign exchange program.

"I wonder why she threw away Hokkaido University's letter?"

Marie did not see the hawk breast feather that fell behind the filing cabinet. Instead, she went to the window to be certain that her novena for her daughter's safety was still lit. She was not Catholic, nor did she follow any form of Goddess religion, as a non-practicing Protestant, but in times of stress she did fall back on old habits ingrained as a child. Her mother had often prayed to Mary, and to Bridget, and seemed to have been a devout Catholic. Marie had preferred not to deal with intermediaries during that short time when she truly had believed, and had gone to a Protestant Church. Things were changing though. In the morning she would pay another visit to Saint Michael's, but first she had to get through the night. No doubt she would only be able to sleep curled up in her daughter's bed, surrounded by abandoned treasures.

In the windowsill burned a tall candle in clear glass, and behind this were pictures of Saint Bridget and Lady Mary. A Celtic cross had been crudely painted on the windowpane in red paint. Arranged before all of these monuments to her spiritual past were several mementos of her only child, odds and ends such as her baby teeth and a small bit of hair from her first hair cut. Kneeling in front of this altar, Marie began to pray.

"In the name of the Father, Son, and Holy Ghost I pray that my daughter be kept safe from all harm and bewitchment. Mother Mary, I ask you to help me bear my loss with grace and to teach me the fortitude to have faith until she returns to me. Saint Bridget, who was once known as the goddess Brigit, I ask you to also lend your aid to my baby as one of your own."

After her heartfelt prayer to all of the powers that she knew of, Marie retired to finally attempt some sleep.

BlowingWind could feel her heart pounding the entire time she had been waiting for the supervisor to be connected via phone to the University. It seemed that everyone in the admissions department was out on lunch or that they were all busy. Yura had also seated herself, obeying her superior's hand motions. BlowingWind was beginning to give up on her dream, when a gust from the ventilation system sent all of her paperwork flying all over the formerly pristine office. She and Yura scrambled to collect everything and arrange it on the desk once more, beneath his disapproving glare.

Between the two women, everything was put back on the desk quickly, including an extra paper that they had not seen when it had fluttered down through the air system when the mysterious breeze had happened.

"Perfect, I will have to have a word with maintenance about the faulty air conditioning after this phone call."

BlowingWind could not believe how full of himself this supervisor was. All of her experience with Japanese people back home had painted them as polite and considerate to a fault, but this guy was making even the crabby old janitor at her old high school look like Miss Manners in comparison. If only there was some way to knock him back down to size. However, Father had tried to teach her that violence solved nothing. If he were here, what would he have done?

He certainly would have done his research before running off to another country. It was an understatement that she was in deep trouble.

At that moment, she paused in her self-punishment after catching sight of something much unexpected. Lying there on the desk in front of her, as innocuously as if it had been there the whole time, was her college acceptance paperwork, and one hawk breast feather on top of the sheaf. Picking it up, she looked incredulously at the very thing that she absolutely knew she had left at home, puzzling over how it could have gotten here when two customs officials said it had not been. By the presence of the feather, she knew that at least one spirit had followed her from home. She just hoped that Coyote had not decided to tag along for the ride.

"Sir, I found my acceptance letter."

She handed the irate man her papers, keeping the feather to herself. After glancing at the papers he placed the black handset on its cradle once more, grumbling about how Americans were always misfiling things and wasting his time.

"You have ninety days to file for and receive a student residency visa. You will also need to file for a visa to obtain and hold a job if you intend to work. If I were not required to let you in for ninety days based on your stated objective of sightseeing then I would send you back to America on the next flight. Consider yourself lucky; now get out of my sight. Yura, escort her back."

"Yes supervisor."

Yura led the young American back to the traveler's area silently. She had apparently overlooked the acceptance letter, and would be receiving a stern reprimand if not actually loosing her job. What was worse, she had lost face in front of her department head.

"So, is that guy always like that?"

The American looked sympathetic through Yura's eyes. She was too young to have been in such a precarious predicament before, but something about her earnestness kept Yura from feeling resentment.

"Yes, but it is my fault for being unobservant. Please forgive me for detaining you in your journey."

"Hey, we all goof up from time to time. It's a good thing you did though, since I didn't know I needed any visas to go to school. And confidentially, I hadn't seen the letter either. Sorry for getting you in trouble."

"Arigato gozimasu."

The women were at the door to the main hallway again, sharing a last look at each other. Nodding, they went through and parted ways. BlowingWind felt an insistent pull leading her onward, and this chafing was driving her further into insanity than she was willing to admit.

Wisdom had been wandering all over Tokyo, chasing down little bits of herself that had been flung about due to the stress she was under. She had already found her physical body at the airport, but watching her own thoughts from BlowingWind and RagingTornado, it seemed that they needed a little time to grow. It had been very irresponsible to move to another country without getting the proper permissions. Perhaps, if she led them on a little chase, then they could all learn to work together.

Having gathered up the bits of herself that her other parts had shed in their nervousness, Wisdom continued on her own mission. She would leave each soul piece in various shrines, temples and churches throughout the islands of Japan. There on holy ground they would be safe until her more dominant aspects either found them once more or learned to sing them home.

Ob shook his head as he navigated the upward flowing passages towards the main vent, to where Fujiyama's office was. As much as he enjoyed hitting a high ranking magma spirit in the haunches with a blow dart, he hated having to report the injection just as much. It was hard to know who hated it more though. Ryu for receiving it, Ob for having to sedate the dragon, or Fujiyama for not having exposed Ryu to a female dragon or even a phoenix strong enough to balance out his yang essence with soothing yin essence.

The hallways outside of the office were studded with globules of obsidian and rough diamonds that had been forced up the ancient volcano's throat by the roiling forces of Earth's beating heart, refracting the light upward from the magma in the central pool far below.

Ob knocked on the door, and the *shoji* slid open quietly to admit the healer dragon. Here in this room the walls were all smoothed obsidian of the deepest black serving as magical monitors for the surveillance of all the processes of the mountain below the skin that the humans saw. Along one wall were rows upon rows of tall black metal filing cabinets that contained the records of offerings that the mountain Gods had received even before he had taken this post. In the center of the room was an array of crystals that fed information into the crystalline matrix of the planetary brain. On another wall was a writhing red and gold tapestry that listed every member of his clan and their relation within it, and nearby this sat a teak desk where an exhausted and worried Fujiyama morosely scried in the mirror of his cold tea.

"He sleeps now Lord Fujiyama."

"Thank you Ob. He is getting harder to control. I am afraid that if we do not find some way to balance him soon, that he will become darkened. He has far too much energy and not enough outlets for it, and you have already seen how little care he has for his own domain at times when in the grip of such excess."

With a wave of his hand, Fujiyama summoned a kneeling cushion for the healer spirit. It was a bothersome thing, and he had already had to prune out troublesome tongues too eager to extend their elemental manifestations to their aboveground territories in the dance of re-creation. Each time he had needed to kill a son or daughter for endangering the plans of Nature he had sprouted at least one gray hair while making those hard decisions. Ryu was his favorite son, and it was heartbreaking realizing that unless things changed he would either have to seal him away or destroy his body.

"Where did I go wrong?"

"You haven't Lord. Ryu is just more Yang than many dragons have been for a long time. The blood of Lord Susanowo flows richly through his veins, just as it does in your own. It is no small wonder that Susanowo-sama's outrageousness is as glaringly evident in one, out of as many broods as you have had. I gave him something new in addition to his usual sedative. I believe that it should be an exceptionally calming influence for him."

"That is good news. Your *sensei* has trained you well."

"*Domo arigato gozimasu.*"

Nodding to dismiss the healer to his normal duties, Fujiyama felt less trepidation as he logged the footage of Ryu's bout of insanity. The great *Kami* that he was directly accountable to, Fuji-sama, Konohanasakura-hime, and Sarutahiko, would not be overly sympathetic. Neither would the other four members of the Great Council of Asian Dragons, that he was a part of, be pleased if he were to lose yet another heir to his important and yet highly unenviable job.

"Ryu, I hope that someday you will understand."

Now that the incident was logged, Fujiyama was free to visit his son. Perhaps having someone to talk to when the boy awoke would prove helpful.

CHAPTER 9:
HOME BASE

BLOWINGWIND found herself overwhelmed yet again as she made her way to the exit. Thankfully, the way out was fairly straightforward. As long as she remembered to follow what the signs on the wall indicated, instead of following the thronging hordes, she was pretty sure she would eventually find her way out.

"Note to self: learn to read Japanese, at least *katakana* if not *kanji*."

Luck seemed to be with BlowingWind today. It was a fairly simple task to win her way through the thronging hordes to baggage claim. If the movies of airport meetings she had seen had been right, then the way out would be close by.

"Awesome! I can see the light. I really hope there are less people out there, or at least some more space between them. I feel like I ran after a train."

BlowingWind slowly made her way down the stairs leading off of the fairway. Her first order of business would be to find a place to stay. In good conscience she could not crash at Shawn's home uninvited. No, she needed a place of her own, a home base of sorts for her operations. Besides, his wife probably wouldn't approve of a strange woman just showing up out of thin air. Marital problems were not what she would consider a proper repayment of such kindness. Similar thoughts rushed the citadel of her mind as she grumbled to herself.

"What am I going to do? I'm such an idiot for coming all the way here without a game plan. Even Angelina, or Willow, or whatever that Big Valley girl calls herself in her mundane life had a plan of attack for when she left home for Southern Oregon University."

While BlowingWind was kicking herself some more for the mess she had jumped headlong into, a semi-familiar call carried over the heads of racing salary-men and gawking tourists.

"Hey! Over here! I'm surprised they let you go so quickly. Customs can be harsh."

Figuring that the shouts hadn't been meant for her, she continued on her way towards the door. She would just have to hail a cab and get to the nearest hotel for now. Once there, she could take a nap, peruse the phone book, find a realtor, and maybe even get some takeout.

"BlowingWind! Just where do you think you are going? You'll be eaten alive out there."

A hand reached out of the crowd and grabbed her elbow, whirling her to the right. How she had missed someone close enough to touch her she had no idea.

"Let go of me! Rape!"

Lashing out with her left hand, she used her right hand to free herself from her captor. Looking outward, the face of her attacker registered a half-second after her fist had slammed into his face. Both parties felt the sting of crushed nerves between opposing bones, and while BlowingWind cradled an abused appendage Shawn edged away as well as he could while nursing a blackening eye.

"Oh my God! Shawn, I'm sorry. You scared me."

"You're vicious! There is definitely Celtic blood in you. Maybe I should be protecting Tokyo from you instead of the other way around."

"I said I was sorry Shawn."

"Shawn, you should never grab a lady, and certainly you would have learned to never let your guard down."

The old voice that had broken into their conversation underscored its point when the owner's cane came down on the young man's head. BlowingWind's eyes followed the weapon to find a deeply lined and craggy face glaring down on Shawn. The light brown eyes were fierce as twin hawks, betraying ancient life knowledge hard won by experiencing life in the best and the worst of times. Clad simply in a pressed black dress shirt and slacks he was a somber representative of all elders, his silver hair cut in a business-like manner, although no indication as to his occupation could be seen.

"Please forgive the boy, he gets overexcited. Shawn tells me that you need a place to stay until you get your feet under you child. You seem to be more stable than others that he has flown with, but perhaps that is only because you are a civilian and war tends to do strange things to soldiers. Do you have any more luggage than that, my child?"

BlowingWind was reminded of her paternal grandfather by this man's straightforward manner. It had been long since she had seen WolfPaw, and the word from RedFeather had been that he had taken to the Star Path only a few months ago. She felt a longing to go back to the Reservation again, to immerse herself in the culture she had known at her birth. Yet here she was, in a land very distant from any that she had previously known. Would her ceremonies still work here, or would she need to learn new ones? Why would her training bring her here?

"Of course I forgive him, I just wasn't expecting anyone to grab me. No, this is all of the luggage that I have."

"Well then children, let us leave."

BlowingWind followed Shawn and the old man out into the drizzling rain. Her leathers were well oiled, but she was still a little worried about how much water they would soak up. It was possible that they would need another oiling before she began her exploration of the country.

An old gold Toyota Tercel waited out in the parking lot amongst many other Japanese cars. She was squeezed into the back with Shawn's bags, feeling rather like a sardine freshly pulled from the sea and dumped into the hold of some ship with tons of other stuff. The old man, who had not introduced himself, darted through Tokyo's early morning traffic, stopping at traffic lights and merging so close to other cars that BlowingWind was certain she would wind up in the Emergency Room.

Having little else to do than to pray to anybody listening that they would not wind up as splatters on the pavement, she watched out the window as they rolled by stores, business buildings, street vendors, and other such common city sights. At one light, she watched a business woman buying a bowl of noodles for her breakfast; at another light she saw a group of sailor suited girls on their way to school. Jet lag was truly a terrible thing, as she was exhausted and the day here was barely begun.

"You children look exhausted. Haruko will have breakfast ready when we get home, and then it is into bed with both of you."

"Ji-san, I've had my four hours of sleep on the plane and was looking forward to helping around the house. I am sure BlowingWind could use some rest though."

The American pulled her eyes away from puzzling out the heartbeat of the city, looking up and into the rear-view mirror at the wise and dark eyes of the old Asian driving the car.

"If you please sir, I have much that I need to do today. I have to apply for a student and a work visa, contact my University, get set up for language schooling, and start exploring."

The old man began to laugh, pulling over to the curb and handing his son-in-law some money. Shawn pulled a list out of his pocket, grinning himself as he ran into the store to pick up some needed items. The old man looked back at the young woman while he waited, giving her some important advice.

"Young One, the first step may begin the journey and the last may end it, but it is those in between that make the journey what it is. Experience each step before you take the next."

"I don't understand sir. Isn't that what I am doing now?"

"How can you see if you are running in a fog?"

"I am?"

"Are you? You are the one who said it."

The old man was right. She was in a fog, and completely lost to boot without a light to guide her home. She didn't know where to apply for her visas, only had ninety days to get them, and the school year didn't start in Japan until April. Her vision quest had only told her to come to Japan. The quest was done now, or at least so she thought, so what came next? What were the steps of the correct path, and why did a new quest start at the end of the previous one?

"My whole life I have been lost in fog, searching for answers and the way home."

"Then walk."

Those two words were oddly troubling, as if she had been running her whole life and still not leaving the same spot. It had all passed her by so fast when she looked back, and as she thought about it she realized she had always been pursuing something just out of sight. Perhaps she had been running after the phantom of Coyote then, but how did one learn to walk on the path of life instead?

"Thank you for your wisdom, sir. How do I repay you?"

"You call me Ji-san or Grandfather, instead of sir. I am no officer after all. You also let us help you begin your new life, and you help Haruko catch up on her chores before you leave town."

"With all due respect Grandfather, you don't even know me. Why are you willing to offer so much help?"

"Why shouldn't I? It is something that the Buddha would do."

At that moment, Shawn got back into the car, carrying two small bags of groceries.

"I've got it all Ji-san, including Haruko's green tea ice cream. Let's go home."

Ji-san pulled back out into the traffic, following the paths of artificial stone that lead out of the teeming city and out into the relatively quieter suburbs that stretched wistful arms ever closer to the most sacred place in all of Japan.

Black braids adorned with the breast feathers of a hawk framed the thin and sun tanned face that gazed out upon the material world he was no longer part of with gold-brown eyes. Clad in leather boots and blue denim jeans that had wandered countless miles of desert, his red bandana and blue ribbon shirt were the only new things that he had worn on the last day of his physical life. It was easiest for him to materialize the clothes that his thirty something body had been buried in, and so that is what he wore when taking his insubstantial, and usually invisible human form. Watching his daughter's progress in her testing and training, from his usual unseen location above and behind the young woman, SoaringHawk contemplated how he found himself so far away from the familiar energies of Turtle Island.

His murder had caused him to leave his mortal flesh at the moment of his death. Ultimately the nuclear power plant that he had given his life to defend his people against had been built, and it seemed that his sacrifice had been in vain. His restless spirit had become one with the air as his body was broken down by decay into its basic elements. His breath had flown all over the world mingled with the wind of Hawk's wing. The fire of his youth was passed on for his next seven generations to draw their own passions from. His body had become one with Mother Earth once more, and the waters of his body had been evaporated into the air to rejoin with the water cycle thanks to the work of the crematorium's transforming oven.

Only one part of him remained tied to the world of mortals, tethered by bonds of love, and regret. Like the ghosts of the other men of his wife's Clan he would find no rest until his wife and child were at peace. For all he knew, he would be restless for eternity, as the curse could well continue that long, with the luck that seemed to befall those of Maeve and Marie's blood.

SoaringHawk was proud of his baby girl, although he felt so guilty for not being able to provide physical comfort as a good father should. Although he had been able to lend a comforting presence from time to time, and to hide the car keys at critical times when Marie had been too distraught to drive the family car safely, neither had been able to see him. BlowingWind had felt him, but she had not developed the gift to see those who lived on in the realms of the dead. BlowingWind had grown into a fine and proud beauty nearly on her own, intelligent and yet as stubborn as anyone could imagine. It was his thought that she took after the women of her mother's family, as those of his family were much more temperate. SoaringHawk had watched with pride as she followed in his footsteps though, her search for meaning surely making their Spirit Animal Ancestors

Snake, Hawk and Coyote proud as well.

With a father's indulgence he had watched when she was befriended by Obsidian. BlowingWind had been a very lonely girl after he had been cast out of his body, and it was good to see someone taking such an active role in her life and leading her on her life's path. The Lake spirit had become her Spirit Guide and Protector, lending her his strength and protection as she grew. Coyote still got her into trouble, and so Obsidian's protective influence had come in handy when BlowingWind had played a small part in Willow's adventures in the spiritual world. His pride and indulgence had turned to concern as His daughter and the lake spirit fell in love though, but their ill-fated courtship had not raised his ire.

Obsidian had been a good boy, as young non-human spirits went, but it was a father's tendency to be a bit over-protective. To Obsidian's credit, he had never made an inappropriate advance. On the other hand though, perhaps it had been the thought of a dead man watching him as closely as a Hawk that had kept him in line. BlowingWind may not have discovered the ability to see her Ancestors yet, but Obsidian had seen their self-appointed chaperone quite clearly.

Gazing at the white cone of Fujisan from his perch on the roof of the Tercel, SoaringHawk admired the godly presence looming over the island of Honshu that was so similar to the commanding presence of Mount Shasta. It was a serene vision, but like the other volcanoes of the Pacific Ring of Fire and even throughout the world, it too was awash with activity unseen to the normal mortal eye. Not even the volcanologists of the world were privy to the hidden activities of the spirits who either embodied the processes of the earth or who were responsible for them. He had been a guest beneath Mount Shasta, and had invaded Fujisan when following the string that Life had been drawing from his daughter. Somewhere beneath that spire of rock and snow was a dragon that hopefully had the courage and fortitude to tame his daughter somewhat.

The spirit was lost in his pensive thoughts for quite a while, enjoying the wind produced by the speed of the car. SoaringHawk had been working hard in the past several days with aiding the Tribal Elders in the search and call for a strong enough spirit to withstand BlowingWind's fierce temper. As if that had not been enough, he needed to be certain that she connected with the right people. Who knew what would have happened if someone had picked her up with dire motives instead of one of the Hawk People? Truly it was something he would rather not think about, and he was thankful to Hawk for having sent Freedom on a little side trip on his own trek

The car pulled off the road again, parking in an ordinary garage beneath a house so similar to others on the street. The green two-story home had a few stairs leading up to a porch enshrining the red front door. The simple porch was adorned with bamboo wind chimes tinkling and dancing in the breeze fanning away the last of the rain shower, and a Japanese and American flag flanked either side of the porch in the same manner repeated by most of the other houses on the street. Diagonal to the door on the lawn, a golden frog faced the home, sending the occupants prosperity. Although each house had overt nods to the country they were in, it was easy to see that this was off-base housing for the American military personnel and their families.

BlowingWind stepped out of the car, her knapsack nervously slung onto her back. He smiled as she grabbed several bags and helped to bring in everything, already beginning to assimilate into what he hoped would become like a family of sorts for her.

"Ji-san please let me carry that for you."

The old man nodded as he turned over the bag of groceries. With two free hands now, Ji-san led the way up the steps and opened the door for the young ones bringing the things in. During all of the shifting in and out, an even older man stepped out unseen to float up to the roof. Long, snow-white hair was lifted up into an ancient topknot, and a carefully combed beard came down to his knees. A white robe clad the elder, stirring in the breeze while the man motioned SoaringHawk to join him. Flowing with the breeze, SoaringHawk joined the other departed human.

"The child is yours Young One?"

"Yes sir, she is my daughter."

"It is far from home that you are, Traveler."

"Yes sir, and long will it be still in my sojourn before my daughter will find a new home."

The ancestor *Kami* frowned, sympathizing with the young father spirit and discarding the formal mode of address. He himself had been an ancestral guardian for centuries now, and his house had been blessed by staying somewhat close to where they had lived for generations beyond counting now. His family had never been high in the governmental hierarchy as they had been mere rice farmers, but it had been enough for them. It surely would be hard to start all over again and even harder for those who were as obviously far from home as these two souls. It was also tiring for Ancestors to follow the living from the Ancestral Grounds, and until the girl wed and was assimilated into a family it would be difficult for following Ancestors to find a place to rest and gain strength.

"The house of Takamura has taken in wanderers before. We will provide shelter for now, and we guardians will entreat Nushiwatarimono-Kamisama, the guardian of wanderers, to assist in the re-establishment of your own house Young One."

"The Mountain Children and Snake Clan of Turtle Island thank you and your Clan for your generous hospitality."

"You are of the Take, the Mountains? Your child must go and pray at the Sengen Shrines then. The *Take-Kami* there will ultimately be responsible for settling you and yours. We are only of the field, but we will do what we can for you."

"I thank you again Mr. Takamura."

"Come now; join me and my people in the *Kamidana* while the living attend to their own matters. Eat of the sacred rice with us and partake of the sake while we rest and wait for our children to have need of us."

The Takamura elder ghosted inside, riding the wind as be became an ethereal orb, unseen to the living humans. SoaringHawk followed, merging with the wind until he was naught but an invisible hawk, alighting eventually upon the spirit shelf. BlowingWind, who had been bringing in the last bag, paused in the doorway for a moment. On the shelf diagonal to the front door, she swore she had seen something pass in front of the small round mirror.

Shawn had gone into the back after putting away his last bag of gifts. He was looking for his beloved Haruko, looking forward to seeing her again after six months of separation. The letters that had been flying back and forth between the pair during his absence had told about how the office was letting her work at home until shortly before her delivery. The wonders of telecommuting were a godsend for them, as Haruko was one of those strong-willed women who felt a deep need to help put food on the table, a necessity now that her father was retired and an assistant at the local shrine. Thanks to e-mail and telephone conferences, Haruko would have extra time to recover before going back to work.

His home was decorated in simple and traditional Japanese style, the pine floors overlaid with fragrant tatami mats. What furniture was here was low to the ground and black. Plants abounded, bringing in a touch of nature to soothe the chafed soul. His wife was proud of her heritage, and her love was reflected in every aspect of the home. Sliding aside the *shoji* door that the Japanese used to save that always-important space, he entered her small home office.

Shawn found his blushing and pregnant bride pouring over spreadsheets at her desk. A chewed up pencil had been tucked behind one ear, and her little square reading glasses had slipped down to the end of her nose. Beside her sulked a cold cup of green tea and a forgotten bowl of rice that had been half-eaten. Long brunette hair had been hastily pulled back into a pony tail, and her long green dress did nothing to conceal her nine month pregnant and very due belly. A longed for voice pulled her out of her work and brought her head up.

"Working so early in the morning, dear?"

"It's good to see you home Koi-kun. Breakfast is waiting for you in the kitchen. I was just finishing up on the Nakamura account before my office-partner takes over during my leave."

"It's good to be home, love. How are you feeling?"

"A little tired, very beat up, and the housework piles on faster than I can keep up with it. Ji-san tries to help, but he isn't as young as he used to be, and he has so much to help with at the shrine."

"I know. It doesn't seem possible that he is a grandfather now, and we are parents. I can still remember when he threatened to kill me himself if I didn't remove the dishonor I had put on your family by merely being your associate and taking you 'to wife' as he had put it."

The pair shared a laugh at the memory of when Ji-san had discovered they had been dating. He had been displeased for weeks, but after the *San-San-Kudo* ceremony he had calmed down again.

"Speaking of disturbances Koi, Oba-san has been rather active the past few days. She has been stealing Ji-san's keys again, and the dishes have been breaking like crazy. I know you don't believe in ghosts, but there haven't been any earthquakes strong enough to knock down dishes from the cupboards, much less rattle them. I can't think of any other explanation than Grandmother."

Shawn sighed and shook his head. Haruko and Ji-san were very superstitious in his opinion. Indeed, it seemed that the whole Japanese Nation was superstitious with its Shrines, Temples, and the various ceremonies they were always doing to appease the spirits. He did not believe in any of it. In his mind, there was always a better explanation.

"I'll check the shelves later on today then. I also brought you some gifts, and I found someone to rent the spare room and help around the house for a bit. She'll be leaving for Hokkaido after she gets her paperwork squared away, but she's got a long way to go before she can make it on her own."

Haruko smiled and shook her head at her husband as she put away her glasses. Shawn's soft heart was going to get him in trouble one of these days, but Haruko had played the mentor before.

"You found another runaway high school student, didn't you Shawn?"

"Not exactly, but close. Why don't you come and meet her. Otherwise Ji-san is probably going to start inundating her with old legends. Remember, when he was telling my last battle buddy about how easily the Earthquake *Kami* is insulted? Fair warning though, her Japanese is very poor, since she just started learning."

"Shawn-kun, one day you are going to see that there is far more in this world than we understand."

"Yeah, like why I keep getting passed up for promotions and

shipped back to the States and messing up my base seniority. Oh well, just a few years left."

A dry wind danced through aspen and pine trees, rustling summer leaves and pulling him back into wakefulness. The fresh air invigorated him, and the blazing sun was a welcome kiss on his skin. Ryu's eyes opened in shock, registering with great surprise the scenic high desert diorama spread before and below him.

"Oh boy, Ob's concoctions are finally making me hallucinate."

Standing up, Ryu looked down from the rocky crag that he had awoken on, gazing curiously over the mountain canyons housing low shrubs and summer-gold grasses. Nestled in the *arroyo* below him near to a trickling stream, feeding steadily into a mighty river, that issued from a connected canyon was an encampment of some kind. The simple shelters looked like rounded and very primitive huts to him, arches of branches interwoven with smaller branches from local shrubs. Dogs roamed through the camp, nosing from group to group, searching for handouts. Young women tended children or smoked meat for storage while young men tended horses or brought in freshly killed deer.

While he was overlooking the camp and listening to the chatter in a language he had not heard with his own ears before, an old woman came out of one of the larger and more ornate outlying lodges. Her iron-gray hair was plaited into two long tails on either side of her face, and it was difficult for him to tell her sun darkened skin from the animal skins that she had borrowed to fashion primitive and yet fine clothing. Other old humans very much like her followed out of the lodge, some in elaborate costumes and others in the simplest of garb. These others began to drum, sing or dance; the dancers ringing around the camp, watched by the young ones who had formerly been absorbed in their day-to-day duties.

The music was a vital beat, stirring the *Kami's* blood. Ancient beyond memory, it was the beat of the earth itself, calling him down from the distant peak and to the natural granite outcropping much closer to the humans' camp. As the others sang blessings for the tribe, their land, and the planet, the old woman walked beside the stream down to where the river met it.

Curious as to what the woman was doing while the other apparent priests of her clan were occupied, Ryu slipped through the foreign landscape behind her. What could possibly be so important as to draw an elder away from such a seemingly important tribal ceremony?

At the river, the woman stopped, bending down to drink of the life-giving waters. At length, she looked up from where she had kneeled, gazing caringly upriver at something that he could not see. Words poured from her mouth then, the language not that of the five ethnicities that had created the people of Japan, unknown to him and yet still understandable thanks to his heritage and the root language that all dragons knew.

"Mountain spirits of distant lands far beyond the Salty Sea, take my Grandchild by her hand and lead her home to me. Shelter our little rattlesnake and help her find her True Direction out of the Watery Lake and back to the Heart of the Mountain. She is lost within a forest guarded by fear. Penetrate and begin her life to gently Steer. Such is the People's prayer, from the Doorway of the Snake; let no need to cut our hair come as our songs we make."

Something stirred in the depths of his being, reacting to the love in the song and yearning to hunt up the solemn river, the unfamiliar and separate consciousness sheltered within him drawing strength from him. The gentle stretching was like that of a tired babe searching for its mother and then quieting at her breast. It was the first he was aware of another being taking up residence inside of him, and he was vaguely aware of it being a yin influence. This feeling, although something he had not experienced for himself before, was not totally unknown. He had heard other *Kami* describing it before, but it had only been those who had been involved enough in the realm of the humans to take disciples to uncover their own spirit nature. They had only experienced such a feeling after the initial possessions though.

The old woman smiled, dancing now back to the rest of her tribe. Twice she swooped down to pluck up a pine branch discarded for her use by one of the trees, and TeachingPine passed by the wondering spirit, who had thought himself well disguised by the rocks he hid within. The prayers of the other Ancients to Creator had worked and

connected the tribe to a spirit of the land that their Granddaughter
had fled to. There was hope for the future of the Clan that the
Rainbow Children would soon be coming. The chosen Keeper of the
Pipe would soon receive her Calling and her Guide. Ryu was left
alone, looking upriver where a roaring of a mighty waterfall could be
heard in the distance.

The being enfolded inside him yearned forward, striving toward
what it recognized as its Source. The nourishing energy of the one
she had been entrusted to was nice, but Ai had to get back to the other
three. The easiest way home to the others would be to retrace the
path to her Source, and with what strength she could muster she
wordlessly attempted to get her point across. Soon though, she did
not have the strength, and so she had to subside and rest within the
body of her somewhat unwilling host. However, she had at least
managed to convey her feelings of loss and emptiness, leaving her
host in confusion.

"Odd. What is this about?"

Assuming his dragon form for increased safety in this strange
land, Ryu began to explore his way upriver. He could hear the calls
of ferocious beasts in the forest, and wondered about what the Elder's
song had meant. As he walked, his vision turned into a dream, and
then the dream faded into wakefulness in his own realm. Looking up
out of the pool of magma, Ryu saw the face of his father gazing down
with concern.

CHAPTER 10:
SENDING NEW ROOTS

T HE long weeks had passed her by without hurry, turning blithely and uncaringly into months. It had been two months now since she had entered this strange and exciting new land, the novelty of new places and experiences taking away the fresh and ragged edge of her loss. She had even worked up the courage to try true sushi for the first time in her life, and had discovered that she absolutely adored raw seafood. There was something about the juicy and succulent flesh that fed her soul in a way that she could not describe, that would have horrified her only a few months previously.

BlowingWind could not say that the time had passed by without event, it had been both as lazy as a dog in the sun and yet as frantic as ants scurrying to escape a flood. She softly hummed a tune to herself as she washed her breakfast dishes, listening to Haruko singing a lullaby to the baby out in the living room. Ji-san had been rightly proud of his granddaughter, and had proclaimed loudly that she would be called Yuki since she was as pure as the snow.

BlowingWind had a special place in her heart for little Yuki. While Haruko and Shawn had been laboring at the hospital, she had been tearing around the house making last minute preparations for the new addition to the family and seeing to it that everything would be simple for the new mother. For the kindness of the Takamura-Bowers family, BlowingWind had only felt it right and proper to help out with the little one. It was a new experience, and BlowingWind had soon discovered that she hated changing diapers much more than she had hated scrubbing the toilet back home. It was alright though, soon everything would be in order and she could move on in her life.

Ji-san had helped BlowingWind to navigate the maze of infinite peril that was more commonly known as the visa application process.

In a few days she would be hearing the decision of the visa department, but things seemed to be sailing on favorable winds as far as that was concerned. Waiting on tenterhooks would do little to speed or affect the department's decision, and so she had thrown herself full-bore into working on preparing herself for facing the wide world on her own. Haruko had helped work on the very shaky foundation of Japanese language that BlowingWind had painstakingly erected, pointing out many mistakes that she made in pronunciation or grammar.

Her hunch had been right, Shawn had been far too easy on her that first day, and Haruko had gotten tired of hearing her struggle through dinners. When she had resorted to carrying around a tourist phrase book in order to survive at the market, Haruko had taken it away and started her out again from scratch. BlowingWind was getting better though, at least she could say that about herself, and soon she would be able to apply for a place to stay in Hokkaido.

Haruko had been very tired when she came home with the baby seven weeks ago. Those first two weeks BlowingWind had been spending much of her time cooking, cleaning, and following Ji-san around as he ritually purified the house to protect his only grandchild from evil spirits. Ji-san was a lay-priest at the local Oinari shrine, and deeply devout in his spirituality. As time passed, she still learned what she could from him on the local practices. It was her opinion that she needed to learn as much as she could about the local spirits to avoid offending them, and the guise of folklore perfectly conveyed the ancient wisdom. Although Shawn rolled his eyes every time that Ji-san began to tell the stories of old Nippon or to teach her a new chant, BlowingWind hung on every word like it was a precipice, thrilled at the fresh view she was getting into the spirit world.

Today, Shawn was at the base. The US President had called for another war in the Persian Gulf area, and as a result of the immanent threat of being shipped out on short notice the soldiers were being required to barrack at the base. BlowingWind didn't understand it, but whatever was going on in the Gulf had to be big. Haruko didn't show it, but BlowingWind also knew that she was afraid that her husband would be shipped off again so soon; or even worse, she could lose him entirely. While the others slept at night, BlowingWind found herself sitting in front of the *kamidana*, praying for the small family with the prayers of her homeland, and the prayers of this new land that she was slowly learning.

Old eyes watched the girl who was trapped in a woman's body as she went about her chores and cleaning up after herself. It was her day off, yet she still insisted on washing her own dishes. He was thrilled with the sincerity in everything that she did, but it disturbed him to see her constant refusal to deal with whatever she was hiding from. Through numerous teeth-clenching exchanges as he had slowly gotten to know the girl, he had found out about how she had been training as a mystic in her own land. Takamura Kenshin had been glad to entertain her with the old stories from the *Kojiki* and *Nihongi*, and to teach her the simple rituals the family performed daily at their spirit shelf. In return, she had told him her ancestral tales of the beings Snake, Holy Boy, and a rather deranged wolf-dog that she called Coyote.

"Scrubbing dishes until the flowers are gone is not going to make the reply letter arrive any faster, my child."

BlowingWind jumped, disturbed from her pondering.

"Oh, *ohayo* Ji-san. Why aren't you at the shrine yet? Isn't that where you normally go today?"

"BlowingWind, the other lay priests and I have been talking, and we think that it is time for you to speak with the *Daitoku*. You told me about your ancestral calling, and we think that we might be able to help you."

"Really? I mean, uh, *honto ne*?"

"*Honto ne*, really. Bring the items that you usually use for your rituals so that the spirits of those objects can be naturalized here, and we have some additional items that you may find useful in your new path."

"Is that so? I am not Shinto though. What if I mess up and accidentally anger one of the spirits that live at the shrine?"

The dish that BlowingWind still held in her hand began to grow warm. Staring incredulously at the porcelain platter, she desperately tried to remember how hot the wash water had been. Surely it had not been hot enough for the plate to retain heat for so long, and it had been cool just a moment ago. Platters and cups in the cupboard began to rattle softly, and the temperature dropped several degrees. As quickly as the phenomena arose though it subsided just as quickly, leaving the woman to wonder why she could not just have a normal life like others did.

"Perhaps you would offend more spirits by not going."

"Good point Ji-san. I think this is the most haunted house I have ever been in."

"We like to keep our ancestors close, here."

She put the plate away, nervous as to what would happen next. BlowingWind had been immersing herself in daily life to escape her pain, much the same as her mother had done after father's death. As the days had passed, she had begun to wonder if she truly wanted to continue on the Blue Road of Spirit. It was getting increasingly difficult to pray or sing to the spirits the old songs without remembering Him. She was cursed with this knowledge that there was more to life than what was seen, and this intense need to drown in it, as if she were not truly meant to leave the past behind.

She had no choice though.

Her father's death had caused the Hawk Pipe to come into her guardianship at the young age of seven, her family, Clan and Nation unsmoked for until the time that she had become aware of her recent loss. It was a long time for a people to go without the medicine of Hawk, and she was now a Keeper of a Sacred Mirror as well. If she were to lay down her burden, whom could she give it to? Who would sing the songs and offer the sage? No, this was her path, what she had been born to do. She had to continue in her training and trust that she would be where she was needed.

Ji-san watched as the child left the kitchen to gather her things. He had not seen spirits before with his eyes as far as he was aware, but he had been able to sense them his entire life. Lately, ever since the child had begun her stay to be precise, he had been feeling more than ever. They seemed to be attracted to her somehow; as if she were a magnet and they were iron filings. It was worrisome, as not all spirits were beneficial and it was well known that some cases of seeming psychosis were truly cases of spirit possession.

She had not completely left behind the mentality of childhood either, and so perhaps it was this innocence, however wounded it was, which happened to be drawing the *kitsune* and other troublesome spirits seeking a home.

BlowingWind was unaware of Ji-san's thoughts, climbing the stairs and turning left to her little room at the end of the hall. She gently pushed aside the sliding door, surveying the cozy enclosure that had become home in its Spartan way. Her futon had been rolled up and stowed away in the closet as soon as she had risen to greet the day, and when she got an apartment one of the first things she intended to put in was a real western bed. Also hidden in the closet were her doe skins with her grandmother's beadwork hung reverentially, to keep them clean for special occasions now that she was in the mundane world. On the wall to her left was a round mirror, and next to it she had hung her old knapsack that contained her holy items.

She closed the door gently, removing the white T-shirt and slacks that she had gotten at a local store as she started her new existence. Reaching out to take up her grandmother's hard work once more, BlowingWind realized how lost and exposed she felt. If she had run home to the White Mountain Reservation, Grandmother would have helped her in her search for truth and reason. But if she had, she would still be in Coyote's territory, and he still had not given up on teasing her until she left Turtle Island. Here, perhaps, she would be safe from him and his tricks.

The drawback was that she had to watch out for new trickster spirits, the *kitsune* or fox spirits that Ji-san said still caused problems to this day.

As she donned her ceremonial clothing, she felt the connection to her people strengthen, a physical reminder that although she needed to find a new guide she still had a purpose of some kind. BlowingWind smoothed down her leathers, relishing the feel of them against her flesh. Her ancestors, both Celtic and Apache, had been warriors and explorers. If she thought about it, she was only following an old path trodden down by countless booted or moccasined feet before her own.

Moving towards the mirror and her sacred objects, BlowingWind could not help but see herself. Her hair and eyes were so unlike the others who were pure blooded, and even the other half-bloods did not look like this. The elders had said that every few generations, there would be the occasional child that was born with light features, even in the old days. It was said that those children showed their spirit blood. It was the only explanation she had for her looks though; as according to what she had learned in Biology by all accounts she should have both dark hair and eyes. This, perhaps more than anything else, had driven her to want to be as great as her father, as the spirits were giving her much to live up to.

Pulling her eyes hastily away from the mystery she had lived with her whole life, she set it aside for now. Checking carefully, she made sure that all was in order in her bag of tools. Obsidian's mirror slept in its wrapping as silent and cold as it had been since his death. She had pouches of cornmeal and tobacco, bundles of good white sage, and gourd rattles that she had made herself, all glaring accusingly up at her for neglecting them for so long. Feathers of various kinds waited for their proper use.

The tanned hide of a rattlesnake was rolled up as well, waiting to be tied around her head. RedFeather had caught the snake himself and gifted the hide to her when he had gotten word of her first moon. Mother had not been able to take her to the Reservation to participate in the Sunrise Ceremony that year, and so she had missed her own welcoming into the ranks of womanhood. The Hawk Pipe waited in its painted leather case, and BlowingWind was glad that this relic only had meaning within her own family. If it had been something belonging to the Nation, she would not have been allowed to Keep it at such a young age. All was well among her tools, and silently she brought out her moccasins, keeping them out to put on at the door.

Quietly padding out of her room and down the stairs with her pack in tow, BlowingWind noticed that Haruko was no longer singing to the baby. Pausing at the door to the living room, she saw the pair sound asleep in a rocking chair in the corner of the room. It was good to see Haruko resting, and it would be a shame to wake her. Instead, BlowingWind went to the kitchen and left a note explaining where she had gone.

"This is the way your holy people dress?"

Ji-san had come back into the house after he had made sure that everything he needed was in the car. It wasn't that he had much to take in all actuality, but what he did need was easily forgotten at times. To his eyes, the leather that she wore was odd, but no doubt he would look odd to her eyes when he donned his ceremonial garb at the shrine.

"Not anymore Grandfather. Most just wear jeans and a calico shirt now, even for the pow-wows unless they are one of the dancers. Even father tended to dress that way, but Grandmother insisted that a Medicine Keeper should look like this one for the ceremonies."

"Admirable. That is the way that things should be. If the old lessons and traditions of a people are not passed on then they die, taking the spirit of the people with it. It is time to leave now my child."

"All right, Ji-san. I am ready."

Two gold eyes watched from under a bush as the pair got into the car. Her defenses were failing to hide her from him as her thoughts began to fall away from the Blue Road and becoming mired more increasingly in the mundane. He had watched her for a long time now, witnessing many of her triumphs and tragedies. Indeed, he and Puma had even kept the girl from killing herself after the boy she loved had left this world, she foolishly believing the love of a child to be the mature love of true mates. Although he was not the girl's Guide, he did feel a sense of responsibility for the girl as her grandmother was from the Coyotero Clan. He had taken the hard journey as a stow-away in her plane, and Thunderbird had not been very precise as to where the child had been running.

Coyote had not been amused to find himself in Japan. Now he had to compete with the native trickster spirits here, the *Kitsune*, *Tengu* and *Tanuki*, among other spirits. How was he supposed to be her mirror to show her what she shouldn't do, if he had to fight his way through a bunch of foxes looking for a host, or trying to earn their daily bean curd? In his opinion, they needed to step aside and let him do his work.

As if this wasn't enough trouble, Hawk and Raven had followed him and had been trying to drag him back. If they would drag her home then he would be happy to go home. He could only hope that

RedFeather would give his wayward cousin a severe tongue lashing when he found out just where she was.

"It has to be the O'Drake influence. My people never ran away from themselves, at least not that I can remember." He ground out.

Running through the streets, Coyote attracted little attention as he chased after the car. The townsfolk were used to seeing wild animals run the streets, as they were often misplaced from their homes, and so the wild dog was no different to them than a crow frequenting the market. Although he could not run as fast as the car did, he would still be able to keep up by catching the wind and transforming into sand when no human eyes were upon him. So it was that he followed her.

BlowingWind had delighted in observing life going on around her as they drew closer to the shrine located at the edge of the sleepy suburb. It was small, but parking guidelines necessitated a short walk of a few blocks to the steps that ascended a small hill, to where the shrine grounds were. The fresh air and gentle breeze invigorated her, and the earth below her was warm and inviting, tempting her to lie down and watch the leaves dance on the trees and the clouds skitter by. The quiet and benevolent power in the sacred site so close and surrounded by the arms of the city without irritation was intriguing, and she wondered why the spirits of her home had not accepted humanity changing the land yet.

Twin stone *Kitsune* stood guard at the base of a red *torii*, the curved crossbar soaring at the top of the gate like a triumphant Thunderbird brewing a life-giving storm. At the sides were basins of water, and ladles for the devout to cleanse themselves before entering the sacred grounds. Ji-san had walked over to one, and so she followed so that she could learn to proper way to enter without offending any indwelling spirits guarding the grounds.

Following Ji-san's lead, BlowingWind silently picked up one of the wooden ladles with her right hand, pouring a little water over her left hand, being very careful for the water to fall onto the gravel and not back into the basin. At his nod of approval, she switched the ladle to her left hand to purify her right hand. Next they switched the ladles back into their right hand, catching a little water in their left hands and rinsed out their mouths. BlowingWind thought this was rather strange, but if it were local custom then she would observe it.

Following his motions, she rinsed her hand again, and then tipped the ladle up to let the remaining water cleanse the handle.

"Is this so that the ladle will be clean for the next user Ji-san?"

"Yes child. It was necessary to remove the unavoidable impurities picked up by daily living before coming before the *Kami*, as impurities repel the beneficial spirits."

"Oh, I see, Ji-san."

Mounting the steps to the shrine grounds finally, BlowingWind could feel eyes watching and appraising her as she climbed. Although she felt the presences, and could hear vague whispers hidden by the wind, she saw nothing. The spirits of this land had not accepted her enough to show themselves to her yet, but she did not know what it was they were waiting for.

Another *torii* stood guard at the top of the staircase, echoes of a well-maintained *samurai* solemnly standing guard, even though the *samurai* class had been disbanded long ago. Another set of *Kitsune* stood guard here, smiling tauntingly at her as she regarded them, each playing with its own spirit ball. White sand poured like a dividing river across the shrine grounds, lovingly raked into waves and graced with stone pathways serving as bridges over to where Oinari supposedly was enshrined in a small wooden building. Ji-san led BlowingWind over the stones and toward the small shrine, speaking like a whispering pine as they crossed over into the grass and stonework courtyard.

"When you come before the *Kami*, you place an offering into the wooden box that we call *saisen bako*, in thanks for the help that you will receive. The shrine uses the funds generated for upkeep. You will then make your prayer, followed by *nirei nihakushu ippai*. To perform this, you will bow twice, clap twice, and bow again. This respectfully lets the *Kami* know of your presence and shows gratitude for Oinari taking the time to help you."

"Ji-san, what if I forget what to do?"

"I am sure that it will not be a problem."

Nervously, BlowingWind stepped up to the simple enclosure, placing a few coins in the box. She wasn't sure what to pray for, or whether she just wanted to offer her respect. She was lonely, of that much she was certain, and it was not a feeling that she relished. Not knowing what to think, she stood there for a moment, feeling the confusion roiling beneath her surface and wishing that she knew what to do. Something stirred behind the wooden doors that she stood before, and jolted out of her reveries she bowed, clapped, and bowed again. Looking once more at Ji-san she saw him talking with a man in cloud white *haori* and powder blue *hakama,* and at length Ji-san motioned for her to come back.

"Taisan-dono, this is MountainChild BlowingWind. BlowingWind, this is Taisan Haku, another lay priest that serves here to assist tourists and worshippers."

"*Ohayo kannushi-san.*"

BlowingWind bowed as she had learned was a polite greeting here, and Taisan bowed back. When the men began to walk toward a larger wooden building, she followed them, not knowing what else to do. Taisan smiled internally at how the child unquestioningly followed, as she was passing her test. He saw no reason that she would not be successful at the Sengen shrines where he and the others who had vouched for her to begin training. There was much time yet before she would need to leave for Hokkaido

A woman in blazing red *hakama* and white *haori* opened the door to the building, bowing as they entered. Each of the men made a small bow to the woman and then a deeper bow into the room, and so she followed suit. She saw nothing out of the ordinary, but there was a presence that told her that there was something else in the room as well, watching and waiting like so many of the spirits at home had until they had become comfortable around her.

"Follow me MountainChild-san. We have been expecting you. Please let us assist you in your preparations."

Following the *Miko* through the building, BlowingWind was led to a small chamber for changing her robes. Her leathers were changed for a simple white robe of snow, fastened shut with a similarly chaste obi tie. The soft cloth discomfited her slightly, leaving her with no worn ties to her own culture. Carefully she packed her clothes into the old knapsack that had served her so well, watching another young *Miko* carry away the pouch after she had secured it. Nervously following the other *Miko* away into yet another room, she heard things stirring behind the thin walls, bringing their attentions back from wherever old spirits go who have lost interest in the happenings of their homes.

At last, she was led into a small plain room, and motioned to kneel before the sole occupant of the small and yet gaping enclosure.

Kneeling softly on the woven bamboo mat, BlowingWind eyed the short man carefully. His costume of the Heian period was a green rivaling new rice shoots, and he himself was folded in a grim and yet flowing manner. His eyes were closed, and yet he seemed perfectly aware of her. They sat in the ravenous silence, each measuring the other in their own way. When he finally broke the oppressing nothing, BlowingWind could feel nothing but relief.

"The seed is to make pilgrimage to the Shrines of the Sengen. It is there that she will find the soil suitable for her roots and it is there that what is missing will be found. In the lower shrine you will stay for a time, and then you will wander the forest to finish your preparations. When you have found your guide, he will lead you to the upper shrine. So says Lord Inari to his humble priest, who says this to the seed."

The *Miko* came back from wherever she had gone, retrieving the greatly shaken BlowingWind. The old priest's voice had trembled, yet it was not with the weakness of old age. No, what had spoken was more like what she would expect to hear from an ancient rice paddy, or perhaps an old river that had no more need of cavorting through depleted fields. She did not notice when her knapsack was pressed back into her hands, or even when she was deposited back in the garden outside. The insistent pulling that she had ignored so much that it had been forgotten had begun once more, and all she could see was a longed for laughing face.

"Father, is that where I will finally find Obsidian again?"

Only the air replied to her whispered question, a small whirlwind skittering over stone and sand to dance with a few discarded leaves and papers.

❁

RedFeather gazed out over the expanses that the cattle grazed upon, hard at work checking on the meat that would feed his family. These cows were not his own, as he was just a poor cowboy, yet as he was paid to take care of them, he was still responsible for them. In his way, he would be feeding his family and Nation, providing for their needs in the way that a warrior should.

Other Medicine Keepers of the Nation had noticed Coyote's lack of overt activity in their lives. Coyote's many children still roamed and performed their own mischief, but his silence had never boded well before. Someone was due for a very large scale awakening by the look of things, and all of the Keepers were nervous as to who would be exposed for a fool.

Other problems had been bothering him as well though. Recently, he had received a letter from his Aunt Marie. Enclosed with the expected graduation photo of his favorite little cousin had been a tear-stained letter informing him that she had run away. Coyote had always been fascinated by her overly adult view of life, and had long worked to fill her life with spontaneity and mischief. RedFeather could only hope that wherever she was, Coyote was letting her get on her feet instead of trying to seduce her or playing one of his dangerous pranks on her.

It was over a month ago now that he and the other Medicine Keepers for both Clan and Nation had gathered in Council over the disappearance of the Keeper of the Hawk Pipe. They had sung and prayed long, some dancing beneath the sky, others within Sweat Lodges. The Seers had sought to find her, but she had been scattered, and all that they could find were bits and pieces that refused to come away from where they had hidden themselves. One particularly troublesome piece of BlowingWind's spirit had even seemed to take up residence with a rather grumpy creature that they had described as a snake with legs and bearing plumes of fire. Where she was hiding was an impenetrable mystery to humans. Unknown to RedFeather, a separate Council was discussing his cousin even as he worried over her state.

"What will happen to my cousin? Please be safe BlowingWind."

A whirlwind passed by after he spoke to himself, and for a moment, RedFeather could almost believe that it was some spirit come to harass his cattle or to addle his brain. With the luck that had befallen his family in the past generation, there was little possibility that the errant wind housed a spirit that would help them.

Three figures kneeled upon cushions in the room, engrossed in the ritual that happened before the actual conference that had been called. Each bowed and greeted the others according to rank. The *Daitengu* and *Tenko*, the leaders of the crow and fox spirits of the land, had asked for audience with Sarutahiko, calling upon his position as the leader of the earth-born spirits to solve their problem.

Daitengu, having long ago lost his personal name when he rose to power over the other *Tengu*, was arrayed in the robes of a simple monk. His red face and long, beak-like nose had once struck fear in the humans of simpler times, and the impressive wings on his back were the furled night waiting to confuse the unwary. His companion and the head servant of the rice god Oinari, Tenko had also lost his personal name in the same manner. Nine tails spoke of how many long millennia the *Kyuubi no Kitsune's* white coat, and flinty eyes, had chased after fools as he listened to his compatriot speak. Kneeling respectfully before their lord, the trickster spirits posed their dilemma, the Daitengu speaking first.

"Sarutahiko-sama, what is to be done about the intruder who followed the *Miko*-child?"

"Yes, that is my question as well my lord. The humans are blaming my fellow *Kitsune*, and me, for many things happening around the child, which are not our faults. The tricks always are aimed at the foreign girl, but humans in her vicinity unwittingly step into them and we are tired of taking the blame."

"The *Kitsune* is right my Lord, and the child will be setting out on a journey through our forests soon enough when she makes pilgrimage to Fujisan. I and the other *Tengu* have no wish to have him interfering in the tests that we will be administering to this girl, who is training as a type of priestess. If he wants the volatile thing he should just take her, and stop making our job as testers so difficult."

Sarutahiko gazed tiredly at the two spirits that had come to him for audience complaining of the foreign spirit who had invaded the soil, while chasing after the strange holy woman, who seemed to bear a trace amount of spirit blood from some unknown source. As far as he could tell, the wild dog held no ill will towards the girl, although he did seem to have a penchant for attempting to embarrass the poor child. Other spirits had followed her on the back of the winds as well, although these two seemed to be seeking to return Coyote home once more.

Now was not an appropriate time for the trickster to go on a world tour, as Nippon had enough problems and who knew how Amaterasu would react to his mucking about in her country.

"I know that you are frustrated, but this will soon be over. As she is now stepping out of the protection of the spirits of the house she has been living in, she will once more be undefended. It will not be long before she is claimed, for good or ill, and then he will have no further reason to stalk her."

The Daitengu's face broke into a series of chasms and gorges, such as could be found hidden in the forests over which he was lord while his pointed teeth glinted in the light. He well remembered the time long ago when he and others would kidnap children and the unwary. He remembered "tormenting" or teaching them secrets until either returning them as half-wits, depositing them in far lands, or the souls of the unlucky leaving their body unable to stand any more of the broadening of their perception.

It had been long since any humans had received the full severity of their tests, but those who had been so favored and managed to keep their wits had become great heroes. Sarutahiko himself had called a halt to the practice, believing the humans to be too frail for such barbarous training as they fell further away from their own spirit natures. Perhaps when this child finally took up the mantle of true womanhood the balance would begin to dip back the other way and spirit-kind would once again rise in dominance over the earth, returning health back to the planet.

"So you will not interfere in her life, no matter who takes possession of her and her abilities? You will do nothing even if

Amatsu Mikaboshi himself takes an interest in such a 'lowly' thing as a human or if any of my kind were to accidentally test her as hard as we have others in the past?"

"Amatsu Mikaboshi is too vain to go after a human woman, too busy pursuing my grandmother, and is too busy working on his latest plan to take over the Heavens at the approaching end of the Age to worry about the happenings here on Earth. Should he acquire the Seat of the Heavens, then the Earth will already be at his feet, and there is nothing that I can do to help in the High Expanse until the Gateway opens once more. As for your training methods, it may be preferable for her to die and exist as spirit than for her body to serve as a link to the material world for a *Kami* with malignant motives."

Neither the *Tengu* nor the *Kitsune* could hide the smiles on their faces as they were given leave to test by any means that was deemed necessary.

CHAPTER 11:
AT THE FOOT OF FUJI, RELEASE!

BLOWINGWIND had wandered after Koji meekly as a child, riding home in a now very familiar sense of unreality. Things were moving again, and she could not shake the feeling of some great machine poised to crush her. The ride home was quiet though, the silken silence only broken when they pulled up in the driveway.

"Ji-san, what am I going to need to take with me?"

"Take your sack. You already have all that you need in it. After that, allow the spirits to guide you."

Nodding her head, she followed Ji-san in, pausing only to collect the mail from the box, drifting in and wondering what would happen next. Sorting the mail, the only thing she found for herself was an official looking envelope. Shaking fingers set aside the rest, and then broke rudely into the white expanse like a snowboard carving through the early morning powder. Removing the letter as carefully as she would a tiny kitten from a hay nest, she felt her future teetering on the edge of a precipice between where she was and the Great Unknown. Finally, she unfolded the fateful leaflet and awaited the decision of the Powers That Be.

BlowingWind scanned the paper, her eyes only skimming the surface. It was indeed from the Visa and Immigration Department. Gathering her courage to herself, she read it properly. Falling into a boneless heap on the foyer floor, the meaning of the words finally sank in.

The thud and shake of a body hitting the floor attracted the attention of Haruko, who had awoken long ago. Peeking out of the kitchen where she was preparing a meal, her eyes became wide as gongs as she saw the young American puddled on the floor. The poor child's face was a mask of shock similar to one she had seen long ago in a *Noh* play, and nearby a letter lay forgotten on the floor.

"Ji-san, come quick! Something's wrong with Buro-kaze! Kaze-chan!"

Both of the natives rushed to Wind's side, kneeling down and attempting to awaken her from the shock. Finally, a slow grin began to spread across her face like the first thread of a summer dawn. Barely a whisper, words breezed out filled with the freedom of relief.

"I can stay. I have to re-apply for each scholastic year I'll be staying unless I want to change my citizenship, but I can stay."

Haruko desperately hugged BlowingWind, holding the girl steady as tremors of relief began to take over her body. Being able to stay in Japan seemed to mean more to the mysterious girl than just going to school, otherwise the reaction would not have been so big. Just as quickly though, BlowingWind's display of emotion was gone, blown through like a small but powerful storm.

"Ji-san, when can I get to the base of Fujiyama?"

"Tomorrow if you like."

"Yes, I would like that very much. Thank you."

"**G**ood morning Sun! Good morning Amaterasu!"

"Kaze-chan! Don't you think you should eat breakfast first?"

"Oh, right. Thanks Haru-chan. Sorry Ji-san, I thought I was running late."

"BlowingWind, don't forget what I said about always running around. Slow down and enjoy life."

"Kaze-chan, must you really go?"

"For a little while Haru. I promise I'll write, and you know that I'll be back before I move up to Hokkaido. Shall I bring you an *omamori*? What charm would you like?"

"Something for the baby would be fine, thank you Kaze-chan."

The young American had eagerly greeted the next day, although

Haruko was sad to see her go. BlowingWind traveled south toward the sacred mountain, half-dreaming of a passionate reunion with the spirit she loved and half dreading the more likely outcome that her entire adventure was little more than a wild goose chase. When they arrived at the shrine, the assistants were preparing for the fire festival that would announce the official beginning of the climbing season. Already, there were a few devotees of the Fujiko here, undergoing their austerities in preparation for the anticipated climb.

"Ji-san, there are already so many people. What is going on?"

"Just the fire festival. It happens every year. Perhaps you could help while you are here."

"That would be great!"

She had a short conversation with the head priest, which mostly consisted of smiling and bowing at each other. With her broken Japanese she explained why she was there and what she intended to do. BlowingWind ended up sharing a room with some female student priests. She gladly made a sizable donation to the shrine in thanks for their help, and spent her days in helping with festival preparations and slowly merging the shrine's practices with her own. Her nights were spent with visualizing her ascent to the peak and sleeping in her thin futon on the tatami mats. Shrine life was quiet, and in her mind it was perfect save for the loud tourists who passed through on picnic hikes up the mountain. Regarding those, she was reminded of the rabble that always seemed to litter the Ski Park back in California.

Another donation had provided for a priest to be assigned to her, teaching her all she needed to know for a traditional climb. He informed her of the tradition of bathing in the five lakes around the mountain, and dutifully she had bathed in them. He helped her to memorize her route until she could practically see it with her inner eye, although she would most likely have little trouble as she would only need to follow the hordes that would be filing up the mountain after the opening ceremony. However, on her hikes she had seen an area that called to her soul, and finally she asked her burning question.

"*Kannushi-san*, what is that area of twisted trees lost among the volcanic rock that has such a strange feeling to it?"

The young man looked carefully at her, the training mystic sitting demurely in the *Miko-san* uniform they had issued her after she had come to train with them. After he was certain that she was of fairly sound mind, he reluctantly answered her apparently innocent question.

"It is called Aokigahara Jukai, The Sea of Trees, The Forest of No Return, or the Forbidden Forest two hundred years ago. That is all that remains of the old forest after Fujiyama's eruption of 1706 to 1707. Legend says that those who enter never return, and for this reason it is a popular place for suicide. The police do a yearly sweep for bodies, but I am sure that many of the bodies are never found. It is a strange place where one is easily lost, and a good place to stay away from."

"I see. We had many places like that at the foot of Shastayama. People would get lost for weeks, mostly tourists. I visited a few of those places, and the feel was always very odd. Why would they feel odd?"

"In the old days, it was said that such places were where the bridge between our world and the world of the *Kami* was easily crossed. Those who crossed over the borders rarely returned, for good or ill. Now, it is said that travelers are so easily lost because the landscape looks the same and the rocks confuse the compasses. I personally do not put much stock in confused compasses from the iron content of the rocks though. Still, I would take great care all the same."

"Yes. I will be careful. Thank you."

Bowing, BlowingWind rose to go and prepare her things. In reality, all was already prepared, but it was always good to double-check everything. However, she also felt that it would be more appropriate if she was in her own clothes. What she was learning of the native faith dovetailed beautifully with her own for the most part, however she also was no *Miko*. She had no wish to remain virgin, even though she was not looking to loose that precious gift at this time. No, she was an Apache shaman even though she had been deprived of a full childhood in that culture; her new location could not change that and only gave her new knowledge and more forces to call on.

"When will you be leaving MountainChild-san?"

"As soon as I am changed and have finished the Hawk Dance."

"Good journey then."

"*Arigato gozimasu Kannushi-san.*"

Ryu stared up at the ceiling of his grotto, floating gently on the heated currents of his magma tongue. For the past several days after he had awoken from his calming sleep, he had felt a strange presence roving in his above land keepings. Most of the time it was beyond his borders, but a few times it had ventured near, pulling him from morose musings into musings after tendrils of cinnamon. When it had moved away from his borders he was in peace once more, or at least relatively speaking.

Fujiyama had come down to visit his wayward son, reminding the fidgety spirit that it would not be much longer before he was free again. Ryu's reclusive dam had even sent word of her encouragement through her mate, even though she herself could not leave her clutch of eggs. Ryu appreciated the sentiment, but he was still rather sore at his father for having wrestled him back into his origins. Things were so dull here, and it had been so sobering to have discovered that although he had reached full size, he still had a long way to go before being as powerful physically and magically as his august father.

The visit had soothed the dragon's nerves somewhat, but he was still on edge. Something was happening, and he did not know what. Being trapped inside of himself only gave him time to stew and wonder, which did nothing but make him even tenser, a bowstring poised to snap.

At last, Ryu felt the magic bonds tethering him into the fiery river loosen their irresistible grip; falling away at last and evaporating like dreams. With a great cry, the magma dragon hurled himself into the air, riding the magnetic currents to the ledge high above him, where his high-seat lurked empty these many years. Landing squarely on the granite, his great claws etched in new furrows with their excitement. Shaking out years of imprisonment, globules of his molten earth sprayed off like sheets of fiery rain or discarded scale. His wild howl still reverberated throughout the hallways, eventually filling the whole volcano with his joy and causing the more unstable deposits to shift or crumble.

His brothers and sisters that were still residing inside of Fujisan no doubt cringed at his exuberance, anticipating perhaps some oncoming practical joke for having not attempted to sneak a visit or smuggle him some fresh meat. Despite the hesitant misgivings of his more reserved siblings, the various other earth and fire spirits who dwelt in his sector cheered along with their lord and master. Dragons, snakes, and salamanders left posts in kitchens, store rooms, onsen, and other areas, joined by lizards and bats from other areas of the division. Healers who were not tending patients at the time left their quarters, and even Mayu, who had just finished arranging the new eggs in her nest, looked up before curling around them again.

"I take it that it feels good to not have your magic enchained anymore."

Ryu snorted in disdain, shaking his head like a dog that has discovered something unexpectedly malodorous, which sent his mane flying madly.

"I will take that as a yes then, my son, and be glad that you seem to be in such a good mood."

Ryu's dark eyes regarded his father's endless night that was his dragon form mistrustfully as a high school student would watch a substitute chemistry instructor. Servants watched with interest at the edges of the chamber while guards released their human shapes for the heavier natural armor of dragon scale.

"What did I do now *Otou-sama*? Or is it what I have not yet done?"

Fujiyama shook his head, realizing that in some ways he did deserve the mistrust of his son. Something was bothering the old dragon about his son though. It was not something that he could place his claw on yet, but something was different. The boy was even more distant than ever perhaps, and the chemistry of the magma that composed the boy was changing slowly, as if the ever-reaching tongue had happened on some rare element it was incorporating into itself.

"Just be careful out there my Son. Even though the majority of humanity does not believe we exist as they do, does not mean they can not do great harm if we allow them to come too close to us."

"Father, you have given us all this talk before. I remember my lessons about Kaguya-hime and the Emperor, and the havoc in both worlds that relationship caused. I will allow no human to intrude inside this holy mountain, I will toy with no hearts, and I will not tell anyone that my father is a hoary old dragon stuck in ancient tradition."

Ryu shook his head as he made his reply, uncomfortable at the thought of his now long distant puphood, but mildly amused at the more recent memory of the conversation with a favorite student that had been the reason his father had chained him in the first place. At the time that he would have said something to hopefully break the tension between himself and his 'hoary old man' that would hopefully result in his complete freedom, thunder rolled through. His escape was now firmly blocked by the summons and invitation of all the resident spirits to the fire festival now commencing as the setting sun painted the horizon fire red. Resigned to perform his duty, he followed his father through upward wending passages instead. It figured, and was his luck, that he was released from his magma just in time to hear the drummers enticing his fellow spirits to witness what was being done in their honor.

Subterranean passageways gave way to the vents at the top and side of the mountain, and various volcano-dwelling spirits took the forms of wind or steam to waft out and alight in secrecy at the shrines around the rim of the craters, or to venture down to the lower shrine. Bells and gongs joined in the wild pulse, and the smells of the food offerings were tempting this year. Down below, the fires could be seen where they would blaze throughout the night, in imitation of the mountain's own fierce inner fire. Ryu knew that the next day the coals would be raked out, and people would be guided across the heated bed to be purified for the next year. Eventually, the stirring scene would lure him down as a shimmer of heat to dance in the bonfire with the others. It was always the same, each year that he was present even in part.

The unusual scent of cinnamon hung heavy in the air in the courtyard of the lower shrine this year, and a laughing voice wound through and above all of the other revelers. Ryu wanted to find the owner of this voice, and this scent that had started to grow on him. A new dance had been added to the usual fare, surprising him, and when the woman swooping and soaring with a feathered blanket appeared to give her offering the voice was gone, replaced by chiming bells tied to the foreign dancer. The *Kannushi* announcing the addition was very excited to have such an offering from a holy woman from another land to present, it showed even through the carefully trained exterior. To Ryu's consternation, paints obscured the face of this new delicacy, turning the human into a very believable hawk. Tendrils of his spirit extended, seeking to brush and explore.

At last, when the graceful bow of the moon rode high and the stars brightly danced in the skies to a more ancient music than that the humans offered, Ryu and Fujiyama answered the humans' plaintively joyous calls and partook of what was offered. Konohana-hime and her sister, joined also by the retired Lady Fuji, descended in invisible forms to send their blessings as well. In the golden glow of gilded festival lanterns as he stalked the grounds and wound between parishioners, Ryu did not notice a leather-clad woman, carrying a simple pack on her back, waft the smoke of the fire over herself after being allowed to scatter a handful of earthy ceremonial tobacco over the coals. Nor did he notice when her cinnamon scent withdrew from the gathering to wander midnight forests on her search for a true purpose, being too drunk on the ambient energy.

Other ancient spirits did notice the presence and withdrawal of the visitor, following her as she wandered from the light and noise into the cloak of the night. Moccasined feet stepped lightly along the rocky paths, following both her eyes and the quiet pull at the core of her being. During her eight days at the shrine, a small piece of herself, infinitesimal to say the least, had slinked back into place during a quiet moment of meditation. It was certain that it wasn't everything that she was missing, but somehow she felt a little bit better, as if she were on the right track.

The bow of the moon was an old friend to her, a familiar face from the time before she had her heart broken and even before she had given it away. Although it did not provide as much light as it would at the full, it was still enough to make out her path by for the time being. As she went further into the forests it would not be enough any more, but she had to escape the noise. She was on a quest, and the living celebration would only have sucked her further into it, holding her back and plunging her into the crowds searching for entirely different answers.

Unnoticed, a small red fox bearing two tails ran past her on a parallel path, and it paused now and then to survey the shaman's progress. Once satisfied, he reached into her mind, borrowing the form and voice of the male most prominent in her mind.

Nubby roots reached up from the ground now to trip her, and the gravel's sharp edges told her that somehow she had managed to wander from her intended path. Regaining her footing once more, a fog began to rise from unseen water sources, twisting like a silken dragon through avenues of jagged stone and twisted trees. A voice from not so distant happy days called out to her in a laughing challenge.

"You can't catch me, Beautiful!"

"Obsidian!"

Her heart thundering now with surprise and excitement, BlowingWind accepted the challenge of the ghost conjured by the magic of an ancient forest, wily *Kitsune*, and a lonely heart. Racing unheeding after his calls into the Forest of No Return as the *Tengu* peeked at her from behind their rocks and trees, neither the shaman nor the dragon that fate was weaving her together with were aware of the challenges that soon would come their way.

CHAPTER 12:
TESTS OF THE *TENGU*

BLOWINGWIND chased after Obsidian's laughing voice, spurred on by her bouncing knapsack and her intense desire to be with her Beloved once more. Mist rose higher than before, first sucking at her ankles, then nipping at her knees, obscuring the already difficult path she followed. Her bearings had been lost hours ago, a thought which brought her up short, to collapse on an oddly shaped rock gasping for breath like a fish out of water.

This natural maze of tree and stone had done its entrusted work well, acting as a barrier to trap its prey for hundreds of years. BlowingWind could not allow fear to grip her now though. Looking around from her moss-covered perch, the nightmarish land was unbroken by any manmade object, save for one. Oddly placed, a wooden bridge painted garishly in crimson arched innocently over what seemed to be a river of dry stones. No trace could be seen of the one that she had pursued so passionately, a sign that once more she had fallen prey to the ghosts of her abundant imagination.

"I really hope I didn't chase Coyote, or a *Kitsune*. Why on earth would there be a bridge over a dry riverbed, when somebody could just walk across? It doesn't look like there has been water in there for years."

Standing back up, she did not notice that the knee-high rock she had been sitting on was carved into the rough resemblance of a double-faced creature, nor was she aware of the mocking leer the sinister engraving was possessed of. Her eyes were fixed on the worn bridge and her hand was outstretched in an effort to verify the evidence of her eyes.

The bridge was as solid as the rocks, and as her hand first touched the rail the wind chose that moment to howl under it. The phantom sounds of a rushing river carried to her ears as she slowly began to cross it.

"What could have once been up ahead for this to be in place so obviously long?"

Now at the other side, the shaman turned around to look back, although she had no idea as to why she would do so. By turning and looking back, the magic of the borderland was activated, and magic sealed the way to the human world without her even knowing she was crossing that fine line. As she consciously expected, she saw nothing unusual, and the fog crawling down low obscured the rising water that she otherwise would have seen. Shaking her head at her foolishness, BlowingWind continued onward, away from the ghostly river and the bridge that was vanishing unseen behind her.

Behind a rock, the small red fox with two tails watched with a small smile. Sitting down, he nibbled on some *aburage* that one of the *Tengu* he was currently and oddly partnered with had left for him.

"Good luck."

Her path took an upward tuck now, and it flitted across her mind how similar this area was to a spirit world that had been depicted in one of the hangings she had seen in the Buddhist temple that shared grounds with the Fuji Shrine. After a short time, she was so tired that she could no longer walk on, far more than she expected.

"It's as if the very forest is sapping my life force. Must be my imagination."

With a groan, she rose, searching out a cave for her seclusion, or a suitable clearing. After a while, she finally found a clear space with enough room, knowing her search would have to continue after the sun rose. The tangled roots of a tree, naturally covered over with soft and fragrant moss, served as a bed and exhaustion soon pulled her into a deep sleep.

As the young woman slept, what appeared to be a wandering *Yamabushi* materialized beside her still form. Simple robes of coarse earth brown wrapped loose arms around an old and wizened figure that was yet unbent by age. A woven straw hat, resembling a mushroom, lurked on the top of his head while a long red nose poked out of his face like a fire-prod. The ringed staff in his hand did not wake her, even though the otherworldly music that it made was not silenced. Tiny black wings fanned the air around him as he bent over to administer the medicine that would keep her in the world of spirit disappearance, instead of allowing her to fade to nothing.

Soft pink lips parted for the hard red berry, grimacing as her teeth crushed the pellet to release bitter juice. The *Tengu* nodded as the human swallowed reflexively. If her tests accidentally killed her then the body would not be found. It was time now for her first test though, that of endurance.

"Run my child! Run as if the hells themselves were burning your heels!"

Although the *Tengu* was an old man, the booming voice was that of a young one. As it roared across the forest, stirring the birds out of the trees, it also stirred the young wanderer out of her barely begun rest. Befuddled by her lack of rest, all she could do was to blink at the rude 'person' who had awoken her, not noticing the obvious signs that he was more than human.

"Run girl!"

Though highly confused, she took off like a rabbit. The tattoo of her feet was the drumbeat that would have been played at her maidenhood ceremony if her mother had taken her to the Sunrise Ceremony in the year she obtained her moon. Night gave way to day, the gray of early dawn resplendent silk as stars faded away. Every time she thought to stop, the strange man was there to yell into her ear the dreaded word. At last, after the longest four miles of her life, the sun rose and she fell beside a peaceful stream. The only other creature with her on the grassy bed was a laughing crow, which seemed to be amused at her plight and enjoying the chance to mock her. With eyes rimmed with the yellow of stress, once more the human sank into sleep.

"Good job *onna*, you pass this one."

By the time that BlowingWind awoke, midmorning had cast her radiant garment on the canopy of tree limbs above. The grass had released its sweet scent thanks to her crushing fall, and the stream nearby tinkled quietly to itself. The strange crow was gone, and she would have thought her headlong and confused flight through the forest a dream if it were not for the ringed staff that had carefully been laid beside her.

"Well, I guess that must have been a *Tengu*. From the way Takamura-jisan described them though, I thought they would look more crow-like. Pretty good joke though, chasing me through the forest and then leaving a fancy stick to lean on. Thank goodness it wasn't Coyote."

Scarcely had she turned away from the bank to continue on her way, but she was shoved roughly into the water. Strong hands held her under as she struggled, and when her head broke water once more she was able to get a glimpse of a crow's head perched on a monk's body before she was plunged back under. Her new staff connected with what BlowingWind desperately hoped was at the very least his gut, which ended ultimately with her release to the mercies of the now churning water. As consciousness stole away once again, the stream, deeper than she had supposed, swallowed her and swept her away to its underwater ruler.

Although consciousness had left her, BlowingWind's body had entered into its own struggle to continue living. Though her soul was broken and aching for release, instinct eventually brought her clawing back into consciousness.

BlowingWind found herself at the feet of a large dragon firmly ensconced at the end of a great hall. Pine needles had lent their green to his great scales, while onyx colored his mane and claws. Eyes the blue of a summer sky gazed with boredom upon the little human who had been forced into his domain. One great claw clutched a giant pearl in its three-clawed paw, lazily rolling it as one would a meditation ball.

"So, the *Tengu* had thought to defile me with yet another human body, but at least this one is still alive. Tell me *Ningen*, what is it that brings you into the *Aokigahara Jukai*, where they still roam free?"

"I am seeking my guardian."

"You do not look like a *Miko*, or a *Yamabushi*."

Clouds narrowed the blue skies into slits as the dragon contemplated whether it was worth his time and effort to devour her, or if he should merely allow her to drown. BlowingWind was glad that Obsidian's shell necklace still possessed its magic protecting her from drowning, but there was little she could do to defend against those sword-like teeth.

"I am neither. I come from another land. There, we perform much the same function although we dress very differently from those you are used to seeing. I am a training shaman and a Spirit Keeper."

"One who keeps spirits? It would make you similar to an *inu-gami-mochi* or *kitsune-gami-mochi*, one who employs dogs and foxes as your magic servants for your evil spells, witch."

"I am no witch, nor do I seek to own anyone. I only want to find my guardian again."

"Lies."

The dragon pounced on her then, wrapping his coils around her, seeking to constrict her so as to more easily swallow her small form. However, at that time the staff that she still had with her sprang to life, driving the *suigami* back with a holy shield while a roar issued from the depths of her knapsack.

"Obsidian!"

BlowingWind's cry resounded through the ancient hall and mingled with the roar, a plaintive cry that knew it would never be answered, even though she still sought after him and carried the torch of memory. The dragon picked himself up from where he had been thrown, shaking in his anger.

"Get out. I will eat no one with a pure heart."

Hurling a much smaller pearl at her than his own, the water god called on the waters to cast her out of his domain. A giant wave tossed her onto the shores of the streambed, leaving her half-drowned and doubting her sanity. During her tumultuous exit from the water realm contained within the stream, the pearl had somehow mounted itself on her staff. These items proved to her that these adventures were no dream, and for just a moment she caught herself missing Coyote and his tricks. At least with him, she knew what to expect.

"What a rude water spirit. I need to find a friendly place. Otherwise, a rock might try to squish me for sitting on it."

Hidden in the branches of a cedar tree, the *Tengu* that had pushed her into the stream nodded in approval, then signaled to the other *Tengu* and the *Kitsune* he was working with that she had passed and survived his test.

❊

Ryu had enjoyed the night's celebration, the carefree air of the *matsuri* recharging him with all of the vivacity that dragon-kind was noted for. He had left as the priests were raking out the coals, a nagging feeling telling him that he had to find shelter for the delicate feminine soul he had been guarding as of late. She was not yet strong enough to take form on her own in the material realm, and although he knew very little about his charge or how she had come to him, his dragon's sense of honor could not leave her unprotected.

"I wish that you would talk Little One. I enjoyed myself, but I hope that it was not too much for you."

Having flown invisibly as a shimmer of heat back to the peak of Fujisan, and then navigated the sundry lava tubes back to his subterranean abode, it was a curious relief to secrete himself once more in inky depths and infernal heat. Glad of freedom once more, instead of plunging into molten rivers of earth, Ryu closeted himself in the chambers that had been prepared long ago for his more mobile portion of himself.

Here, roughly smooth stalactites slowly dripped down the walls to whisper the secrets of water and wood going about their purposes above. Although earth itself composed the boundaries of the rooms, these chambers had been filled with the artistry of Buddhist monks now long dead, and furniture crafted by artisans whose names had never been uttered by the tongue of man.

Kneeling down on one silken cushion, his *Ningen* shape stretched forth an arm, waiting for the little pink orb to shyly come back out of his body, to roll down onto the table. Troubled dreams had led him up the river that had begun flowing in his strange fantasy world deep within a forest he had never known with waking eyes. It was a dark place full of fierce creatures that gladly attacked him on every visit, without even the slightest provocation or warning.

He had fought and vanquished these demons countless times now amongst the twisted and blackened trees invested with their own vengeful life and the scorched rock holding tales of pains of the past. Yet each time that he thought them dead and gone, they sprang to life again, hungrier and more vicious than before. Each demon seemed intent on finding the little soul who whispered and pleaded to him for protection from the fear and pain, and each creature called out to her to give up and return with them to something called a Source and to the protection of a raging tornado.

It was on one such unexpected excursion into the strange world that he had finally gotten to see the little being that had been living inside of him. Ferocious wolves had closed around him as he had been pushing farther up the river in response to her urgings, pinning him into a side canyon and taking advantage of his inability to use his larger form for self-defense. While he had been snapping at one, another, even scrawnier and tawnier than the rest, had ripped at his left flank. With a cry, a little pink orb had flown out and high into the air. Her weak attempt at flight was brought pitifully short though as the wolf's jaws snapped up the morsel that had been screaming something about a Coyote.

Seeing the hapless *tama* quivering in the jaws of the monster, and hearing her high keening, had sent the dragon into a rage that he had only entered into perhaps twice in his life. Fang and claw had become coated with bitter blood as he burst out of the box canyon to attack. Gladly would Ryu have ended it all and eaten the horrid creature, but before his jaws could close around he who had dared to steal a dragon's jewel a giant Hawk and Raven swooped in to carry off the battered and cursing being. The *tama* fell from the creature's jaws into an outstretched draconic claw, and by the laughing of the Raven he supposed that perhaps he had either passed some kind of twisted test or the thing called Coyote was not very well liked among the other demons of the forest.

Whatever had truly happened, the dreams came to him less now, and the little soul was feasted daily with meat and fish, or whatever else the dragon had been fed. The small being rested carefully between a jar of water and a juicy piece of raw venison, bringing Ryu out of the recent past with her tiny and still voice.

"My sisters will be coming for me soon."

It was the first time that he had heard conversational words come from the strange jewel in more than a whisper. Ever curious, he leaned closer to her until his face was level, as if by moving closer he would learn more through a strange process of osmosis.

"There are more of you?"

"Three other souls actually, Spirit. I can feel our approach. The main of us is moving closer, but it will not be until later that she will come. You must take me to the others, please. Her forest is too much for us."

The dragon man and spirit orb silently partook of the food; Ryu thoughtfully sipping some tea while the soul did her best to absorb the energy in the fare. Something was bothering him, and had been for quite a while now.

"Little One, what are you called? I can't keep calling you Little One, Mysterious Jewel or Precious Treasure."

A paler shade of pink washed through the ball, as if someone had set a rose quartz sphere on a light stand, or left it out in the sun for long enough to bleach it out.

"If you don't know my name, then it is not mine to give. Ask the others for my name."

Ryu did not understand what he had said to cause her pain or sadness, but by the dejected way that she rolled back to his palm and settled for sleep again he knew he had caused her great pain. She was quickly absorbed into his being again, shielded from the other much larger energies around them, and he was finally ready to leave the mountain on his own terms.

CHAPTER 13:
MAY I STAY?

AFTER hours of wandering, BlowingWind at last found an
area suitable for her purposes. An inky cavern gaped wide
its hungry maw, waiting patiently to devour any soul brave
enough to venture into the underworld through it seeking arcane
knowledge. A small stream, thankfully a different one than the one
that she had been pushed into with such murderous intent earlier,
wandered down the slope through trees and rocks, and concealed
both sleeping fish and succulent river weeds. Pine trees offered
familiar pine nuts tucked within their prickly cones, while low and
twisted bushes proffered their bright berries. Ferns and moss took
away harsh edges that had survived the centuries of wind and rain,
and at last the wanderer finally felt safe.

Opening her pack, it could be seen that the *suigami-ryu,* or water
dragon-god, had taken his due from her before she had awakened,
and her supply of jerky was gone. He had even taken the store of
dried fruits and nuts that she always kept in her pack for emergencies
and offerings. Luckily, she could go for a while longer without food,
and she was still supposed to be fasting anyway. It was the principle
of the matter that offended her though, that someone had looked
inside and through her things without proper permission.

Further looking through her things, all else was in order. Her
kinickinick was thankfully dry, as well as her sage and other herbs,
thanks to the wonder of plastic bags protecting the cloth pouches.
Her rattle was unharmed, as was the small flute that had been slipped
into her items by someone while she was busy with the *Kannushi* and
Miko at Inari Jinja. The small hand drum that had also been added to
her medicines was still wet though, but a fire would easily remedy
the situation.

The flute was a gift that she halfway could understand. It was a
soothing instrument to hear, and her own culture often would send

prayers upon the back of the wind in this manner. Once, only
Buddhist priests had been allowed to play this particular version of
the instrument, a means of meditation upon the Divine.
BlowingWind had never taken lessons with flutes, having been more
of a stringed instrument kind of girl, but she had been greatly cheered
when the priest mentoring her at the lower Sengen shrine had told
her that the intention was more important than any melody. Still it
was a medicine she did not understand and would need to work
with.

The drum was a gift that had puzzled her upon its discovery. It
was as simple as many that she had seen in the multi-ethnic store
called Soul Connections back on the main street in Mount Shasta City.
However, it still had its own aura of simple elegance giving her the
feeling that it would be sacrilegious for her to so much as tie a feather
to one of the strings serving as a handle. This she knew was not
destined to be truly hers, and yet the energy was already inextricably
entwined with her own.

"What was I supposed to be doing with it?"

BlowingWind took one more look around, marveling at the
beauty all around her. The earth itself seemed to have made a perfect
fire pit in the center of the clearing, complete with a ring of stones
waiting with open arms to embrace wood and fire. There also was a
small natural table of stone that looked as if it were meant to hold
offerings. Following the inner prompting welling inside her breast,
she gave a gift of the sacred cornmeal and some of her fine tobacco,
singing as she made her gifts in the ways of her people.

"I ask to be allowed here, to rest and sing and pray. I seek the
way to steer, so I will listen to what you spirits say."

A wave of curiosity issued out of the fern covered cave, and the
trees sighed as the preliminary verse of her song ended. They had not
sent her away, waiting for something, and this encouraged her.
Setting up camp was a simple thing, and soon she had wood and
tinder arranged for the fire that would be the heart of her temporary
home. She continued, feeling eyes following that were neither
welcoming, nor forbidding, ever increasing just beyond her range of
sight. Rummaging in her bag again, she pulled out the bit of steel and
flint she used for her fires, striking sparks into the dry tinder and

hoping for a catch.

"Fire came to my people through Coyote, Puma, Hawk, through Four Legged and Winged People. So goes the talk. May this fire be as sacred as the first."

The fire caught and roared to life and smiling, she gratefully offered a pinch of tobacco and sage to the flames, wafting the smoke carefully in all six directions acknowledged by her people. The leaves rustled as the trees and other plant people talked among themselves and the *Tengu* hiding in the cryptomeria, the cedars, discussed how they could lead the girl away from her appeasing magic. Still singing, this time in thanks to Creator for her journey, BlowingWind positioned the drum near the fire where the skin could dry and remain properly tuned. Lovingly setting out her tools so that they too could bask in the sacred energy of the place, she additionally narrated the story of each item to honor them, as the medicines were her partners in her journey. She sang of her totems and helpers back home, and invited the spirits of the land to join in her dance.

As she unwrapped her mirror, her song suddenly fell off, leaving the clearing even more silent as rocks and plants kept watching the strange woman who had penetrated so far into the Forbidden Forest's secrets. Memories of Obsidian washed through her once more, and as she gazed into its depths tears coursed unnoticed down well-worn waterways. The insulation of dreams had rotted away at last, and once more she was face to face with the painful end of a relationship that had been so young. She had accepted that Obsidian was dead and gone, and yet it was still hard to move on even after so many months. It was useless to believe that she would find even a piece of him; her shell had grown cold long ago. It was time to go under the sponsorship of another, but even though she had gone all this way she was afraid, and very lonely.

Her silence lasted no more than a moment, and the mirror found a place with everyone else. As she sighed and tried to shake her depression away again, a great *tsunami* of welcome and comfort, rivaling her former dark currents, poured out and over her from the direction of the cave. The spirits had made their final decision, and it was good to feel like she belonged in this forest that was so similar to where she had grown up and yet so different.

He had finally reached the entrance to the ancient forest of which his above ground holdings were but a small part. Most magma beings could very happily exist solely underground their entire existence, but as he was fated to flow completely to the surface one day, he continually strove towards the sweet air. The thought of seeing trees and ferns again so intimately made him purr with pleasure even though he was investigating a disturbance. He could feel the confusion and mixed feelings penetrating the earth even before he could smell the earthy richness of a new blend of herbs. Ryu had been about to boil out in defense of the weaker spirits when he heard her songs and saw her innocently bright face shining like Amaterasu.

"My, what is this then?"

Ryu's draconic vision took in not only her material form, but also all the other shapes that her souls and spirit were capable of. Layer upon layer bore wounds and scars attesting to losses and trials, but it was her innermost being that took his breath away and froze him just within the shadow of Mother Earth's birth canal. Still rough, but slowly becoming tumbled into a round bead of sky-blue turquoise, she was shot through with veins of silver and gold. The human woman was performing a ceremony unknown to him now, lighting a fire and singing of the spirits who had accompanied her and stood ranged about her like old friends.

It was easy for him to tell she was not native to his land. Her red-brown hair was like the iron rich obsidian hidden about the landscape, in his opinion, a far cry from the usual blacks and dark browns of the indigenous population. The pale jasmine colored skin so liberally sprinkled across her pert nose with freckles told him so as well, just as clearly as the cobalt of the heavens that had been fashioned into her eyes inherited from some ancestor and the fringed white leathers now piquing his curiosity. His best bet was that she was American, although he had been wrong on human ethnicity before.

Ryu had been enjoying her dance, reminded of the mysterious hawk maiden swooping and sweeping before him at the festival, painted pink and red by firelight like some phoenix descended from the Heavens. Her voice he enjoyed as well, and performance, in addition to her prayers to stay for a while on her sojourn.

Breaking her performance short, some sub-oceanic tremor below the waters and winds of her spirit set a great *tsunami* ripping through her tiny form. The epicenter seemed to be the polished hemisphere of volcanic glass that she had been dealing with at that point in her ritual, so carefully held as the maiden lost herself within it. The grief and loneliness poured from her eyes told the dragon that it held a very fresh and quite raw memory encased within it in addition to all of the other uses it had been put to. The tiny soul riding within him stirred uneasily, fighting her own grief as silently as a sphinx from Greek Myth regarded its prey. None of the other spirits in the area had made her truly welcome he could see, and something about the woman plucked at a chord deep within him, urging him to protect her. So it was that Ryu expanded his warmth and welcome to the strange little *onna* in a great volcanic eruption.

As Ryu's searing warmth ripped through her frigid inner tides, he was gratified to see whole icebergs trapped within her seas melt away, and the glacier blue of her eyes swiftly warmed to a sapphire shot thorough with olivine. How quickly her eyes changed with her mood fascinated him, and he gladly watched from his lair as movement found the woman once more, and she danced to complete her previous tasks. The smile on her face was all the reward he had needed, but he certainly was not about to turn down free entertainment.

Now that her song was finished, he watched as she sat silently regarding her surroundings, as if she were waiting for something to happen. The normal sounds of the forest continued, but the crack and snap of an occasional twig began to wear on the dragon that waited for her voice to rise once more and soothe his soul.

It was well that she should be on her guard. The *Tengu* that lived in the forest surely would not treat her kindly if they discovered her in the forest. Truly, he could not even understand how she had gotten this close to the gateway into the mountain world. The Forest had kept humans away for a long time, even with the human habitations encroaching upon their borders here, and to even enter into the version that the spirits dwelled within necessitated both finding the dry river and crossing the bridge. If the arch was not passed over, the humans stayed in their own world, and the bridge presented itself for crossing only if someone was pure enough or other spirits were entering into the human world. Such people as never found the bridge merely got lost or eventually found their way home. For those who did cross the bridge though, there were only two possibilities for them.

"How did you come here Little One?" Ryu whispered.

A human, even one who had recently undergone the ritual purification of *misogi*, could not tarry long in the spirit world. Being flesh and blood, the denser vibrations of their bodies would eventually fall back into the human world, unless fed upon the spiritual substance of some edible. As most were unaware of that magical law, many quickly returned to the human world, fading away and remembering their brief sojourn – or not – as may be. If they did manage to eat something, or were fed by someone, then they were trapped in the spiritual world, never to return to the human realm without a guide or being cast out. This young woman was obviously currently guideless, despite all the spirits who were her helpers.

Now that she had formally been accepted into the area by one of the leading families here, the wildlife of the place went back to their normal lives. The birds sang in the trees, a deer crashed through underbrush looking for berries, and the resident fox peeked out at the foreign woman. Time passed by, and the woman picked up the flute to shakily pick out a melody. Her inexperience with the instrument was glaringly obvious, and it wasn't long before she put it away again, much to the relief of his ears.

"I should have stopped to get my guitar before running away. Now I can't share any music except through my voice, or this drum." She shook her head after, heaving a small sigh.

The wind rose as the woman made her statement, swirling up and away, taking a few leaves with it. Then the wind was gone, and a few hawk feathers fluttered down to land on the girl and in the fire. She picked one up and examined it before twisting it into her hair. One of the feathers also managed to find its way to Ryu, and the tiny flutter of joy from the strange soul that he carried with him was an unnerving dance, fluttering his belly with recognition of whatever spirit had just left. Also, the matching of the pattern of the last feather that he had seen to this new one confirmed for him his connection through this unknown windy spirit to the woman now sitting silently listening to the wind.

"Interesting."

Ryu made himself comfortable out of her sight, watching the antics of the newcomer.

The stream flowed on into a river, feeding a sacred lake in the distance. Just like the stream that BlowingWind sat by, outside in the Spirit World, the waterfall that RagingTornado so jealously guarded flowed away from its Source to an ultimate destiny. What it was she knew not, only that two paths would cross in herself to unite two worlds some day, as with any other woman.

The winds in this interior forest were changing again, and the beasts of her forest had told her that a far more dangerous beast than they had infiltrated the dense defenses as of late, following the river towards the Heart. Having peered through BlowingWind's eyes from time to time, she knew it was an uninvited presence.

RagingTornado cleaned her snowflake obsidian tipped spear again, anger coursing through her veins. She wanted to be left alone, to wander these woods and mountains within her mind without a life mate to abandon her at the journey's end. The rumors had it that this beast also possessed a human form, and part of her soul as well. Perhaps it was merely Coyote trying to tempt her out of hiding and back into the treacherous world. This put her at a loss as to what to do. Should she chase out the intruder, or should she stay here at the roaring falls issuing out of subterranean waterways to guard her most precious secrets?

In the outer world, RagingTornado knew that her lighter half was calling for Obsidian, although she refrained from using his name. It would have changed anyway, so what was the use of it? She could also tell that BlowingWind was close to grief paralysis again, as her surroundings stilled and the waters took on an icier note. If this happened too frequently, the river would freeze, and she would have to break the ice again with her spear. If the waters and winds ceased completely, BlowingWind's physical life would end. It had been much easier when the missing two souls were here to help, but Wisdom and Love had been missing for quite a while now.

At first, their absence had been a good thing. Love's endless moaning about Obsidian had ceased, and Wisdom could no longer be heard rationalizing their grief. The quiet had soothed the injured and irritated soul at first, but then it had become eerie. Now, it was becoming harder to maintain the connection into the physical world because of their absence. The winds that had once torn through the valley, to carry the waterfall's mist farther away, no longer blew as hard to water the forest, and no part of BlowingWind's four part spirit had learned yet how to sing back missing souls or soul pieces for themselves or others.

Things got worse though. As to this mysterious beast of obsidian colored rivers and flowing flame, the pine and cedar claimed to have seen for themselves that he held a pink being captive within his own being. Coyote, who she absolutely knew had to be lurking about, had attacked this beast, this four-legged and plumed serpent, and liberated the little orb for a short time. However, the interference of Hawk and Raven had resulted in the dragon regaining control of Love. So then the beast couldn't be Coyote in disguise. Somehow, some creature, some demon of this Land of the Rising Sun, was trying to possess her piece by piece. Perhaps he had Wisdom also then. If so, then she had to do something.

"Was this how Rattlesnake felt when the first humans moved too close to his home?"

Snake stirred on the rock he had been sunning himself on, previously unnoticed by the training Shadow Shaman. Few of her generation followed the calls they received from Spirit, and dark was not always evil. Each shaman had to balance the dark with the light within him or her; it was the use of power that caused a shaman to be good or evil.

"Yes, I felt the fear, anger, and confusion that you feel now my Granddaughter. One must face their fear though, and your forest will not keep him out of the Heart forever."

"What should I do Grandfather Snake?"

"A member of the Snake Clan has her rattle. She should make her warning before striking with fang and venom. However, the solution may be reached within a council with the invader."

"This forbidding forest and the creatures I have placed in it are not enough warning?"

Snake, coiling upon himself to raise his wide head to better regard his distant descendant, restrained a sigh. She lacked scales, lacked fangs and venom, and many of the other things that self-respecting snakes had which made them so beautiful. This human did have a vast mystical potential though, and was probably born a few centuries late. The only physical trait he had ever picked out that might be a sign of the reptilian blood that also ran in her veins, was the diamond pattern in her eyes that resembled his fine diamond-back. Still, she was of his blood, his ugly but beautiful grandchild.

"Sometimes, one must carry the warning themselves to make an intruder realize."

"You are right Grandfather, of course."

Raging Tornado stood up from her own rock, carefully staying away from Snake's personal space. She did not know why her tribal helpers and ancestors were able to reach her from so far away, but there were many things that she did not know yet. Perhaps some of her questions would be answered when facing the intruder. The woman stormed down the river, her dark fringes racing with the breeze. As she left her haven, a sudden wave of delicious summer heat tore through the forest and thawed the once congealing waters. However, her rage had elevated her own temperature so much that it passed her by completely unnoticed as she raced the river and wind.

CHAPTER 14:
A NEW GUARDIAN

AFTERNOON rolled lazily by as her gentle beams slanted down through the trees in reverential and passionate forays into the future. In due course, Dusk came to the volcano's forest spreading behind her the shawl of Night that she was never without. BlowingWind had alternated singing and dancing to the fire's crackling beat with praying and listening to the speech of the forest.

At first, she had come close to the cave entrance with her spiraling circles of life and supplication. Dipping and whirling outstretched arms like those great wings of her father's namesake, BlowingWind had brought to Japan and to a spying dragon the energies of Arizona deserts and Shastayama's winter blizzards. All that she had ever been and was now had been laid bare to the inquisitive eyes of the volcano *Kami* as he peered into her soul, but after awhile she grew conscious of the furtive peeks into her being. A warning tingle had set itself about her belly, bringing her teeth to sharp edges every time she passed near the tempting entrance, as if someone in the cave had been poised to snatch her away into the dangerous subterranean world below. So it was that the young Shaman had gradually and unobtrusively moved further away from the beckoning gateway into the mysterious lair, tightening her circles around the familiar safety of the likewise dancing flames.

Ai could feel the building pressure within the inner currents of her current protector, Ryu's greed to possess for himself such an exotic treasure for his perennial delight. She desperately whispered warnings of the curse upon her family, afraid of the doom of another man through her very act of being. In vain were all her efforts, the whispered warnings falling on ears paying attention only to the songs of the human he watched outside and the music of her rhythmic body, the faint taste of the forbidden having already ripened the interests and possessiveness of the magma dragon.

Indeed then it had been wise for the little thing to back away. Ryu had more than taken a shining to the turquoise soul seated so very tenuously in her mounting of flesh and blood. The glints of pain and longing desire within her being awaked his long-buried desires to hoard and brood. Not all dragons were completely good, if any, and Ryu was certainly no exception.

Patiently the dragon waited for an opening to spirit her away for his own, or to enter her body as a mist and lodge in some choice cavity of her body, but not one decent chance presented itself to him again, now that his mind was set. She was too focused on calling to her mysterious guardian that she was seeking so desperately, even though she refused to call out its name and it was pointedly refusing to answer her. The dragon seethed with his choler against the spirit who had abandoned the tender morsel, as even though he had had no specific worshippers of his own, he could not fathom the thought of leaving such a devout follower to the mercies of the world. Even though he would have no quarrels over territory, it was clear to him that he would be a better guardian than this "He who calms the tempest within my heart."

Finally, Night came to the forest, and this visit gave him new shadows to lurk in, so that he could get closer to his prey. Humans tended to react unpredictably when surprised, and out in this forest was no place for her to take off in a headlong flight to save herself from him. Rocks and ledges were plentiful within this twisted landscape, and a human's body was far more fragile than even the most delicate flower *Kami*. As he watched, the woman finally collapsed into the eager embrace of the loam, mechanically rolling herself into the thin blanket that had been waiting patiently there to hold her in its tender embrace. While BlowingWind hoped to receive at least a dream from Obsidian, Ryu stewed over not being able to use the ground to caress the temporary abode of his shining flame.

BlowingWind's dreams contained no messages from her departed love. Only ancient voices of her ancestors greeted her with the croaking of elderly oaks in a high wind to chant new songs to her, songs that worked into her memory like worms into the earth. The tribal elders of times long gone had been teaching her the old songs during her sleeps for a while now. Their faces were always unseen because of the wild forest that she was lost in, but she knew that they were hidden somewhere in one of the high-mountain *arroyos*. She wanted to follow the voices and learn more of the old ways of her ancestors, eager to have some kind of strong connection to at least one side of her heritage. However, fear of the beasts roaming in her mind kept BlowingWind hidden in the cave that was her stronghold in this dream forest of hers.

As the human maiden slept and learned from the ancestors of her body and soul, Ryu crept close to sit beside the woman and the warm fire. Even sitting so close to a slumbering human eased his crushing loneliness, and her body was a symphony to ears long deprived of the music of living material beings. The slow and steady pound of her heart accompanied the electric zing of her nerves and synapses, while her gentle breath was sweeter than any flute note. Even her smell, curiously like what had been haunting him of late, was something to savor before it faded away with the eventual death of this mortal. It always awed him how delicate and temporary the human and animal kingdoms were, so much more fleeting than the mountains and rocks that his particular breed of dragon were. An hour he managed to pass in what could become a favorite past-time, but his peace was shattered by the snapping of a twig just out of the ring of the fire's crackling influence.

The heavy and acrid scent of *Tengu* drifted to the brooding dragon, offending his nose like the stink of garbage left too long unburied. He had become so engrossed in his entertainment that he had not paid attention to the encroaching presence of the *Tengu*, but his instincts were now unfettered now that her spell over him was temporarily broken. Turning and rising away from the maiden, Ryu began an advance towards the invader in defense of his morsel, but a misplaced foot snapped a larger stick. Though small, the sound resounded through his ears like the echoes of gunshots that had once thrown even the High Plain of Heaven into an uproar when the Western guns had entered into the *Sengoku Jidai*, or Warring States Period. To him, it was even louder than the fateful atomic bombing that had taken the lives of so many *Kami* and *Ningen* in Tokyo and Nagasaki.

Cougar eyes snapped open at the sound, BlowingWind responding to the danger hanging in the air like mist and also to the noisy misstep of her new and as of yet unknown protector. Throwing back the blanket, the shaman flew at the "invader," intent on driving off whatever creature was daring to interfere with her search. Whoever it was had his back to her, and a well placed fist bruised a kidney while her weight and inertia drove him to the ground. Ryu glanced back in surprise at the unexpected contact, shocked that a human who had been so fast asleep was now attacking him. Although he was quite capable of defending himself, Ryu was leery of warding her off, afraid to hurt his new treasure.

It was not the first time that he had tasted dirt, nor the most embarrassing, but it was enough to annoy him. Although part of him did want to cherish and protect this child-warrior a deeper and ingrained voice gained from the long respect that his kind had enjoyed wished to sear away her body so that she would never repeat this mistake again. Doing so would also have the added benefit of freeing her spirit from its flesh to appreciate more fully, even if he did lose the entertainment of her material shape.

Fortunately for the human, BlowingWind was able to deflect his ire. While the ground softened at the impact of the earth spirit below her, BlowingWind glimpsed his face. Her normally pale flesh lightened all the more, and trembling hands gently turned him over to get a better view, although as nervous as the land when the earthquake *Kami* danced or the plains when Thunderbird came visiting.

"Obsidian?"

Yellowed eyes mottled with the browns of confusion as they stared into the chocolate eyes whose shock matched her own. So similar to the visage she knew so well, the minor differences now leapt out at her. His skin was paler than Obsidian's had been, as if he had not seen the sun very often within the past few years. Where luxuriant rivers of deepest currents would have been plaited into streams, short and overlapping spikes of hair wildly waved at her. Pulling back and to the side, BlowingWind hugged herself in disappointment as her eyes took in the now rumpled but still expensive fiery silks. Just as quickly as that, the new hope that had been kindled in her eyes was drowned by the waves of despair. As the spirit sat up, the Shaman questioned him.

"Who are you Spirit? What were you doing sitting beside me?"

"I am Take Ryu, Maiden. You seemed lonely when you came to my attention and I thought to provide you with some company. I also live here."

Somehow, Ryu could not look into those eyes and admit that he had been waiting for a chance to possess her, nor that he had fallen in love with the way she moved and sang. He could see the thoughts flying through her head as she deciphered what he had just said to her, and then formulated what she would say next.

"My name is MountainChild BlowingWind."

"It is a pleasure to meet you then MountainChild-san, even if you did greet me by shoving me in the dirt. May I call you BlowingWind, *onegai*? Your given name suits you so well."

A flush crept up BlowingWind's cheeks, painting them a delicate shell pink, despite her best efforts to stamp it down. She tried to raise her plentiful anger to hide it, but the mask would not fit itself to her face underneath his humored smirk and twinkling eyes. Something deep inside her mind whispered of danger, but the voice was buried deep within and too hard to hear, and the play of emotions on the *Kami's* face was very distracting.

A lock of her cropped hair had fallen over her face during the brief scuffle, and when Ryu's hand swept forward to tuck it away BlowingWind could not stifle her flinch at his touch, leaping several feet further away from the fire. His hand was hot, and her skin had always felt so cold, and touch was not something that she had felt much lately.

For his part, Ryu had been amused at her embarrassment and unnecessary fear of him. However, as she had just placed herself closer to the *Tengu* lurking in the forest he was more concerned with luring her back to safety. She was cute in the dust, but that wouldn't last for very long if the *Tengu* had their way.

"So, you obviously do not come from around here. Tell me about yourself, and where you come from, and use your native language if you wish."

BlowingWind averted her eyes, self conscious of how the warm eyes seemed to note the changes she knew they were going through, and at having attacked a spirit who seemed now to bear her no ill-will. After all, she had attacked from behind, and he had therefore been at a disadvantage. English flowed easily to her lips as she replied to Ryu, wondering just how much she should tell.

"Father was a Shaman, Mother is a carpenter. I'm sorry I attacked you."

Ryu's lips curved gently upward, a fair imitation of some benign Buddha. Returning to the more urgent matter though, his eyes were flints as he looked back to where the *Tengu* had been. Of course, it was no longer where it had been lurking, but hiding elsewhere nearby. The trickster had no doubt merged with one of the cryptomeria trees nearby, waiting for its chance to administer some test or pull some prank. *Kitsune* would not be far behind. The siren song of her injured and weakened spirit would attract many such undesirable spirits for some time unless she began to heal soon. As long as he was with her, he could keep her safe.

"It is nothing, and you were right in what you did, I suppose. The forest is not safe for humans, especially after nightfall. Let us repair back to the warmth of the fire." He struggled to keep a lofty speech pattern, to impress on her some feeling of wisdom or anything that she might look up to. But he felt that resolve failing quickly.

Rising from the earth's embrace, Ryu smoothed his hair, dusted off his robes and rearranged his folds as he took a few steps toward the heat of the fire. BlowingWind had stayed where she was though, staring at the ground. With each experience in this strange country, her hopes of meeting with Obsidian's spirit were raised and then dashed, dwindling away like a candle left to burn. Her gaze had fixed forlornly where Ryu's imprint still was.

Ryu paused to look back at the little human, watching her wallow in her sorrow like a boar at a mud-hole, while one eyebrow defied the other to reach mountainous heights somewhere near where his mane masqueraded as hair. He had expected her to follow him to safety, but whatever had happened to her seemed to make it difficult to focus anywhere but within her own mind, making her ambivalent toward life at the best. However, he knew a historian was a far cry from a psychologist, and only now did that realm begin to raise his curiosity. Taking a few steps back to the side of the child-woman, he bent over to whisper gently into her ear.

"Perhaps I could interest you in a little tea as well as safety, little BlowingWind? I do hope that you have a kettle."

BlowingWind looked up; pulled out of morose thoughts long enough to register the *Kami's* outstretched hand.

"I'm sorry. Thank you."

In a daze, she took the hand offered, not noticing as he began to wrap threads of his energy around her with the touch. The woman was too wrapped up in memories of underwater currents that had sang so gently in such a manner and of long artistic hands that had pulled her through water and sky. These memories contrasted with the forgotten caverns hoarding ancient jewels and mountain winds now murmuring to her so softly, and with the broad sturdy hands that gently worked their way through the earth's crust. Pointedly not looking at the painful reminder of what progress had stolen from her and her former home, BlowingWind followed after the oddly chivalrous spirit as he shepherded her to the fire.

"Forgiven. Tell me BlowingWind, what brings you so far from the realm of humanity?"

He already knew that she was seeking for her former guardian, but to admit his knowledge would be to admit that he had been spying for hours. Ryu also hoped that he would be able to draw her out and find out more about this shattered woman.

"I am looking for someone. His voice told me to come to this country, but I have found no other clues. At a shrine I was told to come here, and so I wander these woods looking for him. What are you doing here? Why were you in my camp?"

The spirit couldn't help but to smile at the naiveté behind the façade she was trying to build, and at how she also was trying to find out the truth of his own story. Grandly seating them on the log beside the fire, he threw more wood on before answering.

"As I said before, I live here. You called me out, so I have been investigating you. Why don't you tell me about yourself? I know that you are far from home little one."

The command had been gently put, but it was a command all the same. Long used to getting his way most of the time, it did not surprise him when she complied. Though her eyes stared into the shifting flames of the fire he had been keeping going during his vigil, she seemed grateful to have someone to talk to.

"Mother came from Ireland, running from Grandmother O'Drake for some reason she doesn't talk about much. In Arizona, she met my Father while he was attending college, even though she didn't go herself. Mother said that a whirlwind chased her into the library that day. Later, I came to be. Dad had majored in politics and law, because he was helping to fight a nuclear power plant that was being built near the Reservation. That project took his life when I was seven."

BlowingWind had no idea why she was telling him this, but it felt good to talk about it as her tale unfolded. Maybe one day she would work through the grief. Falling silent for a bit, she thought about her father while Ryu hid his horror at the mention of nuclear anything. The memories of the atomic bombings were still fresh in his mind, and so many that hadn't been lost to the blast became twisted by the radiation poisoning. After a little, her story continued.

"Father was grooming me to be a Shaman like he was, a Medicine and Spirit Keeper. After he died, the elders had called a council to decide who would take over my training. The Apache survive, but the old ways are dying and being forgotten slowly, or sold for white people curious about 'savage' ways. Mother couldn't stay on the Reservation though, the memories were too fresh, and so we moved. I guess you could say that she ran away from the pain. At any rate, we moved to where Father had always wanted to visit, Medicine Lake and Mount Shasta in Northern California. I think you call it Shastayama, which is what the local *Taiko* group called it.

Ryu nodded encouragingly. They did refer to that mountain as Shastayama or as Shastasan, and he was familiar with the mountain. It was part of the Pacific Ring of Fire, and one year Ryu had the misfortune of attending one of the meetings of the Ring with his father. Caught in the winds of her story like a kite in a storm, BlowingWind continued.

"Despite that move, I became one anyway. That same year I met Him, the Spirit of Medicine Lake. My first night camping beside the lake, he gifted me with this necklace, and my Smoking Mirror."

There was confusion on her face as she indicated the items and tried to recall the shape in the water. She hadn't ever clearly been able to remember it, but it had to have been a dragon since that was when mother revealed Drake's Curse to her. The image was cloaked by Spider in dust-hardened cobwebs though, and would not come forth. BlowingWind's hand gripped her shell, her eyes finally leaving the fire to lock on the mirror still sitting on her altar.

"The lake always had a special magic. Eventually I met a boy as passionate about it as I was. It wasn't until recently that he revealed to me who he really was though, after I agreed to be his. My plans had been to attend a local college back there, pursuing a major in engineering with his support. I put even more energy into protesting the geothermal power plant that was being built, since my duties with the snowboarding team were over. I can still see how irritated Mom was when she woke up one sunny morn to find three 'Save Medicine Lake' bumper stickers on her car."

Wistful breezes fought her amused smirk at the thought of her sticker escapade. As annoyed as Marie had been at stickers on the car, they had stayed. Ryu watched her face with interest, wondering what other pranks she had played in her not-so-distant youth.

"I take it your mother did not like sticky substances on her car."

The smirk widened into a grin with the speed of a sparrow.

"No. She thought the idea of car stickers was a 'tacky American practice that no self-respecting Irish woman would implement!' Mom was funny like that; she gave up her Irish citizenship but still lambasted America and her politics constantly."

Ryu shook his head, not bothering to conceal his own grin. After all, he now knew where she got her swift temper. As she continued though, the smile faded like a dying ember.

"We were going to have kids some day, like in the old stories. I was even going to move in with him after my high-school graduation. I guess fate had other plans. He wasn't invincible, and turbines apparently can kill spirits while using material forms. I wandered the forest around the lake for a while after I was not allowed to kill myself. A bit later is when he told me to come to Japan. So here I am."

Ryu's heart broke. The woman before him was obviously here because of a delusion. Unless she had gone down to *Yomi*, the Land of the Dead, she had no way to know for sure if it was really her former guardian, a trick of her mind, or just a troublesome spirit who had told her that. Besides, not even the Great Ancestor Izanagi had been able to bring his wife and sister Izanami back from *Yomi*. She was not going to see him again. By her depressed state, it was clear that she was realizing this.

"This 'He' you refer to was the guardian you have been calling for."

"Yes, he is. To find him, I am supposed to find a guide to take me up the mountain."

The glaciers rose in her eyes again as twin *tsunamis* of grief and despair tore through her being again. As her hand tightened around the shell necklace, delicate human flesh was sliced by sharp edges, releasing blood filled with the tang of copper and cinnamon. The pain went unnoticed though, although the dragon did not miss the scent. Gently prying her fingers open with one hand Ryu's other turned her chin toward him.

"I will be your guardian and tutelary, and will guide you up the mountain."

The tears that had been forming stopped at the edge of her eyes, and she could not help looking into those murky pools before her. BlowingWind wanted to look anywhere else, but the *Kami's* inescapable grip on her face prevented a turn of the head and his gentle gaze froze her in place.

"You will? Really?"

"*Honto ne*, really."

"When do we start? Can we go now?"

The tears continued now, venting and welling up from some underground spring to release more of the pain that she had been feeling but denying. Ryu had always hated the scent of tears, and the sight of her silent crying caused a guilt to burn within his hardened rock that served as a heart – unlike any he had ever felt stir before.

"Tomorrow, in the morning. For now, rest BlowingWind."

The young American closed her eyes, too tired to lie down for sleep. As her consciousness fled for the land of sleep her body slumped against him, falling against a chest unused to contact with a warm body. Fevered flesh burned into him even through the silks, and he wondered if she was supposed to be that hot.

Ryu could not remember any of his history students at the University radiating such heat when they turned in assignments, and he began to regret his promise to take her to the summit. He had given his word though, so he could only keep it and the hurry her to a clinic afterwards. When he had a chance, he would need to go to one of the numerous *Kami* libraries hidden throughout the country to learn the proper care of a human. He didn't want her to end up like the deer he had taken in as a pet in his distant puphood.

CHAPTER 15:
THE STORM CONTAINED WITHIN

"**COME** on, I don't think you want to sleep on my chest so soon. Here you are."

The short remainder of the night flew by far too quickly for Ryu, who had just bedded down his new human in the thin blanket that pretended to be a proper covering against the night. As the minutes marched into hours, those very same hours painted a distinct rose flush on the shaman's face. Likewise, the waters of her body thought to escape her earthy caverns, erupting to her surface to stream away into the earth below, stealing valuable salts and minerals in the process. On the other hand, it was also passing too slowly for him. Once moving onto one of the major trails up the mountain, he could easily merge the both of them back into the human world.

"I need to either return you to your plane or bond you to me soon. By your body's reactions this is probably not your first time in the spiritual dimension. What are you running from? A spiritual sickness is far worse than any physical malady, and far more difficult to cure, threatening the very present and future of the shining gem of your soul."

Her face creased in the firelight after he voiced his thoughts, but she did not wake up. The malady only slowly increased, and despite her being at rest he could hear the increased labor of her heart.

"Perfect, I finally have my own human, and I have to choose a sick one."

Many similar thoughts had run through his mind as BlowingWind slept before him. Seeing her shivering beneath the blanket had prompted him to shift into his dragon form twice now, each time coiling around her the way a snake would with his prey. Currently he still held both the form and the maiden, but her heart rate was picking up again, telling him she was slowly swimming into consciousness. It was time to release her and to take up the pretense of a human shape once more. As Amaterasu climbed into the sky, Ryu left his human to prepare a small meal.

"Don't you have any food or things to cook with? Your body is part of you. You should take care of it. You don't want to mummify yourself like those tree priests."

Giving up on the idea of tea and boiled rice, Ryu began to gather berries and nuts for the two of them. It was meager compared to the bacon that he had grown used to during his professorship, but it was far healthier and quite readily available. Ryu had taken off his outer *haori* to use as a basket of sorts, leaving only his yellow under kimono to cover the flesh above his waist. Once he had gathered enough, he was unperturbed when he heard the rustles of his human rising.

Her soft voice was hoarse with a need for water and from the morning. "What are you doing?"

"I should think it obvious BlowingWind. I happen to be getting our breakfast. It isn't very wise to climb on an empty stomach, even for a spirit. I hope you like berries and pine nuts."

Ryu settled down beside the American, spreading out their fare with as much flourish as if it had been the *shinsen* offerings before one of the major *Kami*. In his mind, this meal would be closer to the *naorai*, or ritualized sharing of the *shinsen* after the *Kami* had dined, in order to ease the transition back to the human world. Happily he gave his thanks for the meal, his smile a bright beam in the sun's early morning glow as he began to eat. The human seemed to become a fresh shoot of bamboo though, so green did her face become as she eyed what had seemed so appealing just the day before.

"No thanks. I'm not hungry."

BlowingWind went to drink a little from the stream, settling her stomach and easing a parched throat.

That she was not hungry did not surprise the guardian in the least bit, but he was comforted by the thought that he had at least tried. Perhaps he would be able to interest her in eating something later. Having eaten his fill, Ryu carefully tied up his *haori* in such a way as to easily sling it around one shoulder. Extending a hand to provide a firm foundation for the unsteady maiden below him, Ryu summoned his new *Miko* to her first task.

"Come then, and we shall break camp."

An unexplainable force made her grip his hand, her muscles responding to the spirit's command. BlowingWind couldn't understand why her body was responding, and it frightened her in all actuality as it had only ever obeyed her own demands or Obsidian's gentle suggestions. Still, she did not fight it at this time, as they did need to get moving so that she could finish her quest.

The shaman moved about quickly, reverently packing her things and uttering prayers of gratefulness for her short stay, watching herself as if she had been watching a movie shot in the first person point of view. Before long, her few possessions had been stored away, and she followed after the sure-footed form before her.

Forest paths slowly gave way to winding rocky slides posing as trails, while the woman and her self-appointed guardian rose ever higher. Many times Ryu stopped to wait for her, or to help her past the more difficult areas. However, they had a long way to go before they would break into one of the main trails, and the smell of trailing *Tengu* burned the dragon's nose. His suspicious eyes wandered all around, and on more than one occasion his warning growl frightened the very human he was protecting. The two *Tengu* withdrew each time though, and Ryu saw it as a small price to pay in order to win their way unharassed to the humans' paths.

BlowingWind slipped backward in time while following the otherwise amiable spirit, remembering painfully a hike that she had taken up Mount Lassen one summer with her few friends that had included Obsidian. Thusly occupied with memories, it was no surprise that while walking one foot took a misstep, and only Ryu's quick reflexes saved the little human from a very nasty spill off of the rock outcropping they had been navigating.

"Be more careful Little One. The mountain itself likes to trip the unwary, and my elder brother is only granting you safe passage over his back because I spoke for you."

"The mountain is your brother?"

Ryu's eyebrows could not contain his surprise, floating high up on great currents as he restrained his laughter. He continued supporting her, her head cocked like a little child as she processed his words. Wherever her mind had been, obviously it hadn't quite returned completely. Under their feet, the ancient lava flow was also laughing, its very atoms vibrating with amusement.

"No BlowingWind, the mountain is not my brother. The old lava flow we are navigating is."

"Oh. When did you speak for me? I didn't hear you say anything."

She was centered in her body again, so Ryu could safely let her out of his arms once more. He retained hold of her hand though, for the rock was slick due to the fine sand that had been blown over it, and the crow-stink had drawn closer again. Still, having a companion to speak to soothed him.

"Speech is not always through the mouth BlowingWind. I could teach you later if you wish."

The warm smile gracing his face did little to warm her heart, instead it was like he had taken daggers of ice and hollowed out her chest. It was strange to see the face of the one she loved on another, and the crashing tsunami of grief threatened to drown her once again. Ryu sensed the sudden change in her mood and saw clearly the change in her eyes.

"He said something very similar once."

"BlowingWind, a *Kami* always keeps his promises, even if one is not aware of the reason someone else seems to fill it. Stay here with me, don't go where the wave is taking you."

"Ryu, nothing is taking me anywhere, except my feet up this mountain and closer to the Star Path. Stop trying to read my mind."

BlowingWind let go of Ryu's hand, picking her own way up the slope. The red flush of embarrassment had unmistakably opened her petals across the human's face though. What was worse, BlowingWind's doubt had begun to grow even more. Ryu watched his human scramble ever closer to the main trail, listening to her heartbeat and his brother's subsonic chuckles.

Before long, his brother contained his amusement enough to speak in his mind. The voice was deep and stark, fitting for the flow.

"Ryu, our *Otou-sama* will not be pleased to find you are courting a human, especially one who has become occupied by thoughts of death."

"*Aniki*, I'm not courting her. She was alone and unprotected. How could I let a lone woman suffer the 'tender mercy' of the *Tengu* Tribe?"

"But she is still occupied by death, and you have already begun a binding spell on her. I'm sure that you are aware that her spirit is trying to lose her physical body little brother."

"What am I supposed to do about that *Aniki*? She's looking for her guardian, or so she says, but the weak protective energy around her makes me wonder if he even still exists."

"You are too soft hearted *Nii-san*. Let the girl go, she will only cause you pain. That is all any human can or will do to us."

"Elder Brother, how can you say that? The stories below still tell of you as one of the greatest champions in our Clan for the *Ningen*. What has happened since your body was released to here?"

"You will see in your own time Little Brother. Until then, you should worry about bringing life-giving minerals to the soil when you also erupt properly. Stop chasing after the perfect female, for she does not exist. Find a good *ryu-onna* who will stay with you."

Although Ryu had continued after his human during his psychic conversation with the very ancient lava flow, BlowingWind's embarrassment had lent extra speed to her ascent. One small step was all it took to turn that momentum against her and a small spray of rock showered down on the hapless dragon, bringing with it a now very flummoxed woman. Once more his inherited reflexes came into play, and once more blue skies were locked with dark earth. Just as suddenly, the blue skies turned to the gray-green of approaching monsoons, and Ryu was flung to the ground.

She had watched quietly for hours now, perched just behind BlowingWind's eyes and just below the skin, waiting. RagingTornado had tried to warn BlowingWind of possible ulterior motives that the spirit could be possessed of, but their long mourning and state of soul loss was dampening once strong gifts of insight. Something had rankled her about Ryu as soon as she had seen the *Kami*. It was not the obvious reason of his having stolen Obsidian's face, or the rumors that he had stolen one of her souls. No, it was something far worse than that, even though she had no idea what it was.

Perhaps it was his eyes that bothered her the most, how BlowingWind calmed mysteriously every time she locked with his dark orbs. To tell the truth, even she felt their hypnotic power, and it infuriated her that he could even dare to presume such a thing as using hypnosis. If he were truly capable of doing so, there was no telling what he might force her to do later. And so, for her own safety, RagingTornado watched for a chance to strike.

At last, her chance came as BlowingWind tripped yet again, lost between the past and the present. The rocks skittered down the slope before her, shatteringly announcing BlowingWind's failure to stay within one world yet again. Although RagingTornado would have welcomed death before, there were things yet unfinished and cracking her head open on the rocks would only serve to trap her here with no mourners, and no way to move on. BlowingWind fought for purchase on the slippery slope while RagingTornado waited for her chance to take control of the situation.

BlowingWind's eyes locked with those of their captor, stunned by the fall and by the resemblance that was now never far from her mind. It was the chance the shadow had been waiting for, and RagingTornado threw BlowingWind into the psychic forest of their collective mind while wresting control. The rage and sorrow of months spent in various states of dissociation gave RagingTornado strength, and swift hands hurled what she thought of as "The Impostor" to the ground.

"Impostor! Kidnapper! Thief! Give back my soul!"

A calmer and saner version of herself could be heard inside of her head, telling her to stay calm. RagingTornado was not one to listen though, preferring instead to rage and scream at the very confused spirit lying in the dust at her feet. Her desperation to be whole once more had called out to the wind spirits of the area, and her kindred spirits howled around her as forest fires burned in her eyes.

"Miss MountainChild, what in the five ancient lands are you talking about?"

"Oh no, that innocent act may work with my Light, but it doesn't fool me. Give me back Love and Wisdom. I don't know how you got them, but give them back."

Ryu's faced hardened, as stern as the solidified flow that was now his brother below his back. He was not impersonating anyone, nor was he a kidnapper. Like many other dragons he could not claim to have never stolen, but he definitely had no desire to steal anyone's soul. Loosing his affable manner and his patience, one leg snaked out to knock the audacious human back into her proper place.

The woman acted as he expected, but tooth and nail were no match for his weight and training. She had no right to treat him thusly, and if this was how she had been allowed to act before then her lesson in humility and respect was sorely overdue. Ryu could feel his own dark side striving for release, but to allow his violent nature to be exposed would mean the end of the little one now snarling her hatred and other incoherent drivel below him. Other, more powerful *Kami* would have thought nothing of ending her life here and now; however, she was the first *Miko* he had ever claimed. She would pay for her disrespect later, but not with her life.

"Be still human."

His magic called out to the cells and atoms of her body, which all at one time or another had been part of the earth. His weight still pinned her to his brother's back, waiting for every molecule of her shell to come under his control and possession. Her spirit was strong, fighting with tooth, claw, and spear, but he was far older and far more powerful on all levels. At last, she lay still below him, although the fire in her eyes had grown into a true inferno. Sighing, and restraining a strange urge to eat the maiden, Ryu sat back on his heels at her side.

"Explain to me what you are speaking of, slowly. The process of claiming you as my priestess is not complete; therefore I can not yet read your mind well enough to understand your tangled thoughts BlowingWind."

Almost afraid of what would spew out of her mouth, the dragon spirit yielded control of her mouth and vocal chords. One thing was certain; he knew he was going to need a great quantity of hot sake after this to appease his darker nature.

"BlowingWind is a weak and broken woman living in a fairytale. We will never find him again. He has left us. I am the Tornado that all Winds become when fueled by repressed emotions and given only the meager substance of a life lived in shadows. A tortured soul provided the last stress that we needed, and so we broke apart. Four must work as one, but when one or two are gone, the sickness comes and all weaken."

Her eyes continued to smolder, and Ryu thought that surely her fury would have incinerated an *Oni* quite easily. However, only part of his many questions had been answered. If he kept her talking, perhaps her fury would calm.

"Four of you? Four souls like in the Buddhist and *Aikido* theories? And you believe for some reason that I have two of your four?"

"I do not know about Buddhism or *Aikido* thoughts on souls. All I have is my own experience within my spirit. There are four major parts of me. Two are missing and unaccounted for. I have received reports from the creatures that you definitely possess Love. If you hold her, then surely Wisdom is not far away."

"Love?"

As he said the name, there was a stirring where the little soul had snuggled in for sleep, a quiet stretch only confusing the poor dragon more. Shaking it off as perhaps just her reaction to her name, Ryu spoke again.

"If she is a pink orb of rose quartz, then I have been caring for her, although it is a mystery to me as to how she has come into my possession. As to Wisdom, it has been said that completing a Shrine Circuit can bring that."

"Then give Love back to me."

"I don't know how. I can only wait for her to come out on her own, but I will try. However, in return you must stop knocking me to the earth. The ground softens to cushion me, but it still hurts and is not very dignified."

A short silence fell between the two like a lead curtain, and below the pair an ancient rock dragon coiled, waiting for the drama to end so he could go back to sleep. After a while, RagingTornado grudgingly answered.

"I can't promise that. I have a bad temper, but I will try to stop knocking you in the dust. I can't speak for the others."

"I guess that's good enough then. I can see that we are both going to have to work hard at this relationship though."

A wry smile flickered across the *Kami's* face as he carefully placed his hand on the human's chest, hoping that the shy little orb would transfer easily into her proper body. The elder Take would have rolled his eyes quite gladly if he had kept his mobile body, disgusted at his little brother's knack for getting himself into trouble. However, the little orb known as Love was not ready to leave her host yet and stubbornly refused to move.

The pair could have stayed like that for hours, trying to convince Love to return to her proper place, but a low chortle drew their attention away from the task. RagingTornado let her control go in surprise, and BlowingWind snatched back her body from her Dark Side.

"Go away Coyote, I got myself into a fine mess already. I don't need another."

Ryu let go his control of BlowingWind's body, chagrined that he had been so wrapped up in what he was doing not to notice the presence of another spirit. Then again, he was now in his brother's territory, and apparently the elder dragon had not been concerned enough to give Ryu any warning. The tawny canine laughed again, retorting before scampering back down to the forest below.

"Fine, I'll let you figure it out on your own then. I was going to be nice and tell you the easy way."

The dragon and human regained their feet, Ryu frowning after the strange Coyote.

"Should we not have let him teach us the easy way to put her back?"

BlowingWind shook her head, her eyes now a faded end-of-summer blue. Long experience had taught her that Coyote's plans were not always well thought out and could only bring trouble.

"Coyote's job is to be the fool and to get others into trouble. He is a great teacher, but his methods are questionable. Come on, let's go."

Ryu shook his head again, confused at her sudden mood change yet again, and it occurred to him he had done more head shaking in the past day than he had in the past year. When they were done, she was going to see a doctor and a psychologist for her split personality problem. Once BlowingWind had gotten about fifteen feet away from him, she called back.

"We'd better not get too far apart. He might try to convince you that he was me. He is a very good shape-shifter. Trust me on that."

Somehow, Ryu didn't want to know how she knew that, or to fall prey to such a joke.

CHAPTER 16:
THE RYU CARRIES A TREASURE

RYU cheered inwardly when he finally saw the people streaming up and down the main path. Although his human had started with a quick pace, it had not lasted long. Loose rock had slowed her down, and the dust of their endeavor covered them both like a pale cloak. Although he was of the earth, Ryu hated being dirty, and a visit to an *onsen* was now also on his list of things to do. He was willing to bet a considerable amount of gold that Miss Foul Temper would fancy a trip to a bathhouse as well. *Kamikushi* knew that her sweat certainly smelled ripe enough.

"Great Ryu, you really did find it! I was beginning to wonder if you were going to climb to the summit without the aid of a humanly navigable path."

Her sunburned face cracked into a smile below the sun, her leather dress heavy with her sweat. Dust had afforded a little protection for her skin, but the thin film was tracked with little rivulets of sweat tracing their way down her face and neck. BlowingWind carefully limped upward, favoring her left ankle and wincing almost unnoticeably every time she had to put her full weight on it.

Judging by the grin now lighting BlowingWind's face with relief the way a spotlight does the poor soul singing the national anthem at any great sports undertaking, she was even more glad to see a trail than he was.

Looking at the poor thing lagging behind him now, Ryu almost felt bad for leading her around the mountain and to the crater halfway up Fujisan before connecting with the trail. However, this trail was the easiest, and the border was thinner here than where they had been earlier. Ob the healer may have been able to adjust his frequency to meet with the human world, but it was not something that Ryu had mastered. No, he was still stuck using the gates.

"We are halfway to the summit now. We should be able to reenter your world anytime."

"Wow, what a great crater. Willow would kill to get to see this."

BlowingWind limped closer to Ryu, who had the best view. During their climb to this point, Clumsiness had severely beaten the poor girl for her impatience, and the ultimate result was a twisted ankle. The magma spirit had offered to carry her numerous times before, but BlowingWind's pride just would not allow it. As the young shaman admired the gaping and blasted expanse and unthinkingly used his arm to brace herself, the dragon allowed a quizzical look to dance over his expressive face.

"Willow?"

"A girl I used to compete against. I boarded, she skied, we were in opposing schools, but when you see each other several times a week... well. Willow really loved volcanoes, but hardly anybody really got to know what she looked like because she almost never took her mask off outside. She's starting college this year too."

"Ah. You must miss your friends."

BlowingWind turned eastward, gazing out to where she knew the sea and sky shared embraces and beyond to where her home once was. Mother would be up to her elbows in home contracts, and Summerrose probably would be soon starting her business management classes on the days that she wasn't at the bank.

Now would have been the time to visit Medicine Lake and Glass Mountain. That was probably where her shaman's mirror had come from, exchanged for who knew what Lake commodity had been needed by that spirit so long ago. BlowingWind almost began to follow the train of thought further, but a subtle brush of feathers at her neck pulled those thoughts away. Her father's spirit was near, and reflex caused her to reach into a pouch of cornmeal that was currently around her neck, sprinkling a pinch in thanks to her father and in respect for the forces that had formed this gateway into the earth's hot core.

She cleared her throat and tore her thoughts from her friends and mother.

"Yes, but I must continue along my path. Perhaps I will see them again, but more likely not."

Ryu nodded, understanding the sentiment well. He had seen many creatures rise and fall, some of which he had been rather attached to. As he looked around, he scanned for any humans that might see them materialize into their world or other spirits who would make trouble. Most specifically, he was looking for the *Tengu*, who had not been in the range of his nose for some time now.

"The crows are gone, for now. They are probably scheming something though. They always are. Let's get moving."

"Ryu, you sound as paranoid about *Tengu* as I do about coyotes. But since one nearly fed me to an aggravated dragon I'll agree with you."

The duo left the lower crater behind, crossing effortlessly and unnoticed between the realms of the spirits and of man. Ryu strode easily onward, slowing his pace for the pained gait of the human who was now quite glad of the first *Tengu's* gift to her.

"An aggravated dragon? Who else have you been baiting?"

Her harsh eye nearly sliced Ryu in two with all the surgical precision of worked obsidian, so great was her severe unamusement. Ryu's detached joviality had been wearing thin for her over the past few hours, and he had begun to remind her somewhat of Coyote or Raven.

"The *Tengu* tried to drown me first, after a different one chased me through the woods. Creator only knows what I did to piss them off."

"Maybe they just could tell you would be easy to bother. Some of them like to torture people who are easily annoyed. I can't blame them for that; I like to be rather bothersome myself."

"I've noticed. You definitely are not what I expected."

"What? You expected all the spirits here to be old and overly dignified like what some people think is in the *Nihongi* or *Kojiki*? If you really read it carefully, then you'll see the *Kami* mentioned are far less dignified than what many people think, and more human than you might think. Perhaps you thought that your guide would be wrinkly with a long grey beard, or just a mist? Most of us don't live in one form that long these days, or find the elderly do not get as much respect as they once did."

Impatient for the trek to be over, Ryu gently fended off BlowingWind's less than feeble attempts to ward him off, ultimately perching her upon his back where she could continue to pummel his head until she felt her dignity had been sufficiently avenged.

Her outraged squawks attracted the attention of climbing tourists that they had somehow managed to mingle with, as well as a few university students on a geological field trip. However, the attention was only passing, for Ryu's deep laughter at the peeved woman on his shoulders only made them look like a young couple out on a date.

At last, her urgent and vociferous demands to be put down ceased ringing off of rocks and faded to more approximate the deep grumbling of the earth after a tremor.

"You wanted someone to take you up the mountain, and your limping was only slowing us down. Besides, I get to laugh at you making a fool of yourself."

Although she was rather glad to be off of her foot, it was not exactly something she really wanted to say to him, especially after how vigorously she had protested his carrying her. In order to prevent herself from falling off and making a further fool of herself, she had gripped him quite tightly with her thighs, a most undignified position for the modest woman. As her doeskins happened to be a dress it did not make her happy that his very hot hands could be felt where the leather had ridden up in her struggles.

"I can walk, Ryu."

"I would rather carry you though. At your pace, we'll miss both the sunset and tomorrow's sunrise. I'm sure you will want to stay for that. I hope you don't mind sleeping on a shelf if we can manage to get space in one of the inns."

"I think I would have rather taken my chances with the homicidal *Tengu*."

"I could always take you back down, and let them challenge me for you."

"That's quite alright."

Ryu looked up at her, looking into her frowning face with a sparkle of mischief.

"Good then, although I could have used the fight. I can't leave you alone to go roll in the clouds or spar with a storm *ryu* right now. Anybody could come along and take you from me if I am not here to defend you."

"You are going to let me have privacy for personal needs, right?"

"Of course. Do I seem like a barbarian to you?"

Looking back to the trail he was walking on, Ryu frowned at the thought of letting her have any time to herself. After all, he had claimed her as his own property, and being near the girl at least served to take some of the edge off, but something was going to have to happen soon.

He liked the way she felt on his back, how she was lighter than she looked, as if she had a delicate bird's skeleton. Her scent curled around him like a blanket, and the more he smelled her spice the more possessive he became. BlowingWind's personality really needed adjustment, but then again she was spiritually ill and it was spreading into her other etheric bodies. Ryu was willing to wager that she was truly sweet underneath the exterior that reminded him of the cacti that he had seen in Tokyo University's Horticultural Museum one year.

Thankfully, his steady pace quickly lulled the tired woman into a light doze, and so he let her slip a little further down his back to let a petal-soft cheek rest gently upon his broad shoulder. A warm presence settled over the dragon-man as he carried his charge up the sacred mountain, the sun goddess bestowing her blessings on the descendant of her troublesome brother.

"Thank you Amaterasu-o-kami-sama. *Kami* only knows I am going to need all the blessings that I can get when and if Father discovers this adoption. After all, Fujiyama-sama has killed and eaten offspring older than me before."

A frown marred the young volcano *Kami's* face, darkening it so that his expression was nearly as dark as the deepest cavern under his control. Was taking the girl as his own just another risky way of rebelling against his father, and the strict tenets he had been crushed under for nearly his entire existence? Why would fate have brought the two of them together, and how was it that part of her soul was now stubbornly lodged and hiding somewhere in his body? Why had her scent plagued him for months before they met?

"And just why in all of Nippon am I laughing at your exceedingly bad temper and finding it cute? Bah!"

The woman did not answer Ryu's external musing, her sweet breath instead tickling the hairs on his neck that were what was left of his mane and scale in this smaller, illusory form. Amaterasu finally dipped below the horizon, painting resplendent imperial colors of crimson, gold, and indigo across the clouds as the deliberating dragon finally reached the summit of the towering entity that was Fujisan.

"BlowingWind, wake up. We're here."

Weary eyes cracked open as a low moan escaped, cut off as a gasp rushed into her lungs at the sheer beauty of the land spread out below her feet. The awe of the moment caused her to forget all pain, embarrassment and exasperation, leaving only child-like wonder splashed across her face like watercolors on fine silk.

"Oh Ryu, it's beautiful. Thank you."

The *chi* flowed through her body a little faster then, and the notes of her personal harmonic rang a little truer in the ears of the spirit. This was why he had taken the woman for his own, this glimpse of an exotic child hidden behind walls of fire only extinguished by the waters of the earth, sea, and sky. A gust of wind drew his attention away from the one he would cultivate for his own *Miko*, a tawny feather fluttering instead where the shape of a man melded into that of a hawk to rush through him and then away.

"Do you want to pay your respects before we find you a place to stay? Many visitors don't anymore, but it would be wise for you to."

"There is so much up here, like a town. It will be hard to find a properly private place."

Ryu shook his head at the little human, his hair rustling against the tip of her nose.

"You can do it from where you are if you wish, or we can repair to a quiet mini-shrine that I know, if this is still too public for you."

"Please."

Ryu turned off the main path, heading for a barren outcrop of rock far to the side that it seemed few people frequented. BlowingWind clung to her guardian spirit, eyes wide as she concentrated on not falling off, even though she knew he was not going to drop her. As he said he would, Ryu had taken BlowingWind to a secluded mini-shrine, hidden at the base of the forbidding outcrop near the nearly sheer drop. The small pile of rocks was an unobtrusive marker, and exposed as it was to the wind it was one of the less frequented of the many shrines upon the summit, and one of his favorites.

It had an added benefit as well. While the human was occupied, he had a chance to send a part of himself to secure safe and adequate lodgings for the night.

The high traffic of pilgrims and tourists though the area had produced both psychic and physical offal to litter the holy ground, to his great disappointment. A special task force had been created to deal with the physical refuse, but the psychic soot caking the more usual lodgings of the seventh and eighth stations had rendered them highly unsuitable for his purposes. His charge was spiritually weakened from disowning parts of herself, and he did not want to reveal himself as what he was to normal humans by warding off hungry and lonely *Youkai* created from junk all night long.

As what passed for the physical part of Take Ryu stood guard over the human stumbling through her respects in a language that she understood better than she spoke, a shimmer of heat wafted toward an old gray *torii*, the gateway into the upper Sengen shrine at the summit. The old and frayed *shimenawa* and *shide* had been replaced with a brand new rice straw rope twisted together with the sacred paper streamers for the New Year much earlier on. It was there beneath this ritual festoon that a familiar figure had come out of her retirement to greet the young spirit.

As formless now as he currently was, Lady Fuji gracefully accepted the other spirit's reverence. Without words, Ryu communicated with the former head of the mountain his needs concerning both himself and the young woman he had claimed. With amusement, she indicated by the flickers of a secret fire that he was to lead the human to her. As far as Ryu was concerned, that did nothing to procure room and board, but perhaps the goddess knew of a way to help that required the human's presence.

Ryu followed orders, swiftly flying back to Take, or his other half, who was restraining his curious urge to poke through the knapsack left so enticingly upon loose stones. Merging with himself once more, he was gratified that BlowingWind was still only half-awake and that her masks were set aside.

"Follow me. There is someplace we must go."

"Ok."

Tottering as precariously as a hatchling towards him, the dragon spirit wondered just when had been the last time that she had set anything to her lips. He knew for certain that she had eaten nothing this morning and the night before. Her careful and unsteady gait gave him cause to believe it had been at least a few days, and her already thin body did not need much more abuse.

"You are still moving too slow BlowingWind. Here."

Impatient still, he scooped the shaman up once more, internally cursing whatever imbecile had given the humans the moronic idea that not eating would bring them closer to the gods. Gravel crunched underfoot as he walked, and the expected sharp crack with her staff never came. Instead, she revealed how tired she was by leaning into him with soft sighs.

"Sorry Ryu. I don't feel well. I haven't felt this bad in a long time."

Her uncharacteristically languid manner sent his worries to new peaks, giving his feet a faster beat as he hurried to do the Lady's bidding.

Relief filled the dragon as he reached the *torii*, his eyes seeing a great palace behind it reserved for the greater spirits residing here, and only accessible to humans or lower spirits by divine decree. Other humans still moving about at the peak could not see the vast gables sweeping the sky or the golden dragons that were perennially patrolling ancient cypress rafters. Neither could those same humans see the crisply arrayed servant in cloudy silk that waited to bring the dragon and his maiden into the hall, and away from the destructive energies hidden amongst the humans.

If any human had been watching the pair walk below the *torii*, they would have been hard pressed to know if the mist now engulfing the mountaintop had swallowed the two, or if they had merely been an illusion from listening too closely to inn-keepers' stories.

"The girl will need to remove her animal skins before she goes before the mistress."

"Very well, thank you boy. BlowingWind, do you have any other clothes with you?"

The mist boy waited patiently as the dragon roused his charge. What else was there that he could do? His mistress wanted to meet the sick creature before him, although he was unclear as to why the lady would send for such an injured thing as this one that wore the skins of others for her barbaric covering.

"No. I put the feather blanket away with my other things I left in the lower shrine's keeping. I left right after my dance pretty much."

The girl's response was directed to her master, as it should have been. In the servant's opinion the fledgling priestess needed to be on her own two feet.

"If your human has no suitable clothing, then kimono will be provided."

A female servant, clad in the same pure and supplicatory clouds of white as the boy who had admitted them to the palace, stepped forward from where she had been waiting unobtrusively near the wall. It was only reluctantly that Ryu handed over his newest jewel to her care. Said jewel regained wobbly feet when his hand left her body, but she steadfastly refused to be carried any further.

Resolutely, the little human bravely followed her guide away to be changed, and as the scent of cinnamon retreated from him, Ryu could feel once more the rising pressure within his being. Following the boy to be bathed before being admitted before the full presence of Lady Fuji, Ryu hoped that he had done the right thing.

CHAPTER 17:

SHIN'S RETREAT, THE POWER OF A BATH

CREAM colored walls held this quiet place in their still arms, while soft light poured from the floating orbs that functioned here as lamps, mingling with her own softly silver glow. The lovely smell of old scrolls and ancient books mingled with oiled wood and the sharpness of crystals well cared for. Here she had hidden when not checking on the juvenile parts of her being that still fought each other for control, Light and Shadow each wishing to deny the other yet craving balance. To check on them, she had also been avoiding the *Tengu* Tribe and Coyote during her occasional treks. The sun had told her to find shelter on this mountaintop, and so she had come.

A particularly talkative quartz had called to her while she had been pouring over the beautiful ancient script that she could not read. Perhaps one day she would learn, although with the career she hoped to pursue it was doubtful she would have the time. Every once in a great while she had been able to pick out a common character, and that small victory cheered her greatly.

Responding to the quiet pulses of energy, she had picked up the crystal, thrilled at how it unfolded its secrets before her mind's eye with the merest touch. This crystal had not been able to help her learn ancient Japanese, but it had gladly expounded at length on ancient architecture and building methods. She was pulled out of her lesson by the voice of one of the greater *Kami's* formless servants.

"Shin-san, Fuji-sama wishes to speak with you."

"Very well, I will be there. Thank you."

Wisdom, or Shin as these spirits called her in their language of sacred sound and rhythm, gently glided down the halls of the hallowed mansion hidden in a dimension behind the *torii* of the uppermost Sengen shrine. She loved it here, with the high mountain winds and the reclusive sky spirits. Fuji-sama, who was the same beautiful Lady Fuji who was most well known to humankind as the mistress of the mountain, or as the spirit of the mountain itself, had kindly listened to her story. Moved by her story and the counsel of the sun, Fuji-sama had given her sanctuary as she waited for the other parts of her spirit to find their way to the peak.

"I wonder why Lady Fuji wishes to talk with me again so soon."

The soaring ceiling and dark rafters did not know, nor would they tell her if they had known. No servant spoke to her as she passed, merely bowing silently. It was perfectly normal for the spirits of the clouds and mists, who were always so silent in her short experience. Their mysterious ways were comforting, and she was always given time to ponder the questions of her soul here. Polished pine was soft beneath her feet, and the ancient building made her want to bring the old designs back into the world. Perhaps she should be an architect instead of an engineer. After all, demand for houses that were gentler to the environment would be growing soon.

The only thing out of the ordinary, at least in her opinion, was a spirit who had looked somewhat like Obsidian. The male being was paused at the beginning of the male-spirit *onsen* as if she had been the one to surprise him and distract him from some grave task. Shin could not say what had caused her to look down the intersecting hallway for sure, only that there had been an odd pull. The spirit looked about to say something, but froze.

It wasn't him. Shin closed her eyes, trying not to let the tears fall.

"It's all in your head Shin. I'm just seeing things again in my grief. It's just a normal everyday hallucination."

Muttering her thoughts beneath bated breath, she bowed a greeting anyway, just in case she was superimposing faces onto existing beings. Politeness taken care of, she continued on her way to the Lady.

Black lacquered doors slid open at the end of a distant hall, revealing rice paper walls painted with murals of Fuji-san in her four seasons of the year. Directly across from the doors on the other side of the room was a dais of white *hinoki* wood, polished to perfection, where upon green cushions sat the mountain herself.

The young Wisdom entered demurely, bowing to the retired deity and in awe once more of the beauty. Classic Japanese black hair mingled with the little summer snow that was still left in places on the mountain, which were swept up in elaborate coils that possibly only magic could manage. Verdant green grasses had manifested into robes of softest silk for the mountain spirit's summer attire, and Lady Fuji's cool, but warm, manner never failed to put the human soul at ease mixed in with the required and healthy reverence.

"You called, my Lady?"

The spirit smiled, pleased with the politeness and sincerity in the young voice addressing her.

"Shin, I am happy that you answered so swiftly. I have important news for you."

"I await your pleasure, Fuji-sama."

The goddess became somber, the intricate white and black fan that she held coming up now to shield her face from view as she made her decree.

"It seems that your material manifestation has finally arrived. You will be rejoining with the others this night. You also seem to have a new guardian, who is very protective of you by his own admission."

The Lady lowered her fan once more, unveiling a face that had worn what expression? Had it been sadness, joy, caution, neutrality, or some measure of all? Only Lady Fuji herself knew, and would not tell.

"Thank you for your hospitality, my Lady."

"You are welcome. Amaterasu had asked me to see that you were well taken care of. Child, I wish you to sit behind that screen behind me, until I call you out. I may not, but I wish you to be here when I meet with your other selves and your protector."

Fuji-sama gestured to a folding silk screen painted with a very stylized version of the mountain, perhaps the Lady's own insignia. Shin's heart rose in her throat as she moved carefully over to the screen behind the goddess.

"Why would I need to be behind this screen, or even at this meeting at all? Is something wrong?"

She wanted to ask the venerable matron her questions, but did not dare to. When the Lady told one to do a task, it was done. Her questions were replaced on her lips by a dutiful reply.

"*Hai* Fuji-sama."

Light footsteps echoed down the halls, in addition to his own, possibly belonging to some servant coalesced into a more solid form for some unknown task. The ancient palace enfolded him tenderly, the history of millennia whispering tantalizingly to him out of rafters and from relics displayed so carefully in auspicious places. Strangely enough, as the steps drew closer from down another hall that intersected with the one he was in, so too did cinnamon curls begin to taunt his nose, pulling his mind from thoughts of bathing to other, far more tangled and confused, ones.

Ryu would not have seen her at all, had the scent not become unbearably strong and the footsteps drawn to a sudden halt to allow a surprised gasp to dance through the hallway, drawing his attention to the being. So transparent and translucent was she that he thought at first he was seeing a visiting moon spirit, and she had her own silvery glow that reminded him of little Love's glow. The only color, real true color, was in her eyes, blue as turquoise or sapphire. It was eerie, how much like BlowingWind she looked, as if she were the way that fragile human had been meant to look, with her shoulders drawn back and long hair gently waving down her back like a fresh landslide.

He wanted to call to her, to ask her what she was doing there, or if she was a ghost. The words died on his lips though, and his ears picked up the barest of mumbles.

"It's all in your head Shin. I'm just seeing things again in my grief. It's just a normal everyday hallucination." Murmured the spirit, shaking her head.

The apparition bowed mechanically to him and hurried off, her doubt in what she was seeing pouring off of her like ash. The retreating cadence of her rushing feet took with her the heavy swirls of scented torture that was the breeze playing around the woman, leaving the dragon doubting his own eyes. Shivering, wondering if he had in all actuality seen the ghost of who BlowingWind had once been before the calamity that had befallen both her and her destiny, Ryu continued after the servant leading him to the male's *onsen*.

"Blasted *onna*. She must have cast some sort of spell on me so I can't keep her out of my mind. I'm seeing apparitions."

The nameless spirit boy did not reply, knowing that the dragon was speaking more to himself than to anyone else. If that broken being he had seen in the entry hall had indeed cast some spell on the *ryu*, it would not be the first time a *ningen* had sought control of a dragon, nor would it be the last. If the mist boy had been a mist dragon, he personally would have eaten the woman, and been done with it. Quietly, the mist spirit pulled open the doors.

"The baths, sir."

"Thank you, boy."

"The others will assist you now."

The smells of water and heat, mingled with cedar and herbs called to the dusty dragon, and more servants, steam spirits this time, scurried about in preparation and invitation. Entering this haven did much to improve his mood, smoothing chafed pride as sullied silks were removed from his body to be washed. Both forms of his were cared for in the embrace of hot water after the dirt had been rinsed away, skin pampered and scales scrubbed to gleaming perfection.

It was well for BlowingWind that the men's and women's baths were separated. Here in the heat, his urge to wrap around his pet and to never let go had grown greatly. Eyelids heavy, his tongue lolled out as he imagined her slight form polishing his scales or perhaps brushing out his mane, the favor to be returned with the gift of some precious something from his hoard of priceless treasures. He would cover her in nothing but the best silks, and cause her to drip with jewels and gold, turning her into a shining and sparkling *yorishiro* for his use.

Here, as he imagined the specifics of how alluring she would be, sparkling and twinkling to lure him into her delicate mortal body to

gift her with his preternatural abilities and turning her into some
hitogami, or living goddess, did his thoughts pull up short. Hurriedly
he resumed his human shape, letting go of his favored form in near
panic at the newly discovered emotion.

"*Kami*! I've fallen in love with her somehow, haven't I?"

Toweling quickly, Ryu hurriedly dressed in his freshly laundered
kimono, grateful that the task of laundry was so much swifter here
with magic than in the human world with their noisy clothes washers.
Love was not something that he had precisely counted on, at least not
so soon, and could very well endanger the grand plans he had already
been sketching out for her life.

"How can I make proper decisions for her if my personal feelings
can get in the way?"

This thought rebounded in his head, growing louder and
unlocking other thoughts. Ryu now knew how he had grown so
patient and intrigued with her rash outbursts, why he felt so
possessive, why the mere thought of any Tengu anywhere near her
would cause him to growl so menacingly. A final question, and
perhaps the one most important to him, danced out of a dark and
dusty corner of his mind as he padded soberly away to meet with the
goddess.

"How could I have fallen in love with anyone, or so quickly? I
never thought it would happen."

The palace of the myriad gods had fascinated BlowingWind, just
as any other holy place did. Although she plodded tiredly after the
attendant, her eyes roved along, devouring everything and
committing it all to memory. At last, the quiet spirit drew open a
door and bowed her in.

"The baths, mistress. I will return with new clothes for you while
you bathe."

"Thank you. I appreciate it."

The cloud spirit looked up in surprise, grey eyes wide and
inquisitive as a squirrel.

"You do? Lord Ryu's *aniki* sent part of himself up earlier asking the Lady to remove you from his custody because he was afraid that one of you would hurt the other, and because you were so disrespectful towards his *nii-san*."

"If you had been stuck with him for as long as I was, and he had done the kinds of things to you that he has to me, then you would have been angry with him too. But my anger is usually short lived, and it is hard to stay angry for long with someone who has carried you halfway up the tallest mountain in Japan. Ryu is a lord?"

"Oh yes. Ryu-sama is Fujiyama-sama's favorite son, with massive holdings and a very active magma tongue. When his father steps down from managing mountain affairs for the other *Kami*, everyone suspects that Ryu will be the one he passes the duties to. He is rather known for his flamboyant personality though, as you seem to have discovered. Perhaps not the best spirit to be a bride to, but you could have done far worse."

"Bride?"

"That's what a *Miko* is, bride and handmaiden, a link between our world and your own."

"You mean *Miko* are not just assistants at shrines?"

BlowingWind wilted further than she already was, resembling so closely a lily floating in the water that had not sent her roots down deep enough yet. The spirit frowned a little, thinking very hard, her whole body becoming grayer the harder that she pondered.

"I myself have never been as far as the shrines where the people frequent, so I am not entirely sure of the functions that a human *Miko* performs these days. I only know that in the old days when our kind intermingled with your kind and affairs more fully that the role of bride was fulfilled in its entirety. They say that a newly chosen *Miko* died to her old way of life and became someone new, belonging entirely to her *Kami*."

"I see."

The spirit saw the woman grow silent and thoughtful, turning with all the sorrow, regret, and perhaps anger of a soul being led down to the Land of *Yomi*, to drift instead into the *onsen*. Wondering what had come over her to say such brash and forward things, the diminutive cloud was ashamed, no matter how true her statements had been. She had brought pain and sadness to a human already very sick and obviously untold by her "guardian" what her payment for his services was to be. Still, something about the young woman was so innocently trusting, that perhaps to have left those things unsaid would have been an even greater disservice.

"Are all humans as paradoxical as this one who had been reported to be so fierce and yet was so gentle?"

Whispering the question to herself, the cloud spirit left to find clothing that was considered proper here that would fit. She would have to go through the things that belonged to the Take Clan that were left here for anyone of that family who had need. Meanwhile, while the faithful attendant was gone, female steam spirits rinsed the *ningen-onna* delivered into their care before carefully assisting the tired and unsteady innocent into the steaming waters.

No one dared to interrupt the thoughts streaming through her head, so tangled together were they, and the human's face was as tightly closed as any geode found in the rough. All had heard the conversation at the door, and gave what comfort that they could through scrubbing, aromatic oils to cover her human scent, and the arrangement of her hair that had begun to grow out of where she had butchered it to.

"Thank you."

Her whispered words brought all to a pause, including the mist spirit who had slipped back in, unnoticed, to lay out the blazing scarlet *kimono* and golden *obi*, that had been graced with a symbol that BlowingWind knew she had seen somewhere on Ryu's clothes. Memory would not reveal where to her, but she absolutely knew she had seen it before. She was nothing but property in the eyes of the spirits in this land it seemed; yet these kind beings in this room had done what they could for her regardless.

Then again, as servants they were property too. So then they knew how she was feeling right now.

She dried and dressed quickly, receiving help from the spirit women with the complicated work of donning the strange and intimate garments correctly. When they were done with tying her together, one raised a mirror for BlowingWind to appraise their work.

"Do you approve?"

BlowingWind was not sure if she completely liked what she saw. The woman in the mirror was breathtaking, yes. Like some ancient Japanese princess, some *Hime-sama*, she was a pale wisp in the flowing garment, fragile looking as any flower. She much preferred her trusty doeskin dress, or even some good sturdy denim that was ready for anything, wild, down to earth and strong. Her leathers had been cleaned and packed away, unsuitable for the presence of a goddess, as the *Kami* shunned death, and the things resulting from it, as a matter of course. It was small comfort that her grandmother's handiwork was safe, and her short hair now bound by a complicated series of buns was lacking.

"It's nice, but something is missing. This is not me."

Going to her bag so carefully placed in a corner, she searched for what she had seen in the thought that had passed through her head like a summer breeze. Quickly, she found the woven cloth, unfolding it as the others crowded around to see what the little human would bring out. The small breast feathers of a hawk had been safely stored in the bright cloth, just as she remembered them. As the spirits saw them they caught the thought from her head, and the glimmers of happy memories that were attached to these, and the more recent memory of how she had worn them in her dance before a bonfire. Acting on it, one of the steam spirits could not help but comment happily.

"That does look better mistress, working them into your hair to brush so gently, as if you were part phoenix. You must hurry now though, you are ready and the Lady is waiting.

CHAPTER 18:
LOVE AND WISDOM,
SHADOW AND LIGHT

SIMPLE black lacquer doors welcomed Ryu into the chamber where Fuji-sama waited to meet with him, sliding open gently, as he knew they would. Before this most respected goddess had been arranged many trays of various succulent foods, and also places for himself and his beautiful little shaman who was and would become his *Miko*.

"Ryu, don't be so shy, come in my child. Sit."

The warm and smiling voice beckoned just as strongly as her magic and her delicate hands, and Ryu quickly moved to follow her commands. Bowing reverently from his place, Ryu could see how his father's allegiance had been so strong when she had been the Headwoman of the mountain, and why he kept relations sweet with the spirit.

"*Arigato Gozaimasu*, Fuji-sama."

"You are welcome as always young Take. I can feel you casting about for your charge. She is quite safe, and will be here soon. While we wait, perhaps you can tell me again what your greatest concern for her is. Knowing the essence is one thing, but hearing a perception is another."

"I want to heal her. She is so sad and broken, and it hurts to see her like that. I think that maybe even all of her anger is a mask to hide her pain. Fuji-sama, I want to help her, but I don't know how. There are no chants or motions that I know for it."

The dragon could not help his frantic gestures as he spoke, repeating what he felt was the most crucial part of their earlier conversation when her *mitama*, or separated spirit, had greeted his own at the *torii*. He would not allow himself to slump in despair before her, but the telltale droop of his usually unruly locks was more than enough to communicate the feeling.

"If she is missing Love and Wisdom, *Ai* and *Shin*, then you must give them to her."

"That's what I don't understand. *Ai* has been safely in my keeping for quite some time now, even though I still have no idea where she came from. But when I tried to pass her back to BlowingWind, *Ai* completely refused to go. She clung inside my heart like to be removed from me was death!"

A shifting slide sounded behind the screen that Lady Fuji sat before, as if someone were slightly bored or extremely uncomfortable sitting still. Cinnamon hung heavy in this room, shrouded by Lady Fuji's crisp snow and ripening fruit.

"She had been angry at you, you had also said, O child of Fujiyama. Perhaps she could not accept *Ai* at that time, or both must be together to facilitate this transfer. Or perhaps," the musing afterthought slipped from her lips, "Perhaps she feels unworthy of love."

"She really doesn't seem to like me very much. She tolerates me, but even this seems questionable to me. She only calmed down because she was weary, I think."

Every line of his body spoke of his frustration while Lady Fuji looked serenely on. Such a scene she had seen many times before with other courting dragons, her own children of the mountain, and the occasional human. Lady Fuji had also seen it in well established marriages that had been made out of custom and necessity, instead of desire.

"Do you know how you feel about this human?"

"I would give her everything if it would make her happy! My very scales even would be hers if she asked it! I want to keep her safe, and I'm afraid of what will happen if she slips away. I've fallen in love with the woman, or at least think so my Lady, and when I am near her, I feel... calmer."

"How do you know it is love, and not just a passing infatuation or mere lust? Others before you have taken *Miko*, making them full brides, and then moved on after only a few months to leave them alone and with child."

Horror at the thought painted the spirit white while anger narrowed his eyes to knives and thinned Ryu's lips as he replied.

"I would never hurt her like that. I would never abandon her. I, Take Ryu, would commit *seppuku* before dishonoring BlowingWind like that."

Though his voice had not been loud, the vow carried a binding magic that seemed to swell it to monstrous proportions, filling the room and drawing a gasp from the witness politely hidden behind the screen. Startled by the magic of the vow, the witness was equally startled by the gossamer strings wrapping her, but as Lady Fuji had not yet called, she remained hidden. Trembling with rage at the thought that anyone thought he would commit such a crime, Ryu stared at his food to avoid challenging the Lady any further.

Lady Fuji looked away from the dragon, who was now thrashing about with an invisible energy tail as he tried to do away with his anger. Hesitant footsteps had paused outside the *shoji*, and though oils had been well applied, the decaying scent of a living human was still detectable.

"Come in my child."

The door slid open to reveal BlowingWind, hand still stretched out to move the door herself. Ryu began to purr lowly at the sight of his treasure safe and in the robes of his Clan, reacting before he could seal away his *aramitama*. The human came in shyly, as if sensing the possessiveness of his dark side and not knowing what to do in the presence of such a well-known spirit as Lady Fuji.

"So shy, come and eat Daughter of Man."

"Yes ma'am."

BlowingWind bowed before sitting down on her mat, the humbleness and respect of her tone and gesture stupefying the dragon that she had previously shown such supreme disrespect for earlier. The three ate silently, Lady Fuji silently watching the quiet interplay between the younger *Kami* and the human. It was amusing to the mountain spirit how the human sat as far from her guardian as she could, and yet carefully watched him for cues as to how to eat the various dishes. Once, Ryu had caught her watching him, and the smirk that played on his face turned the human an amusing shade of magenta while she tried to pretend she had not been watching him.

Before long, the food had been eaten and the human did not look so wan. The meal had been small and light, but it had gotten something into her, though tying her more firmly into the spiritual world she was now trapped in once again.

"I hear that you have had some *tamashii* run away from you child."

Lady Fuji had said her statement noncommittally, as if she were talking about the weather or the cherry blossoms. BlowingWind gazed back at the ancient goddess, calm since she was not talking to the spirit that chafed at her memories and had tricked her into such a compromising position thanks to her lack of knowledge of the customs of the land.

"I have found Love, she is hiding inside Ryu. I do not know where Wisdom is though."

"I see. Do you have any idea of where to look for Wisdom?"

"Ryu thinks that maybe I can find her on one of the Shrine Circuits."

"Quite possibly. It would be a logical place to start looking. I have also heard that you had difficulty in getting Love out of Ryu. It sounds like she is quite comfortable where she is."

Choking sounds now came from behind the screen, as if whoever was witnessing the goddess' meeting with them tonight was inexperienced, had not been able to swallow their tea, or possibly was trying to swallow laughter. The Lady continued on, unperturbed by the minor interruption and her eyes sparkling as if she had been privy to some joke with the hidden chaperone.

"Do you have any idea why she would not return to her proper place MountainChild-san?"

"Because Ryu doesn't really want to let my soul go?"

The person behind the screen could no longer swallow their laughter at the angered statement. BlowingWind's blue eyes washed yellow in a flash, glaring angrily out upon the world as Ryu turned his own incensed eyes on her. He had tried to the very best of his ability to coax out and return her wayward soul, but Love had dug deep and held fast, just as stubborn as the rest of the woman. Lady Fuji only smiled gently at the pair, as if at two children rowing over a tattered doll.

"I don't think that is it. He wants to give you Love very much. Shin?"

"Hai, Fuji-sama?"

The curious voice rolled from behind the screen, the owner leaping to her feet and coming out swiftly to look enquiringly at the Lady. As she did, both Ryu and the shaman rose to their feet, breathing the same exclamation with one breath.

"You!"

Shin calmly moved her gaze from the spirit that had so kindly taken care of her, transferring it disinterestedly to BlowingWind, then freezing when her eyes came to rest on the spirit that she knew could only be Ryu. Paying no attention to the outburst at all, Lady Fuji only directed Shin's attention back to her.

"In your opinion Shin, why would Ai not want to return to her body?"

"*Ara*, our Shadow, is very hard to live with. She is always angry and hurting. Our Light does not want to deal with our Shadow, and so they almost never work together anymore. It is very tiresome."

"That's not true. I'm not angry and hurting all the time!"

"*Ara*, come out if you are going to shout at me. You are confusing our guardian."

"Kidnapper more like."

Despite her grumbling, a dark amethyst orb issued from BlowingWind's chest, forming herself in her normal image with her blackened skins. Standing there cockily holding her spear and defiantly staring down Shin, RagingTornado stamped her foot at the tired and sad Wisdom.

"You don't know what has happened. We've managed to become his bride while you were hiding up here."

"This anger is what makes you unable to receive Love and I back into our body. Is it so bad to be someone's bride? Obsi-."

"Don't use that name. Never use that word as a name again! He's abandoned us and gone Home, leading us to this foreign country with what must have been the last of his energy. And you just accept it and soak up what you can of this place! You are even speaking mostly Japanese now while the rest of us still speak mainly English."

RagingTornado raised her spear, shaking it at Shin as if threatening that she would throw life away and run her through with it. Wisdom, taking advantage of the spiritual realm they were in, called upon her resources to produce a bronze shield with the Celtic Dragon that was the symbol of the O'Drake Clan worked carefully into the surface.

"If it makes you feel better, I won't. This is not the place for another power struggle. I was merely going to say that He would want us to be happy. We promised Him that if anything happened we would Live, and that's what I want to do."

"But both Shadow and Light are crystallized with our grief, and are refusing to move on so that we can too. Thus, we cease to Live, although we Exist."

The new voice, the same as the others though from a different quarter, startled the other three parts of BlowingWind as well as the two spirits who had brought her pieces together. Ai, the little pink orb, was perched carefully on Ryu's shoulder, as if one wrong move from anyone would send her diving for the safety of dark arms within the magma spirit once more.

"Now you come out. Why?" BlowingWind, or the part of her still occupying her body, quietly asked her question.

"Wisdom is here now. What good is Love without Wisdom, or Wisdom without Love?"

"And what good is the Light or Shadow without us? The two of you are still fighting for control. We have to accept each other to heal, as well as what has happened. It's an initiation. Into what secret I don't know, but it is anyway and Great Spirit must have some reason for it."

Shin had finished Ai's thought, while Light and Dark glared at each other and Ryu wondered how much *sake* he would need to recover from the sheer shock of the situation.

"I thought that we spirits had personality problems with two main parts. It seems to be really hard to be human. Does this kind of thing go on in your collective head all the time?"

RagingTornado opened her mouth to growl an answer to Shin, ignoring Ryu's question and trying to honor the promise she made to him even if she still did not like him.

"She's weak, and always invests me with anything that she doesn't want to deal with. I am created of all her pain, rage, hate, fear, embarrassment, lust and everything else that she wants to hide. I'll accept her when she fully accepts that I am her and starts helping me with all of these unresolved issues."

"I am not weak. You really want me to admit things like lust, hate, and pain, such base things?"

BlowingWind had ground it out at her Shadow. She was not weak; it was just that she did not know how to deal with her darker feelings other than running away from or repressing them. No one had ever truly shown her how to work with these things, and she was not about to admit that to anyone yet.

Shin threw up her hands, letting her protective shield fly into the air to dissolve with her exasperation.

"You are both so immature. We all know why you won't deal with your Shadow. Love and I will come out when you are ready to accept us."

She shrank into an orb, looking like a silver moon, to hurtle into her protector along with Love, seating herself deep in Ryu's heart.

When the time was right, she would come out, and there where the others could not hear, they plotted with Ryu's own Shadow a way to break down their *Ara's* resistance, creating yet another bond with the spirit. Meanwhile, RagingTornado reentered her body with a huff, muttering about how half of her spirit seemed to be abandoning their past and turning Japanese at heart.

Ryu himself was horror struck.

"No human healer can fix this problem!"

Lady Fuji, thoughtful and serene as any painting of her physical manifestation, replied while BlowingWind merely sat with bowed head, tired.

"No. I suspect that only you hold the key Ryu, but now you at least know more of what you are dealing with. I see that I certainly can not release the child from your side if I tried. We shall perform the bonding ceremony now, to give your human more time."

"*Hai* Fuji-sama."

"Does my opinion count in all of this?"

BlowingWind's small voice drew the attention of the spirits to where she looked up at them through sad and frightened eyes, rather like the doe as she watches the semi-truck bearing down on her. It was clear by her huddled form that the poor girl felt like that proverbial doe as Fate and Destiny smeared her on the highway of life that had hacked through her peaceful forest. Lady Fuji shook her head sadly.

"I am afraid not. My Lady Amaterasu and Lord Sarutahiko instructed me that if you came to me I would act in your best interests. They are that you are bound to Ryu, who will protect you and share his All with you gladly. You have a duty to the Future, not the Past."

Tiny waterfalls sprung from the eyes of the human as she began to tremble like the land in an aftershock. Ryu chewed on his lip nervously while Lady Fuji poured the *o-miki*, the consecrated *sake*, into three small cups to perform the ancient ceremony that had wedded both spirit and human in the Land of the Rising Sun since time immemorial.

"Why are you so frightened BlowingWind?"

"The women of my family have brought only disaster. Please, I'll stay under your protection, but please, don't make me your wife, not in all the physicality that brings so much trouble!"

Ryu reached out slowly, gently blotting away her tears.

"I will not force you into bed if that is what you fear, but if we are not wedded, it will leave you open for spirits far worse than I. Also, since fully half of yourself is hiding within my heart, this is the best way to reunite you, for now, however tenuous it may be."

Lady Fuji gave the pair the *o-miki*, helping the shaman with the ritual exchanges and making her both an official and true *Miko*. Gathering BlowingWind's tiny body to himself, he waited as the ties binding them tightened. Her pain and heartache was his as other and more subtle exchanges occurred between them, pulling him into her energy matrix as surely as she was mingled with his. She attuned to him, becoming a channel for his powers when the need arose and he became her anchor in the world of the spirits.

At last, when the room stopped spinning for the pair, the deed was done.

"You are not fully bonded, and will not be until the day that your union is physically consummated, if that happens at all. Yet you are one, which will give you time to heal BlowingWind. Ryu, you must take very good care of her. Perhaps time together in the Sea of Trees will help remove the blocks between you and strengthen this weak tether."

"*Hai* Fuji-sama. I will."

Ryu stood carefully and cradled his Treasure to his chest tenderly as she drowsed against him from the magic exchange, waiting for a servant to show him to the room he knew had been prepared. The servant waited at the door, bored, and annoyed that he would be the one to lead the 'filthy human' and her guardian to their quarters, though he hid it well. Before he was out the door, Lady Fuji called one last time to the dragon.

"Ryu, remember your promise to her. As time passes, you may find that hard to keep."

"Yes Lady Fuji, I will remember. Thank you for your help."

"Go now my child. Rest."

"Hai!"

Bowing over his precious cargo, he backed respectfully out of the room to follow the retainer.

CHAPTER 19:
THE DAY AFTER

SCALED coils threaded through the gossamer strands of her dreams, while the combined calls of perhaps dozens of animals made themselves known. Vague impressions of centuries past danced through her mind while a soothing voice whispered secrets to her in a language of cadence and tone. As her mind grew accustomed to the odd dream sounds, meaning came across and stories unfolded for her.

"Receive healing knowledge when you acknowledge the partnership of *Miko*, my *yorishiro*. Gain perpetual health and unending wealth, with an eternity of safety. I bring life and death, in the same breath across the lands for those that understand."

It was a flowery and embroidered tongue, that of the *Norito* she had heard intoned at the shrines that she had visited so far. Promises enticed BlowingWind to cautiously poke her head out of her cave, a wolf surveying the lands outside of her den. The speaker was unseen, but the nearness of his voice was a mystery. He whispered gently into her ear with sinuous syllables of his native language, and she realized that every word she understood.

"R-ryu? What are you doing in my dream?"

Turning around and around, like a spindle that she had once seen a woman use to spin thread, she scanned the cave for him or for anyone. No one greeted her eyes, yet she felt his gentle touch and heard his quiet song.

"Sleep in my arms safe from all harm. My fierce monsoon, heed now this tune. The roiling earth from deep below longs to feel the harsh wind blow, cooling his incessantly raging passions of the inner fire from which he's fashioned. A golden cup, a golden bowl, a boisterous one to have and hold, halls of stone soaring high beneath the ground and spreading sky."

Caverns of volcanic wonder were painted around her, the treasures of the earth sparkling with the light of the molten tongue that was somewhere farther back in the passage. In all this time that she had frequented the cave in her inner forests, it was the first time that she had been aware of how much more there was to it. The mixture of dark and light beckoned to her, and the warmth eased her weary muscles.

"I didn't realize I had used so much energy in just hiding. I wonder what's down there."

A purr filled her being, vibrating her atoms, and the invisible hands turned to strange coils again, gripping and holding her still, inescapable.

"Sleep here in my coils. Forget now your toils. Rest and relax, you've been overtaxed. Send down your roots. Like the pine it suits you to reach deep into me to rest and to sleep."

"I hate it when people think they know what's best for me."

The dream faded, though the pressure of arms increased in the dark, holding her, comforting her, but still restraining her after all.

"Mother used to hold me this way, when the nightmares came and I fought Daddy's killers in my dreams. I won't give in."

Gradually, she grew aware of her own breath, and the smell of rich new earth, and a firm and enticingly warm chest, but still without the heartbeat of a truly material creature. No words came from his lips, but the song still whispered in her mind, keeping her lids heavy. It was tempting to drift back into sweet sleep, but pride could not let her stay in the world between wakefulness and sleep any longer.

After a long war, her eyes finally opened.

Flawless and seemingly poreless skin, like sun-warmed marble greeted her, sickening in its perfection. A familiar aristocratic nose jutted out as if to spear the air around them while the innocent mask of sleep graced his face. His sleep-tousled hair dared her to rumple it further, and BlowingWind found it was difficult to restrain her hands.

"Dear God, I've been knocked out and drug into a cheap romance novel! How long have I been sleeping on your chest? What have you done to me?"

As BlowingWind sat up to glance wildly around the room for anything to disprove her theory, Ryu gave up his feigned sleep, choking on his laughter.

"You do come up with the oddest theories!"

"What did you do to me while I slept?"

The wind howled in the form of the enraged woman, carrying far and wide with the power behind the voice. Flesh met flesh through silk as she drove her fist into his gut in her anger and frustration, bringing groans of pain bubbling up from the battered spirit.

"It was just an observation. What a foul temper you have. Look, you're under the covers and I am on top. I haven't done anything!"

"You were thinking it. How long have I been asleep?"

"The thought never even crossed my mind until you brought it up. You shock me, O Blustery One. You have slept most of the night, and the sun will rise soon."

Ryu had grumbled his answer, massaging his stomach as BlowingWind examined the bare traditional sleeping quarters and the flowered quilts covering the shared futon. He was right; she was under the covers, much to her chagrin.

"Sorry."

"I said I would not force you. Have you changed your mind? Is that why you ask? Should I be testing my limits?"

His face was that of the curious child as he watched her trying to piece the night together, but his mask was shattered by laughing eyes that BlowingWind honed in on without any effort.

"No! You pervert! Get out!"

The phoenix and the dragon had long been a symbol of marital happiness in Asia, but also a symbol of war. Like the phoenix that she unknowingly now represented, she too had a fiery temper and was not being tamed. Like the tiger, she was capable of taking her anger out on those around her and so now the battle of Tiger and Dragon ensued. Her hand found the pillow that had held Ryu's head, re-uniting with it once more and in several other places as she chased him out of the room, while he cackled at the baitable human.

"It was just a question. Are you going to beat me for our entire honeymoon, my little *hitogami*? Perhaps we should leave soon then and let the others have the peace they are accustomed to."

"You... you... Coyote! Argh!"

The *shoji* slammed shut in his face as BlowingWind tried to find a suitable name for him. More laughter bubbled up out of him like the springs at the base of the mountain.

"You started it."

"Jerk."

"You wound me Wind-chan."

BlowingWind stuck her tongue out at the door, refusing to play along with him any farther and sulking like any child who had been teased. For his part, Ryu had his hand on his chest as if he truly felt wounded, but the devilish grin and sparkling eyes put the lie to his previous statement. He had been perfectly happy to hold her and listen to her sleep.

On the other hand, he was beginning to enjoy watching her eyes flash as she tried to beat him. Still, he didn't want to push her yet, there was plenty of time to play with her later. In an entirely serious tone and manner, he tried to mend the situation.

"I'm sorry. It was wrong of me to tease you. I have never been very good at holding myself back, and sometimes become far too exuberant. There is no coffee here, but we could go get some tea before we take our leave, if you like. Please don't stay angry with me."

The door slid open just enough for one baleful eye to glare out like Medusa rounding a corner.

"No coffee? What about chocolate?"

Ryu brought his hand over his heart once again, holding the other out to show that he had no crossed fingers, a gesture he had picked up from watching students back at the University's Quad.

"None. If I'm lying, you can make a *shintai* for me to reside in and bury it upside down in your protest for as long as you wish."

"Do you realize how long it's been since I've had either?"

"I take it that you want me to promise to get you some later if I want any chance of you accepting my apology."

The eye continued to bore into him relentlessly, silent and venomous. It was an eye that held promises of many things, imaginative and terrifying. Ryu began to wonder if maybe he should start protecting the *Tengu* Tribe from her, now that she had access to a small portion of his magic.

"Fine. When we go to human civilization then I will personally take you to the finest shops and let you choose what you want."

"Promise?"

"I promise Wind-chan."

The door opened the rest of the way, and the human shuffled out to look up defiantly into the spirit's amused face.

"If you don't deliver, into the mud you go."

"With all speed Little One. Now, let's get some tea and something else warm into you, and then we can say our goodbyes to our Lady and go find how to fix you, even though you are already looking much healthier."

Taking her by the hand, Ryu gently drew the woman with him down the corridors to where he knew Lady Fuji would be waiting to breakfast with her guests. With every step, Ryu watched as her mask gently melted away, replaced by that quiet and impassive face of a woman lost deep in thought. Once more they passed through the lacquered doors, and once more Lady Fuji greeted them.

"Good morning children. A little early for marital spats, is it not? Have you possibly brought a Tiger into your home young Dragon?"

"According to my *Otou-sama*, a Tiger in the home would burn out some of my excess energy so that I do not run ahead of schedule."

"Your Father is perhaps right. You have far more energy than many of the females of your kind."

Lady Fuji's laughing eyes and light tone gently mocked the young dragon, producing a reaction that BlowingWind had not known him capable of. A red tinge, barely noticeable at first, spread across his nose like ink across paper, growing more vivid as he realized that BlowingWind had seen it. Schooling his voice and manner, it was the only sign of his embarrassment.

"It is a simple early morning miscommunication, nothing to worry about my Lady."

"I see. Just remember that rice paper walls hide far less than your usual chambers of hard stone."

"*Hai* Fuji-sama, *gomen gozimasu*. I am sorry."

"It is only to be expected with two as young and vigorous as you. Even Susanowo took a little time to settle after his first wife was gained. BlowingWind, can you eat something more this morning?"

All arguments were forgotten as simply as that, and the Lady was gesturing with the appropriate elegance to the daintily presented dishes. Steaming bowls of rice and seaweed embraced bits of sweetened and fried tofu, to tempt the still turbulent stomach into the realm of hunger. Although the request was gently put, it held all the command that BlowingWind's own mother used every morning, and so she meekly sat at her cushion and tray.

"Hai Fuji-sama."

BlowingWind could only pick at her meal and sip at her tea, while Ryu quickly finished his with both grace and speed, to wait patiently for the human to empty her bowl. Lady Fuji nodded as she watched, having slowed her own pace in respect to the human. Finally, BlowingWind was done, though something was still lacking in her nourishment. Listless and frail as a hatchling that had not received its first meal, she quietly sat beside her *Kami* as the mountain goddess looked on.

"I would suggest that you eat some meat soon. You will find that because of Ryu's specie and the unusual way that you are bound to him that you will require meat far more often than you once did. I am sure Ryu is looking forward to a hunt after so long, and it will give you an opportunity to learn how to work together. Fare well children."

"*Domo arigato gosaimashita*, Fuji-sama."

"*Sayonara* Fuji-sama."

Ryu bowed deeply, folded double on the floor while BlowingWind copied his demonstration of gratitude. It felt more natural than before, and she realized that she herself was speaking easily in the Japanese tongue. As they left, Ryu began to move with a restrained urgency that she soon matched, her staff tapping in tandem with their pace.

"We have to hurry. After sunrise the entrance to the human world is sealed. It used to be open all the time here, but after people started to climb the mountain... well. Not all *Kami* are as accepting of humanity as the Lady."

"I see, Ryu."

They had passed under the *torii,* just as the red sun rose in the sky with her rays of life dancing over land and sky. Turning around, BlowingWind watched as the palace faded from her eyes.

"It's gone, just like a dream."

"Just like any ghost castle or monastery, of which the country is still full, for the right ones. Come on, let's get back to the forest."

Ryu started off, expecting her to follow, but she was rooted to the ground, breath stilled and eyes wide. To her eyes, the very spirit she was searching for stood in the air just past the end of the ground, smiling and beckoning. Ryu's eyes saw nothing, but he could tell that she did. A smell raised warning alarms to him now, formerly dismissed as only some disguised *Youkai* pilgrim making penance for some misdeed.

"I smell a *Kitsune.* Don't move."

BlowingWind did not listen though, enthralled with the vision conjured before her eyes. She was faster now, and calling on her resources she bounded for the arms of her love. Caught by surprise, Ryu had not moved fast enough to stop her, pounding hard after her fleet toes. Her foot came to the edge, and what had appeared to be a rock threw her high and over the precipice, the illusion vanishing without a trace as BlowingWind hurtled through the air. A scream tore from her throat, warbling and clear.

"Oh God!"

The frigid morning air roared past as she fell through it, gravity pulling her downward and her forward momentum carrying her ever outward. This was the end as far as she was concerned, and so she closed her eyes, not wishing to see the red stain she knew she would make. Falling was a far cry from flying, and she knew that the ground would make its mark on her body soon enough. The roaring increased, and then died away, as did the cold. Surprised, BlowingWind opened her eyes.

Red filled her vision, great waves of a soft warm mane materializing from nowhere.

"Well, are you going to just keep falling, or are you going to grab on? Eventually you will fall if you don't."

The voice was familiar, although it had a deeper and more gravelly sound now, as if some great beast were questioning her from the cavernous lairs of her mother's campfire stories. Two great horns curved back through and above the wild forest of fur, onyx spears that her hands wrapped around on instinct.

"Good. Now hold on tight. I've used an invisibility spell so the humans won't see us, but I have no guarantee that some *Kazekami* will not push you off."

The towering pines grew ever closer, reaching out for her as if to catch or impale her with their venerable boughs. The serpentine creature below her writhed in the sky, gracefully swimming an invisible current that she could feel, but not see. Here where there was no land under her feet, the freedom that she had remembered came rushing back, if only for a short time, and she could marvel at the cities, the wilds, and all that lay in between. As all things must, this came to an end, and the dragon silently descended into a favorite hunting ground in his territory.

BlowingWind slid silently off of the great dragon, awed by his sheer size and the graceful sweep of his body. His ebony scales gleamed in the sun and his midnight fur embraced his wolfish face. Now she could see that the scarlet waves surrounded his head and licked down to the end of his tail like fierce flames, never resting, always moving. Twelve sabers were on the tips of his toes, eager to rend the flesh of enemy or prey. A mouth full of swords curved upwards as the dragon watched her.

"Please don't eat me *Ryugami*."

"Are you done ogling me now, or should I roll over so that you can see my underbelly?"

"I'm sorry, I didn't mean to stare. I have just never seen such a..."

"Fine specimen of a dragon?"

"*Hai*. When I fell off the mountain, I left someone behind. I need to tell him where I am."

"I wouldn't worry. I'm sure he knows exactly where you are."

The dark eyes were laughing as the dragon preened before her, and he rumbled his amusement as he spoke to her. The voice was even deeper now, and yet it sounded almost like her *Kami*.

"Ryu?"

"Yes?"

"Why didn't you tell me you were a dragon?"

"Your mind works very fast when you are awake. I never told you because you never asked. Now, shall I go and find us some game? Perhaps you would like a deer, the meat of longevity? Or would you rather that I fished for us?"

"It doesn't matter. Is there someplace that I can lie down for a while? I'm a little dizzy still."

"Of course."

Ryu gestured into the woods at the edge of the clearing, his tail curling majestically through the air. Now that the shock was wearing off, her surroundings were making themselves known. Where the grass melted into the trees lurked a small hut, the clean lines and simple framing harked back to ancient days, although it was clear that it was a fairly new construction.

"This is one of the places that I go when on sabbatical. I've led several human 'lives' under several names. So I have found it convenient to have a place to go when I am working on historical manuscripts or just need time away from the city. You should find all that you need therein."

"Thank you."

Ryu nodded his great head before meandering into the forest, and BlowingWind paused to watch him before she carefully entered the hut. The dragon Ryu moved with the same pressurized fluidity as the other form that she had known, and the volcano itself seemed to lend him her internal drive.

"So, now I've finally met a dragon face to snout, and he happens to be my husband. What else can happen to me? Eat your heart out Murphy."

CHAPTER 20:
CONFRONTING THE INNER DEMON

RED, gold, and black coiled upon each other in grand sweeps of heat on the surfaces that bore paint. Elsewhere, bare wood made its brazen appearance in the vacant spaces where books had not – and martial arts equipment had – been carefully arranged, waiting for their master's return. Period after period flowed relentlessly on upon the bookshelves, preserved in both texts and an assortment of curious curios. The odd blouse-ripper romance novel and paperback manga collection had also found their places to rest, poorly hidden by sandwiching with some equally tattered notebooks.

"It figures that he would read cheesy romance novels and *shoujo* manga. Judging by how ragged they look, he's read them several times, too. I would never have pegged him for a comic book reader, much less the romantic kind. I guess I expected something related more to volcanoes. Well, this really finishes shattering my image of most spirits."

BlowingWind left the bookshelf after fingering the least delicate items in the array poised there, examining instead the mahogany desk and seven-year-old computer. They humbly tucked themselves into one corner, as if they were ashamed to be in the same room as the vast library of historical literature and the museum quality items. Lesson plans and a half finished manuscript waited patiently for a final review, and though obviously old had recently shed any dust that might have built up.

"Where's the dust?"

"What kind of servant would I be if I let Master's possessions get dirty?"

"Who said that?"

BlowingWind looked wildly around, scanning the cabin for the source of the voice. Nothing moved, and everything was still and inanimate as stone. Her hand drew up against her chest, a gesture she had not made since she was very small.

"I did. What are you doing going through my Master's things?"

"Ryu dropped me off. He said that I would find all I need."

"Then get it and go."

The owner of the voice still hadn't become obvious yet, but BlowingWind had tracked it down to the vicinity of the doorway.

"After falling off the mountain, I don't think that Ryu would be very pleased with me if I took off into the forest alone right now."

"That is no concern of mine. Take what you need and go. Some of Master's things are very delicate, and it is my duty to care for this place while he is away."

Standing at the door, she cocked her head to one side, a curious little girl trapped in a woman's body and shining through like a sacred jewel.

"Am I talking to a doorpost?"

"How rude! You are talking to the Spirit of a doorpost. Now get out before I leave this *goshintai* and carry you out myself!"

"Well I never! I was just curious, Doorpost-san. Just when I start thinking that maybe being married to Ryu wouldn't be so bad, I get ordered about by a talking doorpost! When Ryu gets back, you can tell him I went to bring down my own game. Good bye!"

Blowing out the door, she deposited her bag beside it, not even once thinking about how lucky she had been to have kept it on her back, her walking staff beside it. She also did not even think about how difficult it would be to hunt anything, given the fact that she still wore the formal kimono she had recently received. Tripping over her hem on her way down the wooden steps her current state of dress came crashing down on her with the force of her last mid-term.

"I can't go out like this!"

Spinning on her heel, she stormed back up the steps and through the door, picking her bag up again as she banged through.

"What are you doing back?"

"Changing. I can't even fish in this, much less hunt."

"Change? You bear Master's crest upon your clothing and you want to change? You dare to insult the noble house of Take in such a manner?"

"I don't want to get it dirty, alright? I'm not changing out there, it would be my luck that there's a *Tengu* waiting to run off with my top, chase me through the forest again, or try to feed me to another dragon. Where's the bathroom? I know he's got one."

A sigh came from within the wood as the door shut seemingly on its own.

"I suppose you may as well stay since you seem to have some respect for Master's house. If he truly has gone hunting '*Mistress*' then he will not be gone long. I apologize for my rudeness. Master has never allowed anyone here before other than me, for my care-taking abilities and the fact that he cut my tree down."

"No one?" She calmed as she asked her question. "I'm sorry too. I have been under much stress lately, and I never really learned any other way to deal with it. I guess I need to try harder."

The desk chair rolled back on its casters, turning around to present its cushions for her use.

"Please sit down Mistress. I will bring you some tea. While we wait for Master, perhaps you should sort through your feelings. From where I stand, that hunt is more important."

"Thank you."

Drifting to the chair in a daze, she was barely aware that the caretaker was using his spells to put the new addition to the house he served in order. Sinking down into the chair, her bag slipped back out of her hand and her eyes slipped closed. Soon, she was fast asleep, leaving the doorpost *Kami* to unpack her things as the rest of the cabin came out of its magical hiding.

"I still have my doubts you have married my Master, but if you have then you are my responsibility while he is gone. Sleep well, and please take my advice."

BlowingWind fell through soft layers of foliage that caressed her with ferny fingers, delivering her once more into the relative safety of the cave hidden in the forest of her mind.

"What am I doing here? All I did was to sit down. How did I fall asleep so fast?"

"It's just as well. We have a hunt to go on."

A quick look around revealed her shadow-self sitting on a rock beside where the new part of the cavern begged to be explored with its heated glow.

"What do you mean? Ryu's bringing some game, and we have feelings to sort through that I have been trying to divorce myself of."

The Shadow shook her head.

"The game we have to bring down Ryu can't hunt for us. As your Shadow I am also Gatekeeper of Initiation. I can't wait for you to be ready anymore. I need help now."

The Shadow calmly picked up her spear, handing BlowingWind one that had been tipped with worked quartz crystal. BlowingWind followed RagingTornado out of the cave with her heart in her throat, the bellows of a great beast ranging over the forest like a desert storm.

"What was that?"

"Our feelings. Time to truly face the beast we have been running from."

"But what if it kills us? We can die here. What about Ryu? What happens if he comes back to find our lifeless body? What would that do to him? I don't want to put anybody through anything even remotely similar to what we're going through."

"Have you found a reason to live then BlowingWind? All the more reason to bring it down and eat it, before our pain, fear and confusion drive him away. As annoying as he is, I don't want to be left alone again either."

The Shadow darted off toward the sound, her Light racing at her heels as her *kimono* melted into her white doeskins. Darkened and twisted trees reached for the hunters, urging them to lay aside their weapons and sleep, to stay on the known side of the door into a realm where few ventured very far. Whispers and chants rattled along with gourds that fear spirits fiercely wielded to defend the great beast that dwelled within every person, but neither paid any mind, swept up in great rivers of adrenaline and the thrill of the hunt. They were Shaman, and instead of fighting to return the soul and health of another they now fought to retain the power and life they had been granted.

Above and beyond the terrible death rattles calling the life from their bones, the chants of the Elders of ages past and present wove and danced, reminding the pair of the eternal dance of Dark and Light. The broken wails of BlowingWind's mother twined in with the rest, begging a God she did not know for certain truly existed to be with her baby and reunite them again. Guilt ran slimy fingers over her at the cries. As the duo dodged the reaching grip of branches and brambles, the triumphant calls of the Beast continued as it laid waste to yet another part of her being and the subconscious constructions that protected her.

At last, the forest yielded its greatest test, drawing back suddenly from a ravaged and bloodstained battleground, revealing a field of horror and death. Formless and black as the most ancient of demons, her greatest fear waited to gobble them both in body and soul. Embers served as eyes, burning her soul as it laughed cruelly.

"Hello BlowingWind. It's about time that you faced me. I have been slowly devouring you for months now without a fight. It's a pity that less than half of your spirit has come to me though. You are very shattered. You may regret allowing that."

BlowingWind rooted herself to the ground, determined not to give into her fear of the shapeless mass that had been poisoning her for so long.

"Name yourself."

"I am That Which Kills."

"That's not a name, that's a title. Cheater!"

RagingTornado had spoken this time, shifting her grip on her spear and inching closer, fire filling her eyes with life. BlowingWind readied herself and asked again.

"What is your name?"

The inky mist congealed as it laughed, giving birth to two forms within its charged confines. The familiar shapes came to the edge of the mist, rotted and pale as the corpses they were, worms eating at their defiled flesh as they shuffled from the Deeps.

"I am your Greatest Fear."

The mists parted, and BlowingWind locked eyes with the clouded eyes of the spirit she loved, and the spirit she had become bound to. Icy fingers squeezed her heart and stole her breath, while at her side her Shadow hissed in pain and clutched her own heart. Finally, the pain overcame the fear, and BlowingWind screamed as the sleeping spell broke.

"No!"

❧

"Wind-chan, I've brought you some venison. I hope you have been comfortable."

"Welcome back, Master."

The door swung open for Ryu, who entered carrying several parts of a butchered deer. Blood on his robes told the tale of how he had rent it himself, bleeding it as he worked to preserve the much older robes that BlowingWind had been given for their wedding. Behind him, the servant shut the door.

"Thank you, Ku. You fell asleep in the chair Wind-chan? You must have been tired if you didn't finish your exploring, or at least make it to the bed. I'm surprised that you didn't find the instruments."

"She didn't fall asleep Master. I enchanted her."

Laughing, Ryu walked past the desk into the kitchen, through a door that had not been visible when BlowingWind had entered.

"Let me guess, she wanted to hunt her own meat, and you didn't think it appropriate for a woman."

"She also wanted to remove your robes. I did not think that appropriate since she claims to be part of your house now."

"Ku, you're more old-fashioned than my *Ototo*. He at least lets *Omoto* hunt her own game."

"A woman's place is in the home or at the shrine."

Ryu opened the freezer and the refrigerator, putting the meat away before glancing around his modern kitchen at the new conveniences that had been manifested by his human's presence. Pinewood walled the room, contrasting with the steel and black of the stove, dishwasher, and freezer/fridge combination. The coffeepot brought a wider smile to his face.

"I still have to go and get her the coffee and chocolate I promised her. You didn't let her see the bedroom, much less anything else other than the living room. Just what did you think I was going to do to her if I found a comely female asleep in my nest?"

"I wasn't sure of her, Master. She is a human, and though she claims to have married you, I wasn't sure what type of bond you had entered into with her."

Ryu leaned against the doorjamb separating the kitchen from the living room, frowning as he watched his shaman's troubled sleep.

"For now, she is just my *Miko*. She isn't ready to be filled yet. The poor girl has so many demons of her own to face. I can't ask her to give clues about my own yet, much less coil within her inner springs."

"So why her?"

Ryu sighed and moved across the room to the door leading into the bathroom.

"Why not? She needs someone to take care of her, and maybe having someone to care for will help with my own problems. Now, I'm a mess, I am going to bathe and change before I move her. Eating my own kill is much cleaner than preparing it for use by another. If she wakes up before I am done, you can let her know I am back."

"Yes Master."

Ryu opened the door to the bathroom, and then frowned at the billows of cloudy white lace that had taken over his simple bathroom, and the powder blue towels that had replaced the ones he had left for later use.

"Ok you two, everybody out, and please don't completely womanize my whole cabin. This is far too much lace."

Two chuckling orbs disengaged themselves to float behind him. Neither had the slightest intention to leave him alone now that it had been confirmed the cabin conformed to the thoughts and energies of the occupants.

"I can see what you will be like as a ghost. I don't suppose either of you are interested in going back into your body?"

"No, not yet."

"They should be ready soon though."

Ryu wasn't sure which of the orbs had said what, but decided not to let it show.

"Father was right. Females make no sense. I'm sure you would like a long, hot bath too, but it's rather difficult without a body, and I'm not letting you share mine for this. If you filled it with frothy lace, who knows what else it will cross your minds to do to me."

With that, Ryu waved his hand, reordering the room to include his Jacuzzi bathtub and black towels, and then closed the door behind him after he was sure they had seen. From where they floated, the rushing stream of hot water as he rinsed in the shower and filled the separate tub called as loudly as the waterfall within their body that they needed to return to.

"Oh, he fights dirty, Love."

"Ryu's right though, since he won't take us with him for that, and Wind and Tornado aren't ready yet, it will be a long time before we can soak."

"Man, I want a bath after Ryu's hunt. He makes it look so effortless. It sure beats a gun, bow, or trap."

"Mmh. Wisdom, how are we going to know it's time?"

The silver orb floated over to the sleeping woman while the pink one settled carefully on a bookshelf next to a small model of an ancient Chinese weapon neither could recognize.

"I don't know. I am free to go at any time, but there is some connection between you and Ryu that won't make it easy for you to reenter. You've become dependent on him, and however he got you is going to have to be reversed to put you back. Can you remember anything yet?"

"No!"

BlowingWind's scream brought Love hurtling off of her perch in a panic while Wisdom dove into her body to find out what the problem had been. At the same time, the bathroom door slammed open to reveal a dripping, and towel-clad, Ryu.

"What's wrong?"

BlowingWind's eyes focused on the room, her ragged breaths a panted testament to the spiritual battle she had awoken herself from. Ryu knelt in front of her, ignoring for a short time the trembling form of Love huddled in a far corner, waiting for the clouds to finish clearing from her eyes.

"BlowingWind, what's wrong? What happened?"

"I can't. I can't stay here. You'll be hurt. Not again."

"What are you talking about?"

Ryu eased the trembling woman into his lap, watching for any sign that she would bolt. Wrapping her in his arms like she was a child, he pillowed her head on his chest. Love rolled over to the pair, slipping unnoticed into the dragon.

"I don't want it to get you. You don't deserve that. You've been kind to me, even though I have been a real witch to you."

"What don't you want to get me?"

"My greatest fear."

She slipped into sleep again, innocent and soft as the child she had once been, tired and trusting as she gathered life energy to herself.

"You must be facing your demons finally. Don't worry Little One, they won't hurt me. Let's get you into bed."

Ryu smiled as he lifted her, feeling his heart begin to beat in tandem with hers as his bond to her tied him more firmly into her world.

"Be strong."

CHAPTER 21:
STARLIGHT SPIDER WEB

THE moon had risen and set seven times, getting smaller every trip she made across the sky after Amaterasu had set. Ryu could no longer remember why the sun goddess and her brother Tsukiyomi fought, but it served to denote the passing of time. BlowingWind still had not awoken again, lost within his volcanic coverlets upon the bed.

"This isn't what I meant when I told her to sort her feelings Master."

Ryu sighed.

"Ku, she recently lost someone she loved very much and now finds herself my bride, however minor a consort others would consider her. That is something that takes time. For her peace of mind, I am glad that her cycle I now know, but I hope she wakes up before her feeding presents a danger."

Taking a sip of water, he gently passed the life giving fluid into her mouth and watched as her body reflexively swallowed. A sip of the venison broth that he had laced with healing herbs chased the sip of water. His saliva that mixed with the items finished the spell, nourishing her soul as much as her body, and thankfully unable to kindle life within her, at her current point of her cycle. Drawing back, he watched as her eyes fluttered, and then opened gently as spring blossoms.

"Well, it seems that Shin decided to rejoin with you finally and you are back at my side. I hope you are well rested."

"Ryu?"

"*Hai.*"

BlowingWind struggled to sit up, still exhausted by her first encounter with her inner demon and from the stress of reassimilating part of herself.

"Stay down. All you've had the past week is water and broth."

"Well, now I know how long I've been asleep. I'm afraid to ask how you fed me though."

"You wouldn't be very happy if I told you, especially if you know much about my species."

"That's what I thought. I did read something in a mythology book about dragon saliva having fertilizing and healing properties. If you've made me a mother already, then you are in serious trouble. You're a scaly coyote, taking advantage of me while I was asleep like that. Thank you for feeding me though."

"I don't think that will be a problem, but we will watch you for a while anyway. I have some rice sitting on the stove, Wind-chan. I had mixed some venison with it, but I can pick it out of your bowl if you don't feel up to something so solid."

"Venison sounds delicious Ryu."

"I'll be right back then. Stay put."

"I've been asleep for a week!"

Ryu's answer drifted to her from the kitchen.

"And you were fasting for only *Kami* knows how long before you came to me, with only small meals with Fuji-sama after that."

"Fine. But I don't have to like it."

She took advantage of his absence to look around the room, noting how once again everything was a swirl of lava, rich earth, or blackest night interspersed with bronze, copper, or gold. Her red kimono had been carefully folded and stowed on a shelf, as was her doeskin dress and precious knapsack. Ryu had a shelf for clothing as well, and in the closet she could see a normal teacher's slacks and dress shirts peeking out along with shy oxfords and some casual *yukata*. A night table beside the generous bed held the small bowl of broth that he had recently been feeding her from, and a cup of water. Looking down at herself, her under *kimono* was missing, replaced by a white cotton T-shirt that was oversized on her.

BlowingWind groaned and blushed when the implications hit her.

"Ryu, why did you undress me?"

He reentered the room bearing a black ceramic bowl filled with the promised meat and rice, along with mahogany chopsticks.

"Would you rather I not have cared for your needs? I didn't think that you would have appreciated waking up in a crusty pool of blood. At least I know why you were so testy."

"What other embarrassing things have you done to me?"

"That's all. Now open."

Ryu sat down on a chair beside the bed that she had somehow missed, smiling and stifling his laughter at her discomfort.

"I can feed myself still Ryu."

"Alright, I guess I should let you keep some dignity. I've seen worse though."

He handed the utensils over reluctantly; watching as she carefully brought each bite to her lips and spoke between mouthfuls.

"Worse? That's right, you're a spirit, and have probably seen quite a bit."

"I've watched countless human battles, and fought in wars among spirit kind that humans have no knowledge of. I don't mind the rainmaking battles, it's interesting to watch the *arashi-gami*, but I would much rather attend to your needs than to help patch up another friend wounded in pointless fights over the fate of humans in relation to the land."

"Are we really that bad?"

"No. Spirits get scared of what they don't understand, just like humans or anything else. Others become jealous of what you humans have made or taken, and so want to fight for possession. Others are just started because some of us are twisted. Most are just skirmishes of minor spirits against defenseless innocents. It is easy to forget that humans are children of the Ancestral *Kami* too."

"What about the other battles?"

"Territory disputes, perceived slights, breeding rights and courtship rituals, the occasional malcontent seeking to overthrow a dynasty... It seems that the only worlds of peace are the Heavens. But even those I sometimes doubt. You are doing well."

BlowingWind sheepishly put her empty bowl down.

"I hate to admit it, but you're a good cook."

"Was that a compliment?"

Ryu's smirk played on his lips while BlowingWind blushed.

"Yes."

"Since you seem to be feeling so much better, would you like to go for a short walk? We had a small rain shower a little while ago, and the raindrops still look like diamonds on the leaves."

"I do get to get myself dressed, right?"

"I'd have to maim and eat anything else that saw you in what you are wearing now, including the house guardian. If you need anything, either call me or concentrate on what you need, and it will materialize. Here anyway."

Ryu rose, taking the finished meal with him, and gently walked to the door. She watched him go, and caught the flicker of a spectral tail as the door shut behind him. When the rushing water in the kitchen told her he was occupied with cleaning the dishes, she quietly rose to pad over to her shelf.

"At least I don't need to check my underwear. No pads or bandage means that I'm already done for at least a day, unless he had tampons kicking around for some weird reason. I can't believe he did that though, how embarrassing. Can it get worse?"

Pulling down her doeskins, BlowingWind breathed in their earthy scent. "Grandmother, you have no idea how much these mean to me."

Pulling on her dress quickly, she frowned, "With sleeping for a week, I must look like a wreck."

A golden mirror and brush materialized on the nightstand, and she cautiously pulled the brush through her hair until it shone like silk and the tangles had fled in defeat. "More magic. I wonder if I'm in the Spirit World still, or if this is just a retreat in the Human World. Well BlowingWind, I guess that's enough primping for you. It's just a walk, not a date."

Steeling herself and squaring her shoulders, she put down the mirror and brush, watching as they faded back to wherever they had come from. "This could seriously put a damper on my self-reliance. I need to be able to provide for myself. I hope he doesn't intend on keeping me here. School starts in March after all."

Opening the door, she was greeted by the sounds of Ryu humming an ancient melody to himself in the kitchen as he worked, and the voice of the household servant.

"I hope that you found everything that you needed, Mistress."

"Yes, thank you. How is it that things fade away when they are not needed?"

"You refer to the brush and mirror, Mistress?"

"Yes."

"I transferred them from the bathroom to the bedroom, then back. A simple process really, but one that Ryu-sama has not mastered yet. He is still quite young after all."

"What haven't I mastered?"

Ryu stood in the kitchen door, watching as BlowingWind jumped and his servant answered.

"Object teleportation, Ryu-sama."

"At least I'm getting better at it though, Ku. You look lovely BlowingWind. Are you ready? Your moccasins were put by the door, as were your *geta*."

"Thank you."

Silently she pulled them on, feeling much better after putting on the familiar gear that now covered her feet. The door swung open as she stood, revealing dusk bejeweled with stars peeking through the haze of rice paddies and city pollution and shining liquid diamonds filling in for the stars upon the earth. A light step fell behind her, sweeping her out the door into Nature's embrace.

"I thought this would put you at ease and soothe your chafed spirit."

To her right Ryu walked beside her, gently tucking her hand into the crook of his elbow. A warrior's soul streaked through the sky, falling to earth from the Star Path and pulling a gasp out of a still numb heart.

"It's so magical."

"Nature always is."

A spider web had trolled the air fruitlessly for flies, displaying the jewels of life that had been caught instead from the deeply purple sky that was now almost velvet black. The sight of the sodden spider resting under leaves at the edge reminded BlowingWind of how trapped she truly was.

"It would have been better to let me die Ryu."

"I guess I'm a sucker for difficult situations. I don't understand why you keep saying you only bring trouble though."

"I don't want to talk about that, not yet."

Another star fell, blazing brightly and then dying bravely far from its goal. The wind danced in the trees, which sang low songs known only to them.

"I'm not a psychologist Wind-chan, so I don't know much about healing the mind, and I can only hear very strong thoughts from you, so I'm not really psychic either. It is distracting to listen to you constantly blaming yourself. You weren't even with him when he died."

"I know."

"Then why are you so scared?" Ryu had slid behind her easily as a shadow to enfold her softly in arms that had taken countless lives, and would devour many more in the course of history, as he whispered his question to her. Ryu instinctively nuzzled at her ear, subconsciously imitating the way his parents had soothed him as a pup.

"I can't tell you. No matter what we do, Fate will have her way."

A tear slipped down her face, unseen but smelled by the salt marring the mountain's forest night with its seaside tang. Warm lips brushed the nape of her neck, sending shockwaves throughout her touch-starved body from that hot epicenter of flesh as a blush erupted onto her face.

"I will do what I can to mitigate your pain."

She turned in his arms, drowning him in her melancholy pools lit by the jewels of her soul from the deepest currents of her being. His heart sped as the starlight showed how pale she was, a child of mountain winds now but a lost and colorless thread in the Grand Tapestry.

"I'm so lonely, Ryu. It hurts. I want to heal, but I don't know how. My Fear is great, and even if whole I don't know what to do to defeat it. Every time I think I have my life together, it changes completely, and little bits of myself are lost."

As suddenly as the wall was down, it rose again, although considerably weaker than before, a lone fortress instead of the Great Wall of China. The defiance burned in her eyes like watch fires, as if by admitting her weakness she was afraid of loosing a decisive battle. Ryu found himself drawn to the gateway of her lips, ghostly *sakura* blossoms in the night, but dared not invade.

"There is much I can do about that, if you would let me in. Just because our marriage is binding in the spirit realm does not mean we are legally bound here in your realm. If you will let me, I could court you properly. Even if you will not allow me to woo you, you will still not be alone."

Laughter floated through the trees, mocking and wheedling at once, like a magpie.

"Of Love BlowingWind is afraid. Is not a warrior bold? Is not a shaman brave? Why keep your heart so cold? Tuck your tail my *Coyotero*. Slither away, infant Snake, and hide. Hunter, draw your broken bow. Step into where Mystery abides."

The chortling song faded away as the spy danced through the night, the echoes melting away like soy paste into *miso* soup.

"That Brat. He told me both to accept and not accept. Now I know I'm in trouble whichever way I go. That Blasted Trickster Coyote! Your wife will have your hide when you get home!"

Nature continued to whirl in all her beauty, the forest dancing with itself, uncaring of the countless dramas being enacted within its bounds. The romance of the night had died a bloody death for the pair below the chattering sword of Coyote's taunts.

"Come along then, we might as well go inside before some *Tengu* decides to test my patience or an *Oni* smells you, Wind-chan. After what things they have gone through, they aren't all friendly."

"Please don't tell me you expect to be sleeping in the same bed again."

"Of course. Why not? We are married."

"I want something sharp dividing us."

"Don't you trust me?"

BlowingWind glared at Ryu, putting her hands on her hips.

"No."

"Ouch. That hurts."

"I'm not falling for it."

"Please let me hold you? I promise my hands will be good."

Ryu's eyes pleaded with her as he held his hand out toward her, but she danced back after smacking one.

"I barely know you!"

"So? Not very long ago, you would have had no say in who you married."

As BlowingWind walked through the door, Ryu caught a new spark in her eye. He followed her inside, receiving as his answer a sharp crack over the head with her *Tengu* Staff.

"Ok, that's it. You have to learn who is chief here, little girl."

Sweeping her up over his shoulder, her shrieks soon turned to laughter, confusing the dragon as he carried her to their bed.

"What's wrong with you?"

Fingers dove into his armpits, drawing a surprised yip from him as he dropped her to glare at her still convulsing form.

"What in the seven Hells was that for?"

"I'm very ticklish! I was getting my revenge."

"Oh? Are you? Then I'll be taking my revenge now."

Ryu descended on her now wriggling form, and their peals of laughter carried into the night as they fought for supremacy.

CHAPTER 22:
SORTING SEED, GRINDING MEAL

GOLDEN gleams cut back through the night, darting between rock and tree as if they were sagebrush and shadow, back where the shaman he considered his grandchild had been born. Taking on one of his many human forms, Coyote peered through the window of the small cabin the girl had lain in for the past week, mumbling to himself and Creator.

"Matchmaking really isn't my profession, but there are others to mirror that I am neglecting."

A second set of golden jewels joined the first as a shadow winged down to roost upon his shoulder. Both spirits of Turtle Island watched the questioned pair sleep, separated by a sword that knowing the girl, had been meant to keep wandering hands away.

"What is she so afraid of Coyote?"

"The curse isn't gone you know Raven. Her father's murder was a result of it, but Obsidian knew he was going to die early even before he met this girl. It was his misfortune to have inherited that lake, and his misfortune that White Man could not have found a more friendly way to situate that power plant."

The dragon was still, barely anything vibrating, the normally lively dance of his soul paused as if he had reentered the egg, or stone, his dragon shape had hatched from.

"He's so still. Are you sure he's a natural dragon, and not just some human wizard that's learned shape-shifting?"

"Raven, have I ever been wrong?"

"Coyote, think about that."

"Go ahead and rub it in then, but I'm not wrong about this."

BlowingWind stirred, shifting her face towards the open window, but fell back into the arms of sleep when Ryu moved slightly towards her.

"You would think that getting back part of her soul would give her more energy."

"She slept a week straight Raven, and he took care of her. He passed sustenance into her as if she were a very young pup being taught how to eat, and used a great deal of his energy to help her bind that part of her soul back within her body. They are both rebuilding their stores. It probably doesn't help that she started a tickle war with him over a really stupid thing."

The raven shook his head at everything and nothing in particular.

"BlowingWind had always been unpredictable. Are you sure this plan of yours will work?"

"You and I both know she will sneak off sooner or later to think, and how long she wanders when she has no commitments to worry about. Like a moth to a campfire, he will go after her. After all, he's still got part of her soul, and oddly enough, that part happens to be her heart."

"With how deeply he's sleeping, I don't think you will need any sleeping songs to keep him knocked out for her head start."

"Yeah? Who's the idiot that kept the sun in a trunk?"

"Fine, but Hawk and I are taking you home soon."

The shadow leaped into the air in a silent flurry, melding back into the shadows, unaware of the *Tengu* watching from the pines at the edge of the clearing. Coyote's song rode the wind, winding around the dragon now dreaming of winding around his prize, pushing Ryu deeper into sleep with the magic of desert and mountain.

The new day peeked shyly over the horizon, pearl gray warming into rose and gold as the sun goddess climbed into the sky again for her daily inspection of the world. Birdsong wove into heavenly choirs as Amaterasu's warmth roused them from sleep, and twin blue skies opened to view the starling singing on the windowsill of the bedroom.

"Good morning, Little Brother."

The starling preened, and then started singing again as it flew away, drawing a giggle from BlowingWind. Her eyes fell downward, observing the tousled head that pouted in his sleep.

"I see you were good last night, the sword is still between us. Thank you for that concession, Ryu."

Ryu replied by groaning at the sun and pulling his pillow over his face. Another giggle slipped out as she got up and stretched.

"You would be more energetic if you hadn't spent so much of the night watching me sleep, or tickling me half the night trying to get me to give in before bed. So much for well-behaved hands."

Wandering out of the bedroom and finding the kitchen, the shy smile dripped away as she fell into thought, pondering Ryu's last proposition.

"I have a lot to think about. Either way, I feel like a traitor. I guess that's what I get for following one of Coyote's illusions. I suppose he meant well, Coyote isn't bad, just a little foolish like all of us."

"What's wrong, Mistress?"

Sitting on a chair at the kitchen table, BlowingWind rubbed her forehead while studying the close grain of the wood.

"He asked to court me last night. Who asks to court any more? It's sweet in an old-fashioned kind of way. But he asked to *court* me!"

"Is that bad? You are already his chief and only wife."

"I was very attached to the last spirit that had courted me, and lost him. I'm cursed you know. I'm afraid of what will happen to Ryu."

"You are already bound. Master's fate is already sealed."

"What if it isn't? What if I can still save him from me? I feel like I threw him in a blender and hit frappé."

BlowingWind held her face in her hands, shuddering as she pictured what had happened to Obsidian.

"Mistress, I think you should eat something. It will help you see reality."

"Ku? Please stop. My name is BlowingWind, not Mistress. I'm still American, and we didn't do this ranking nonsense there. It makes me uncomfortable. *Onegai?*"

"If that is what you want."

"*Arigato.*"

BlowingWind got up, prowling through the kitchen for anything that caught her eye. Most of the dishes she did not recognize, but the indispensable pot of rice was easily found. Nothing appealed to her though.

"I think I'll go for a walk."

"It is not safe."

"It's no more dangerous now than it was when I first set out on this quest of mine. The only difference is my increasing doubt that I will find what I was searching for, and wondering what I was really looking for."

Abandoning the kitchen, she went back to the bedroom, carefully putting on her knapsack. Pausing by the bed, Ryu's now uncovered face caught her attention, his eyes staring at her though clearly they were still sleeping. Kneeling beside the bed, she studied him.

"I wonder if that's normal for you. Ryu, if you can hear me I'm going out for a little air."

A soft peck on an upturned cheek caused his eyes to slip shut once more, succumbing to the ropes of slumber that were ever beckoning. An odd throb in her heart confused her body even more than the mind already was, and she drifted to the door. After tying her moccasins, BlowingWind silently padded out the door to join with the wind, following once more where it blew her.

Her feet danced through grass and over stones, light as deer along their tracks. Cedar and pine coated her with their sweet perfume as dew washed her legs. The beat of her heart sped as her legs flashed percussion for the incessant chatter of the birds. As always, the wind seemed to feel her mood and it sighed her twisted thoughts throughout the primeval forest.

"Ku's right. His fate is already sealed, just like Obsidian's. If the legend of the curse is real, he might not die like Obsidian did. If that's so, I might be with him for life. But is he who I want for an earthly husband?"

Blue peeked though a curtain of trees, the smell of sweet water calling to the woman who had once freely roamed distant lake-shores. The ground sloped toward the lake, as if it too felt the primordial pull of the ebb and flow of the Elixir of Life. Picking her way down the steep and eager incline, she continued her voiced musings.

"Ryu's sweet, and he's saved my life and taken care of me. Without him I would probably have been one of the so-called suicides rotting out here. But something about him irritates me."

She had won her way to the water's edge, sinking down on a rock and praying her perch was uninhabited. Clasping her hands the way her mother instinctively did when she felt something evil was about to happen, BlowingWind felt the familiar sense of cold heat when her spirit was shielded.

"I let the Light Protect me."

The wind danced, making waves play upon the once glassy surface of the mere.

"Maybe it's because he is so irritatingly direct. It took Obsidian years to kiss me, although I had wanted to since I was twelve, and it was only ever on the cheek. What kind of woman does Ryu think I am?"

The wind rose and fell, as if it wished to sweep her up in intangible arms to rock it all away.

"What kind of woman am I? I'm spiritually married only months after Obsidian's death. What would he say? And I've not been able to tell my mother that I'm safe. I wonder if she got the letter I sent when I was at the Takamura's?"

Reaching down, she picked up a pebble, skipping it far across the water over the caps. Tears began to wash the beginnings of streams into her face.

"The worst part is that I'm actually attracted to him. I barely know him, but I have been wondering what it would be like. I never actually thought about that with Obsidian. He was so placid, but Ryu is like a smoldering ember. I'm so terrible! That sword I requested was for me as much as to keep him off of me!"

The wind dropped away, as quickly as if she had caught it up in a knot on a red string like her Celtic ancestors supposedly had been able to.

"What would Obsidian really want me to do? I don't want to abandon him. I don't want anyone to take his place in my heart."

Another stone found its way into her hand to fling itself out across the water to release some of her anger and drown it in the frigid depths. A guttural cry rose from her throat, ululating up to the Heavens and down to the very roots of the Earth, carrying her sorrow and guilt upon wings of confusion. The wind picked up, released from its shock, embracing her in whirls of earth and leaves as a human spirit took form long enough to embrace his only child.

"I know you will do what's right Wind. Follow your heart and be happy."

"Daddy? I'm so scared and confused."

"A stag's antlers have more than one point, and Rattlesnake's tail has more than one bead."

The arms dissolved and the winds rose directly into the distant sea of the sky, her father returning to the sky realm again, leaving a feather clutched in shaking hands remaining upon the fertile earth.

"Follow my heart?"

A beast chose that moment to rise, roaring its hunger to the forest.

"I guess right now I should follow my stomach before it eats itself. Hey, those berries look tasty."

Haze retreated to the horizon of his mind, releasing him again into the land of the living. Nightmares had tormented him throughout the night, feasting on the insecurities he had hidden so very carefully from his fragile human bride, and causing him to spend much of it watching her sleep. He had fought them easily when she had been assimilating herself, when he had been free to hold her in his arms or wind her into his coils and feel her living warmth. For reasons completely unfathomable to him, she had insisted he unsheathe one of his antique swords and place it betwixt them.

On discovery of her weakness he had exploited it, but her hands instinctively had found his own ticklish points, resulting in a draw. So, the sword had slept with them.

Morning sun greeted his eyes with her golden glow, painting everything into a warm panorama of peace. His nest was cold and empty though, his bride having removed herself hours ago.

"I thought I was dreaming when she said she was going for some air."

Sauntering to the closet, he quickly stripped out of the formal robes he had worn for so long in her presence, glancing at the window vaguely hoping to see a feminine shape frozen in surprise. No such form materialized for him though, and in disappointment he pulled out a simpler cotton *yukata* in his red and yellow.

"I'll go back to modern clothes when we are done in the forest. I hope she remembered to eat something."

Prancing to the bathroom, he checked on the state of his countenance and his hair, grumbling when he began to pull the brush through his hair.

"Why does it always look like I tried to eat an electricity imp in the morning? I probably barely even moved, and it still looks like this."

"Master?"

"Yes, Ku?"

"Mistress BlowingWind has been gone for quite some time now. She said she was going for a walk, but that was hours ago."

"Exactly how long?"

"The birds had only just begun to sing."

"That is quite a while. Did she seem distressed to you?"

"She had been talking aloud to herself about someone called Coyote. She was also distressed that you asked to court her."

"I knew I shouldn't have asked. It's obvious that she hates me and only tolerates me because I have been protecting her."

He dragged himself dejectedly into the living room, flopping forlornly into his desk chair to stare at the sketches of her that he had done as she slept. The angelic face pouted up at him, mockingly innocent.

"Master, she likes you very much. She is suffering under some foolish delusion that her curse is going to make her hurt you."

"Yes, we've been over that."

"Master?"

"It's nothing. I should go and collect her now."

He strode out of his front door, hiding once again all traces of uncertainty. Showing weakness in the forest could be death, as many had found out the hard way. The solemn forest waited for his entry, and he lifted his nose to the wind.

"It shouldn't be too hard to track such an unusual spice through the forest."

"You would be surprised, Young Dragon, how difficult it can be to find her when she wants to be alone. She led her poor lake spirit on many a chase through her home forest when someone had annoyed her."

Ryu's eyes narrowed as he turned to see where the owner of the voice lurked. Tawny fur disengaged itself from the shadows around a shrub, laughing eyes pinning the dragon.

"Coyote. Don't you have anything better to do than to haunt the poor girl? You seem almost as bad as a *Kitsune*."

"I am not haunting. It's my job to show Medicine Keepers and others what not to do. Creator himself gave me the job. This time though, I am actually worried about my grandchild."

"So you confuse her?"

"No. I merely showed her what not to do. Now you have two choices: show her exactly how much you care, or let her slip away. No matter how much she might try, she can't stop walking between worlds. I'm sure you know what happens when someone like her has no strong tether on either side."

"They go mad. Every spirit knows this. She's well on her way already."

The frown that had found Ryu's face etched itself deeper, beginning to look like the floor of a lava tube. Coyote laughed at his distress, leaping into the forest and following the traces of BlowingWind's trail.

"Don't be a cowardly dragon! She's waiting for you. Perhaps you could sing a love song and charm her clothes off."

"Come back here you flea-laden mini-wolf! I don't care if you are a grandfather to her, I'll garland my high seat with your intestines, and your teeth and claws shall be the *magatama* for my innocent *Miko's* rosary!"

"You would be surprised at how she really is if you knew half of the things I've heard her discuss with her childhood girlfriends."

A dark beast stirred, roaring his fury and fully stretching into his body. Take Ryu claimed his entire self as he took off into the forest, fully ready to enjoy the blood and flesh of the one who had spoken of removing his innocent maiden's clothing. The dragon took his real shape, a river of black and red death rampaging through the forest, easily capturing his prey and rending him into bloody pieces. A feral and wild cry echoed through the forest, capturing his attention before he could finish with his threat.

"BlowingWind!"

Continuing through the forest after the source of the heartrending shriek, Ryu left his prey. After the unbalanced dragon left, Coyote's broken body slowly pulled itself back together.

"Thank you Creator for making me always able to return to life."

CHAPTER 23: LISTENING TO COYOTE

THE forest had pulled her farther into itself as she quietly walked along, in search of berries, or small game that she could easily bring down with a rock. Midmorning poured through Nature's cathedral to light her way, and soothe her soul, as the wind whispered secrets in its ancient language.

Unknowingly, she slipped between the worlds of spirit and man, flickering like a ghost and startling a monk that was making a circuitous pilgrimage around the base of the mountain, the woman silent as a shadow, stealthy as a mountain lion. He watched in wonder as she faded in and out before his eyes, murmuring a *sutra,* believing that he had seen a forest demon. The apparition paid him no mind though, flashing through the forest intent on her errand. Minutes later, a fallen sapling lay across her path, drawing her to a stop.

"That could make a good spear. Thank you for giving yourself. You are already dry for me even."

A moss mantled stone sat by the edge of the path, and there she sat to work her tool. Digging into a small medicine pouch around her neck, BlowingWind carefully pulled out a small flint scraper she had found on one of her many childhood walks through the woods.

"It looks like you will be put to work again, Little One."

The outer bark fell away quickly below her hands, and soon light fingers were smoothing the sapling, as she remembered Obsidian's words when he had once tried to teach her to make a simple spear. The scent of the fire came back as she swept back in time.

"You want to use a straight sapling and the straighter the better. Even the straightest need straightening and it takes a whole day to dry these buggers. Arrows are quicker since you can use reeds, but it's the same process really. If you heat the bend over the fire, you can use your hands. Hold it until it's cool and move on."

"It's hot Obsidian! What happens next?"

"You smooth it. A steel knife is okay, but a stone, bone, or piece of glass gives a better result. You won't take big chunks out that way, or at least you'll be less tempted to so you don't cut your hands."

"That stick doesn't look like it's going to kill anything. Are you sure it's almost done?"

The bottom of the lake had sparkled in his eyes, laughter singing below his surface as he held the willow shaft in the smoke and heat over the coals of his fire pit.

"Pointed right and cured well, this is as deadly as any spear tipped with stone or metal. If you ever get lost, you can use this process to procure a means of obtaining your meat. If you make a forked one, you can fish much easier than grabbing the Slippery Ones by hand. They also make it a lot easier to harvest apples."

"Wow Obsidian. Your parents must be survival buffs. I don't know if I have the patience for doing this though."

"They are something like that, I guess. It beats throwing rocks."

The memory faded as she returned to the present, a wistful smile flitting across her face.

"That was a long time ago, before he told me his big secret. I must have been fifteen or so then. I wish I had a fire to cure you properly, but let's see if you'll do."

Frowning at her feet, she inspected the leavings of her project.

"I shouldn't waste anything. I'll bag this up for fire starter for later."

Putting the shavings in an empty pouch quickly, she then rose to continue her hunt when a rustle to her right returned the knowledge that she could also be prey for a larger animal, like Bear. Staring hard where the noise had been, she waited for an attack, but nothing came.

"It's probably just a squirrel then. A spear is overkill for that. I know I'd miss."

Walking farther through the forest, another path intersected hers through the screens of bushes, bearing the tracks of a lone traveler, a silent haiku waiting to be heard.

"Deer."

Following the tracks onto the weaving secondary trail, the utter silence of the forest raised the hairs of her neck.

"I still feel like I'm being stalked."

Quickening her pace, she ran along after the tracks, silent as a ghost and light as a leaf in the wind.

Barest hints of cinnamon were the only confirmation of his human's passing to the edge of the lake. The dragon irately prowled the area she had once sat in, chafing to whisk his prize back to their den.

"A little air my claws, this is at least a four hour hike for most humans. This is where her scream came from though. Where did she go and why can't I find her scent leading away? There isn't even a track!"

"I told you she could be hard to find. All my harrying has taught her how to hide herself when needed."

Coyote sat on his haunches beside the lake, blood still matting his fur as he eyed the frigid water, before leaping in long enough to rinse it away.

"You! I killed and dismembered you! How is it you are alive?"

Coyote sprayed the area with jewels of water before answering.

"Didn't she tell you? I always come back to life. It is Creator's will. What would the world be like without me?"

"No wonder she doesn't like you."

"No. She's still mad at me for getting her in trouble with her mother when she was seven, so that she did not get to spend her father's last night with him. What she doesn't realize is that if she had gone to that rally with him, she probably would have been shot too."

"So you saved her life then?"

"Unintentionally. I was more focused on getting a playmate."

"Leave her alone."

Brown eyes flared to red, glowing embers and blazing fires ready to devour the tawny beast.

"Soon enough I'll be heading home for a while. You still haven't found her though. Her unconscious illusion is too strong for you?"

Ryu took a step closer, his teeth gleaming in the light as he locked his more reasonable aspect away.

"I wouldn't do that, young dragon. I have a secret charm that will allow you to see her. Without me, your prey will get away."

"Give it to me."

"You have to promise not to kill me when we meet again."

"No deal."

"Fine. She'll find her way back to Man's civilization without you then, and drive herself crazy with her grief."

"Very well then. I won't kill you next time, but I can't guarantee after that."

"Good enough. This will only work one time to find her. If she sees you while you wear it, it loses its magic and can't be recharged. You can recharge it using the standard procedure."

Using his jaws, Coyote pulled a burr out of one of his matted tangles. Trotting over, he swiftly encased it in Ryu's waving mane.

"You're sure about this?"

"Never fails. How do you think I've always been able to find her? Good hunting."

Cackling, Coyote took off into the forest in search of Raven and Hawk, eager to get away from the mess that would surely ensue from his meddling. Before Ryu could wonder why the Coyote had gone so easily, his quarry's scent cleared again and her tracks became plain.

"There you are *Koibito*. Let's see why you are hiding when I still have your soul. Or is it that you wish me to pursue you like you were a *ryu-onna*? You did attack me again last night after all."

Her path wove through berry bushes and under trees, stopping here and there where something had called her to graze. Stalking quietly, the thrill of the hunt tingled through his nerves and sped his blood, the challenge of bringing her down beckoning to him and blinding him to the monk that was still chanting *sutras* where he had spotted the demon woman fleeing the dragon. The monk, frightened by seeing a dragon in its true form, chanted more *sutras* with more fervor than he ever had before, hoping to ward off the ill omen.

Finally, Ryu found her, a smiling *Tennyo* working a dead bit of wood into a new creation. Lovingly the sapling was stroked with her stone, while her misty eyes watched a memory only she could see.

"I wish I could see your memory Little One. It will be good when our bond is strong enough that your strong mind can not repel me anymore, my lovely."

His thought coincided with her return to the present, her wordless song dying away, absorbed by the spear.

"That was a long time ago, before he told me his big secret. I must have been fifteen or so. I wish I had a fire to cure you properly, but let's see if you'll do."

She looked down at her feet, muttering vaguely about a fire later and putting her mess away before leaving.

"So she is running away! I won't let her."

He tensed to pounce, his tail flicking a bush as he shifted his weight. The sound attracted her, and she stared cautiously but without fear at where he was hidden, a warrior prepared for whatever was necessary. Her true face froze him, spellbound at the strength she displayed. Held still for ages, he relaxed when she laughed at herself.

"It's probably just a squirrel then. A spear is overkill for that. I know I'd miss."

She continued along the path, stopping only at an intersection where she leaned down to examine tracks in the softened dirt. Her scent changed, excitement swirling heavily and hooking his nose on great whirls of something close to possessive desire as she whispered to herself.

"*Kami!* She smells almost good enough to eat. No wonder Father likes to stalk Mother so much when she hunts."

"I still feel like I'm being stalked."

Her eyes narrowed as she spoke to herself, and when she shot off he gleefully followed at a leisurely pace. There was no need to rush, her tracks were plain, and although he had hunted recently, he had never hunted this type of quarry before. The dance was complex and his pride could not allow her to win.

"You are mine my BlowingWind, but yes, let us dance. We should do this right."

Stealthily padding after her, ancient desires roiled within him, building pressure with every step as her scent told him she thought nothing pursued her anymore. Her pace slowed as she caught up with her own prey, focusing instead on becoming one with the deer.

In a green carpeted clearing the buck grazed, the wind bringing the dragon its rich scent and the pounding surf flowing in its veins. He watched as she slowly hefted her spear, and then released the shaft like one of Susanowo's lightning bolts in a battle. The weapon traced a graceful arch, flying straight, but ultimately falling short of its mark, the arm propelling it unused to such tactics. The buck leaped for the forest, breaking down a panicked path where none had been before.

"It can't be fish I'm craving. No, it just has to be deer liver. At least it's not monkey liver. Yuck." Muttering to herself, BlowingWind collected her spear, and then tensed when the greenery shifted. "What's out there?"

Ryu had moved before she could see him, flashing after the buck faster than a human eye could travel and leaving little trace of his passing with practiced ease. BlowingWind could find nothing that would have made the noise, returning instead to the more fruitful prospect of pursuing her meal.

"At least the path will be easy to follow, but I'll have to get closer next time."

Ryu brought down the deer easily, reveling in its scent of terror and thanking the keeper of the deer for his generosity. Easily breaking its neck, he retreated and left the prize catch for BlowingWind. It was not long that he waited for her to find it.

BlowingWind rested the haft of her spear on the ground, looking down at the deer lying dead on the ground.

"It seems someone has already taken my prey. I'd better not touch it in case it's a trap, or whatever spirit killed it returns with butchering tools.

She took a step away, freezing when a great beast growled its displeasure at her. Blue skies widened and yellowed in surprise, and the increased beat of the drum that was her heart called to the beast within him as he watched her struggle to thaw and whirl to face the rocks he had hidden behind.

"I've been hunted!"

The woman brought the spear up; angry for having gotten so wrapped up in her hunt that she had been the quarry for another.

Again, the growl rose as Ryu fumed over his advance being rejected. Fear rose from her body in great billows as she fell easily into the classification of prey, exactly where he did not want her. He wanted to hear her challenge fly up to the sky, initiating the next step in the ancient dance. All he could do was growl and roar as the color drained out of her face. The roars shook the earth below him, and distantly he could feel as his molten river below the mountain rose several inches in his great frustration and his counterpart Take protested the display of temper. The changing pressure underground triggered another small quake, registering on the ultra-sensitive seismometers in Tokyo University's Geophysics department and gently setting the ground to roll like waves on a lake.

In fear, BlowingWind fled through the forest; desperate to escape the unknown rock beast she had angered.

"Rock demon! Ryu! The rock is gonna eat me!"

"What? What rock demon?"

His growls stopped, frozen by the shock of her terror as she fled. The raucous laughter of a Raven floated through the trees, grating his ears and spurring the young lady faster.

"The young Wind is no dragon, rock demon! She poses no threat to you, and she does not understand this is what part of you meant by courting."

Roaring before taking up his kill in his jaws, Ryu exclaimed, "I've been tricked! I never should have listened to Coyote."

CHAPTER 24:
HEART OF A SHAMAN

HER heart was a racing drum as her feet pounded out ancient rhythms upon the skin of the earth. Swift as Rabbit, she fled between the towering sentinels of pine and cedar, darting around boulders and stones, leaping living roots, but no burrow large enough for her was in the range of her endurance. Soon enough, a root reached out to trap her foot, and grasses eagerly embraced her falling form.

"Ow. I guess I'm still a little weak. I can't believe I chickened out back there. And I'm such a wimp I screamed for Ryu. He's back at his retreat miles away, there's no way he could have heard me. What's happened to me?"

Rolling over onto her back, BlowingWind gazed up into the sky through the canopy of interwoven trees. Cottony white clumps of down skittered in the airstreams overhead against a backdrop of turquoise, paying no attention to the young shaman on the ground.

"At least I out ran it. I still want deer liver, but maybe the liver of something smaller will work."

Sitting up, a chipmunk peered at her from on top of one of the nearby rocks that was hugged by the gnarled fingers of roots. His cheeks puffed out with treasure, even this creature could present a challenge to capture, but no more difficult than a lizard.

"Here, Chip."

Flinging herself at the chipmunk, BlowingWind did not hear the snapping of a branch as Ryu hid himself behind a tree, or his muttered gratefulness at storing his catch in one of his caches. The chipmunk chattered reprovingly at her as it scampered up the tree and her head introduced itself forcibly to the rock.

"Ouch. Just one bite, please? It won't hurt, I could kill you quickly."

Ryu, in his human form, stifled his laughter at how she gazed hungrily up the trunk, like a pup still too young to hunt on its own. Hidden behind a bush, he continued stalking his target.

"Fine, I'll eat somebody else."

A rabbit hopped lazily through the glade as it foraged, unafraid of the still panting and physically weakened shaman. BlowingWind threw her spear when it came in range, but once again it fell short and the bunny hopped mockingly along.

"Coyote must have been the one to fell this sapling, my aim has never been this bad. Let's try something."

Collecting her stick, BlowingWind looked for a suitable target.

"I'll aim for that clump of grass ten feet away since it only seems to have a ten foot range."

Taking aim and then releasing, her spirit soared with the primitive spear, then fell as it obstinately flew ten feet beyond her mark.

"Yup, I either suck at spear hunting, or Coyote bewitched the stick. I've got to get some meat, and it's too far to head back to Ryu before eating something better than nuts and berries. Why does it have to be liver?"

Ryu's heart soared to hear that she was considering returning to his side, and he could no longer contain his laughter at her childish antics. At that moment, the spear dissolved, and now weaponless, BlowingWind whirled around to face her stalker. Before she could turn to see him, Ryu laid out the deer liver on the large maple leaf he had kept it wrapped in, retreating behind another tree.

Nothing greeted her, save for the liver offering itself. Timidly as a fawn, she approached the oddity, carefully not touching it. Looking around from that vantage, the woods still did not reveal her pursuer.

"If you are hunting me, just get it over with. Stop playing with me."

"Your aim is off because you are hungry, although it seemed that the spear had a spell playing off of that."

"R-ryu?"

By the time she turned around to his new hiding spot, he had already moved to a completely different one. In transit he removed the burr from his hair, slipping it into a pocket of his *yukata* to protect its magic, if she did manage to set eyes on him.

"If I had been a demon, you would be dead now. You should eat."

Turning around again, he watched as the blushing rosebud closed on herself, shaking her fist and taking the challenging stance that had begun to fire his blood.

"Ryu, I can hunt my own deer. I don't like talking to things I can't see. Come talk to me properly."

Ryu stepped silently from the tree he had darted behind, which she had drawn up beside in her searching wandering, creeping up on her until he could wrap his arms around her, twirling her around and watching in satisfaction as her breath was easily stolen. As she tried to regain her dignity, she turned in his arms to face him, to challenge him with her polished turquoise.

"Like this, *Koibito*?"

"W-what are you doing Ryu? This isn't right! Let go!"

"Now, why is it that when you know I am around, I only ever see you grieving, even when you play? I watched you go through many emotions today. Why won't you show this lonely Ryu the other faces you possess, instead of hiding behind your masks?"

She was off-balance, clutching him for support as his hungry eyes drove her even further backward than his body did.

"It isn't right for me. Don't you understand? My betrothed is dead and you are working to make me forget him and to put you in his place. Why shouldn't I grieve his passing?"

"Why shouldn't you accept what your life has to give you? Have you thought about my proposal?"

Her eyes searched the meadow desperately for a distraction as the color rose higher on her face. Ryu leaned closer in, trapping her back against the scaly black pine behind her.

"I see you have. Would you be so cruel as to keep me waiting for an answer? Of course, I suppose I have been cheating, as this is how we dragons court, but I would like to court you the way you have been accustomed to, instead of you triggering my instinctual responses."

The dragon closed the remaining inches between them, crushing her into the venerable pine and devouring her lips as he poured through her Red Lotus Peak and into her Jade Spring, drinking deeply of the clear waters welling from that sacred place as he stole her first kiss. He felt as her eyes closed and the wall around her heart crumbled at its weak point when Love passed back out of his mouth and into her rightful body, allowing their hearts and minds to join as their fates were spun tighter together. The sounds of the forest faded, and together they fell through frigid mist as the sounds of a roaring waterfall cascaded into their heads.

Releasing her lips, Ryu opened his eyes again, cautiously looking around at the unexpected teleportation.

"Where are we? I didn't know you could teleport."

"I can't."

"Well, I can't either. I have to use the crystal network or other means to travel long distances."

Blushing, BlowingWind pulled away from Ryu, leaving him growling his displeasure for her to hear.

"Oh stop. Are all dragons so possessive? To answer your question, this is my Source, where my spirit enters my body."

"And it's about time you and Love got here too. Did you have to bring the dragon with you? Hasn't he stolen enough of our secrets?"

The Shadow stepped out of the waterfall, white bandages on her arms and legs contrasting the smoke black of her dress as she eyed their suitor.

"Oh honestly, *Ara*, you act like you're afraid of giving him your heart."

Wisdom stepped out of a pine tree that had been growing near the pool, her silver dress gleaming in the sun filtering through prismatic mists. The Shadow shook her fist.

"Stop calling me that, that's not even close to my name and you know it, 'Shin.' Love's already given him her heart for taking care of her, and you gave your mind for what he can teach you. All that's left is BlowingWind's body and my secrets. And when I faced our demon, she ran away and neither of you even showed up to help us until after that thing had me in its grip."

"But who saved you and bandaged you when BlowingWind called for help?"

The Shadow closed her eyes and sat on the water-soaked rocks she had been standing on to pout. The water rolled down over her, veiling her from sight as she wallowed in her annoyance and muttered to the Stone People around her. Shin rolled her eyes at the other aspect of her self, waiting for the time their Shadow could release the mask she still was trapped beneath.

"You hold the body as your gift BlowingWind?" Ryu stood in the breeze, watching as she knelt to drink out of the pool representing the unity of her spirit.

"As the dominant aspect, yes it seems I do. It also seems that I had already given you the most important parts of myself. No wonder it was so hard to even think about going away."

A cherry tree stirred in the wind, the being finally returned home and reveling in the air filled with the liquid of life. Wisdom laughed as she walked over the grass to pat the slender trunk,

"Welcome home, Ai! Are we being shy after Ryu was your generous host for so long?"

Although the wind did not increase, a gracefully laden bough dropped her fruit on Shin, who continued to laugh.

"What are you worried about? Our plan to get you home worked didn't it? The kiss broke the barrier that Fear had erected, and we now also know why He refused to kiss our lips until the wedding."

A rock winged its way to hit the tree, followed by several that pummeled Shin as BlowingWind continued to drink peacefully, and

Ryu watched the fight with disbelief. The woman hidden in the *sakura* hissed at the attack, as Wisdom called her shield once more. The Shadow emerged fully from her waterfall again, standing instead upon the turbulent surface of the pool.

"You two planned for us to fall in love with the scaly coyote? If I wasn't still hurt I would hog-tie both of you!"

"Is it always like this here BlowingWind?"

"Welcome to my mind, Ryu. I miss the times when the only voice inside my head was my own. So close to my Source I can't lie, no matter how much I try."

A sly look slithered across his face before being hidden behind a smile, like a snake plunging into a hole. "Tell me then my dear; would you like for me to court you?"

"Yes."

The answer slipped out before wet hands clapped over her mouth, the single word a bomb that ended her internal battle even more suddenly than Hiroshima and Nagasaki had ended World War Two for the Japanese. The two souls that had stepped out of their astral representations hurriedly retreated.

"Thank you, Miss MountainChild."

The scene faded, replaced by oppressive heat and eternal darkness that swallowed sensation and threatened sanity.

"Ryu!"

"Over here."

He oozed easily through the unmitigated void, long practice with the gate and crystal systems lending him serenity, the transference between minds complete when he took hold of her trembling form.

"You aren't very fond of limbo I take it. I'll do my best to keep you out of that then. You showed me yours, now it seems I must show you mine."

Ropy ground formed below their feet and walls could be felt close around them, although no light penetrated the subterranean womb. His hands holding hers, he attempted to draw her with him, but fear had rooted the human to the ground.

"Come with me, Wind-chan."

"I can't see, Ryu."

"That's no problem."

Her slight form was light as an *origami* bird to him, cradled carefully against his chest as he swept her off of her feet. The darkness unfolded her secrets to his eyes, nothing in his realm being able to hide from him once he had decided to search for it. Soft footfalls echoed through the ancient tubes as he carried her closer to the heat, and slowly a fiery glow made itself known.

"Ryu! Stop! I can't take the heat."

Sweat poured off of her body as the underground fire sought to conquer the water flowing in her veins, and her breath came in weak gasps as her still living spirit struggled to maintain its connection to her body in the outer world.

"I'm sorry, I forgot that mortals can not approach me without special charms, even if I bring them myself. We'll stop here then. I forgot that you and I are not bound tightly enough yet to give you even the least of my heat resistant magic. I'll have to let him come to us then."

"Him?"

Racing footfalls echoed a frantic rhythm only heard when the crust rolled and bucked in response to the emotions of his family, growing louder the closer they came. A shimmer of heat moved at the end of the tunnel, slowly gaining form as it drew near, wavering in the heat and congealing into a form that mortal eyes could see.

"Sorry I'm late Ryu. Some of the vassals had a disagreement and attacked each other while you were stalking poor BlowingWind. Your temper tantrum didn't help matters either, you wouldn't believe the paperwork you made me file, and I had to smudge the truth a little bit because of you."

"Thank you for trusting me so long in protecting her Take. As you can see I have not forced her."

"I didn't really have much of a choice since you took over when

Coyote taunted us. I hope you mauled him."

The spirit before her still panted slightly from his exertion, grinning as Ryu answered him, until he heard the whole reply and a scowl erupted momentarily.

"I had literally strewn him along the meadow, there were parts everywhere. The blasted canine came back though, and took a bath in the lake as if nothing had happened!"

BlowingWind murmured, "Well that's annoying." She eyed the twin to the one called Ryu, watching carefully for any tricks. Ryu chuckled and put her down.

"BlowingWind, this is Take, my *nigimitama*. You could say that he's my better half."

Take bowed to BlowingWind before taking her hand and raising it to his lips.

"I do hope that my troublesome *aramitama* has not been accosting you too badly. He does need to learn patience, although I must confess that I need to work on that lesson as well."

"He did steal a kiss."

The blush on her face showed clearly, despite the glow painting her from the orange light. Take glared at Ryu, who smiled back unabashed.

"Did he? That is a memory he had better share then. I wondered what had happened when Ai disappeared."

"Take? Where are we?"

"We are close to my heart. My magma is at the end of this passage. Perhaps someday you will be able to see it while still in your flesh, but the charm that will allow that will require a sacrifice you will not give to me yet. Well, we're not really there, this is the copy of my realm that exists in my mind, but the physics are the same. I could show you other, less passionate, parts of myself if you wish."

"Is this the passageway from the cave in my forest then?"

"Perhaps, would you like to walk the other way and see?"

"Hey! What about me? Didn't I prove I can be trusted for a few hours?"

"I suppose so, but you were still a thief."

Sighing, Take pulled Ryu into himself, the essences melding easily together, their heat swirling around the shaman until they solidified once more. Take Ryu smiled down at BlowingWind from his place before her, no difference to the eyes, but warmer than he had been.

"I'm sorry I interrupted you. Shall we find out now?"

The former flush had run away long ago, fear now painting her white.

"I am afraid. There is a demon prowling that forest, and part of me is still injured and not ready to fight it."

"When you are ready, I'll help you fight your demon. You are not alone anymore."

Ryu's lips softly came down on hers as he leaned her against the warm wall of the lava tube. Neither one could keep their eyes open as their spirits overlapped slightly, lightly as darting dragonflies. Vertigo claimed the pair as the world shifted around them, and when they opened their eyes they stood once more in the Sea of Trees. BlowingWind gasped for breath in surprise as Ryu gently gazed into her wide eyes.

"Really?"

"What kind of *Kami* would I be if I let my *Miko* battle demons without some help? More importantly, what kind of boyfriend or husband would I be?"

"Can we at least go slowly, please? What should I call you now anyway?"

"Whatever you wish."

"I'm so tired Ryu."

Exasperation darkened his visage as he bored into her eyes.

"Of course you are! You need to eat more than nuts and berries now, and there was plenty of food at home. Instead, you went for a walk and decided to go hunting along the way. Speaking of that, you need to eat the liver before it spoils."

"Too late Lovebirds, this bottomless pit ate it. That was the longest kiss I've ever seen. It's a shame I don't carry a camera." Raven's harsh voice crowed, shattering the moment like a sledgehammer through glass, and then fell into laughter as the two returned their consciousness to the outer realm.

Coyote tried to hide the evidence of his latest theft while a large hawk held a weary wing over his eyes.

"I'm tired of seeing Coyote parts thrown around, but maybe if you rip him apart the trip home won't be filled with these Trickster's arguments. I'm sorry child, but he insisted he check on you one final time."

The shaman burst out of Ryu's arms, running to the branch that Hawk had perched on.

"Will you be going to the Reservation?"

"I don't know yet where Raven and I will drop him, but probably somewhere with sharp rocks. You would like me to tell RedFeather and the Elders that you are safe?"

"Yes please Grandfather."

"Very well Granddaughter. You should visit civilization soon and write your family and all of your friends soon, before you go much farther in your training. Snake regrets that he could not come as well, but perhaps you will see him in dreams soon."

"Yes Grandfather Hawk."

Hawk reached out to caress her with a wide wing, and then leaped into the air, catching the wind and rising. Raven repeated the movement from a rock he had hopped onto, and the pair gripped Coyote by the scruff of his neck. Coyote's yips and yowls of pain carried well as they disappeared into the currents.

"Ow! I'd rather stow away on another jet and freeze!"

BlowingWind shook her head as Ryu wandered up behind her, the shaman giggling as she pictured Coyote breaking open luggage for warm clothing.

"That explains why he was able to tail me for so long."

"We should get home Wind-chan. You need to eat, and we have your future to plan. Tomorrow we'll go back to civilization and take care of the needed things, and purchase your coffee and chocolate that I promised you. Then we will come back for a short time so that I can help you learn what you can do now."

BlowingWind leaned back into his waiting arms, gazing into her past.

"It's been a while since I could say I had a home. We will need to go to the shrine and pick up the things I asked the priests to guard for me, and I still have to get an *omamori* for my landlady's baby. It's late afternoon now though. How are we going to get home before nightfall?"

"I'll carry you."

"Carry me?"

BlowingWind turned around to determine if her *Kami* was joking, but by that time he had already taken his dragon form.

"I will fly above the treetops, and I'll use invisibility so that the humans will not see us, if any are wandering out here."

He lowered his head, lying down so that she could easily mount him as his whiskers twitched in his excitement. Timidly she clambered up behind his head and grasped hard horn as he shivered in pleasure at her touch.

"Don't you dare pull any stunts, you scaly coyote!"

"Of course not dear, you haven't had much practice riding me."

"Don't count on it becoming commonplace if you can't behave."

"What makes you think that I am misbehaving?"

With that, Ryu leaped into the sky, riding the air as the forest streamed along below them. BlowingWind's scream of fright at their sudden lift-off echoed through the trees, changing into howls of pleasure as the wind freed her spirit once more.

VOLCANO SPIRIT

AUGUST 2005

Eyes of burning fire
Tempting me into the pyre
As I toe the wire
While climbing ever higher.

Red obsidian skin
Holding earthly heat within
Molten you have ever been,
Ye volcanic *jin*.

Magma robes rustle
As you dance and bustle
Bidding me to hustle
Stretching spiritual muscle.

Laughing, you jump into the crater
Daring me not to wait 'till later.
Such a mischievous baiter,
O spirit to whom I cater.

Liquid fires deep below stir,
Causing racing pulse to whir.
In I leap, stung by a burr,
Now the rocky throat blurs.

THE DRAGON SONG

FEBRUARY 23, 2003

Dance beneath the Sun.
Sing beneath the Moon.
Come and have some Fun.
Hear the Dragon's Croon.

Snow cloaks the Mountain.
Laying soft and White.
Filtering through to Fountain.
Again to see the Light

Deep within to find be I.
Heart so bold to seek Me.
Come to me, Be not afraid to Cry.
I stand in the Wind plain to See.

Let me Coil within your Soul.
I'll chase your Fears Away.
My eyes, black as Coal,
Keep Watch both Night and Day.

Do not Fear me Little Maid.
Beautiful You I'll never harm.
I am the Force that hither you Bade.
Come to be your Strengthen Arm.

Stroke my furry Cheek.
Pat my scaly Hide.
Truly, I am quite Meek.
Let me take you on a Ride.

We'll Swim through the Rivers.
I'll Fly you over the Seas.
Please, don't get those Shivers.
Sweet Maiden, Trust me, Please.

Beneath this Sacred Mountain,
Lies a Place Lovely and Fine.
Therein too, the Sacred Fountain.
These Waters here are Mine.

'Tis true I have not Wings.
Gentle Woman, can't you See?
I have no need of such Frail Things.
My Power is at full, when you are with Me.

Wise Little Priestess, Hidden in Plain View,
That Mystery that you have Sought to See,
Hidden deeply in the Caverns of You,
I am You, and You are Me, Together is Your Key.

DEDICATION

THIS revision is for my readers, my dear Vadise, and my children, who all still love dragons. Also to be remembered is my father, Ben Garcia. I am glad that you were alive for the first edition, and you will always be with me.

Thankyou also to Hushicho-san, my dear friend, and to Hayao Miyazaki for his inspiring works.

Many thanks go to my school chums Harley Myers, Tia Roberts, Candy Kilcrease, Brian LaFazio, and a few precious others. For Mike Morgan, I salute you buddy. I write this also for my Internet friends knowing me as Lady Rain StarDragon, among other names, and my teachers not only from school and college, but also from all the communities I am or have been a part of. Finally, I write this for a very special friend, Goruden-sensei, whose support, figurative and literal kicks to the posterior, as well as insight greatly helped me.

And one cannot forget Faith, Angel that she is, for having been my editor so long.

A WORD FROM THE AUTHOR

OVER the years, I have had several questions as to why this book of the series dealt so little with Marie O'Drake, and spent so much time stuck in BlowingWind's head. I have been told, from time to time, that her preoccupation with herself is annoying. I have to admit to being glad of that, as when writing, I had wanted to illustrate the way that such a severe loss can disturb the mind. So, I am happy that I achieved that.

As for why Marie's methods of dealing with her daughter's disappearance were not gone into much, I had wanted to save her portion of the story for another book, as it will be tying in so much with why she first ran from Ireland, and then from her husband's death. Yes, it is a cycle that will be broken.

There have been a few readers that have told me the storyline confuses them and that they have had to go back and re-read. For those that have not figured it out by reading, time between the Sprit Realm and Mundane realm is not hard and fast. Anyone that dreams will have experienced this. This is part of why the timeline might feel to be 'loose' to some. It is supposed to be. Imagine that you have slipped between timelines. Now imagine that this is a common thing for you. Time as we know it then looses meaning. It is this effect I have to capture in the stories of this series.

Some of the capitalization may confuse some readers. If you see a word capitalized in the middle of the sentence, it is intentionally so more often than not. Place special emphasis and consider why I have chosen to do so, then you'll catch a different layer.

Book Two of Dragon Shaman series, "The Smoky Mirror" takes BlowingWind through another world and time slipping journey, wherein she will begin to win back her self confidence. Book Three of the series "The Forge and the Well" follows Marie's story, and how that ties with her sister Marcella, her neice Jewel, and Marie's stifled and forgotten past.

I project the tale of the family, and how they overcome the curse, will spread over eight books. It could be more, or less, depending on how the characters themselves reveal their stories. There is more than only their tale in the series though.

The new cover of this work is done by Victoria "Salaiek Tuaraan" Davis, who is the one that did my cover for book two of this series. The original cover can be found in the extras section of the ebook, put not the print version. Those who purchased the first edition via Smashwords will be able to have both editions of this work. Those purchasing via Amazon, I am unsure of how it handles multiple editions.

If you have enjoyed this story in the series, I am looking for a narrator for an audio version. You can find more information on ACX.com by searching for the title. I am also looking for someone willing to translate into Spanish for a Spanish edition. Both of these will be royalty share arrangements.

If you have found something that you think is a typo, by ALL MEANS feel free to email me with the location, the way it reads in the edition you own, and how you think it should read. If I find you are correct then it will be updated in the ebook, as sometimes things that are supposed to be fixed (and get fixed) do not save the way that they should.

ladyrainstardragon@hotmail.com

Please don't forget to put a subject, such as "typo"!

ABOUT THE AUTHOR

TERESA Garcia is a 30-something mother of two children with special needs, raising them "alone" in the small mountain town of McCloud, CA. Just because she is on her own though, does not mean that she is "alone." Many thanks are due to the McCloud Community Resource Center, to her brother and his family, and her mother, for all their help.

When not drowning in university coursework for her International Relations degree, and chained to the computer, she loves to text role play with her long distance mate Vadise, write stories, hike, paint, meditate, and play games or read with her kids. She also writes quests for, and helps to maintain, the online browser-based RPG Dragon Hearts.

Sadly, her university courses devour most of her time like a jinkiniki devours questionable substances, or an akaname licks all available surfaces of the bathroom.

She was raised in another mountain community, which she visits as often as she can spare time and gas, though not nearly often enough for her wishes. Her parents always encouraged her writing and artistic talents. In 2005, she decided to pick up the dream of writing and publishing a novel once more, having shelved that (and the "Shadow Chronicles" manuscript) in her early college years due to the time constraints of motherhood at the time. In 2006 she released to the public her first novel in the "Dragon Shaman" series, "Taming the Blowing Wind," and has since published a second book in the series and a poetry book.

Currently Teresa has several manuscripts to work on, such as her "Dragon Shaman" series of novels and her current favorite serialized story, "Selkies' Skins."

More about her works can be found at
https://www.smashwords.com/profile/view/Amehana

and http://www.thgstardragon.com.

She also can be found on twitter at
https://twitter.com/#!/AmehanaArashi,

or on the THG StarDragon Publishing Facebook page.

Her personal blog is located at
http//rainstardragon.livejournal.com

She also happily accepts snail mail:
THG StarDragon Publishing
Attn: Teresa Garcia
PO Box 249
McCloud, CA 96057
USA

or email: ladyrainstardragon@hotmail.com

Please fill out the subject line, to prevent it from being thought to
be spam.

BONUS STORY MATERIAL

THIS edition will include some short stories that were never released in the original book, but were posted separately as stand alone stories or removed from the original manuscript. As you read, see if you can pick up the clues as to where the shorts are placed in the timeline.

The ebook edition of this volume contains several bonus images related to the story, and their backstory. I have decided not to include them in the print version.

THE CHILD WITHIN THE WOMAN

THE foreign child gazed into the deepening blue sky from the forest around Fuji-san, contemplating the mysteries hidden within their clear depths. Untold beings lived their lives there, seen only to those who had the eyes to see. The night-time winds ruffled her closely shorn auburn hair, fondly as a parent would to a cherished offspring. For this short span of time, she was genuine and unguarded, letting her heart flow freely and her troubles to abate.

Ryu's breath was taken away at her unshrouded beauty, watching BlowingWind's own open skies close to savor and preserve the moment in her memory. The traveler's tears ceased their relentless course down her face as he watched from his hiding place behind the rock high-seat. The winds swirled around her slight form ever tighter, as if some spirit from long ago were trying to communicate a desperately needed secret.

The air within the human's form began to dance with that which was drying her tears so tenderly, producing an unearthly song of innumerable feeling compressed into a ball for so long to unravel and spin out into the rest of creation. Unaware that the mischievous, and often troublesome, spirit that insisted upon shadowing her was even there the woman-child began to gift back to Creation a dance from the heart. Mimicked movements of hawks and cougars mingled with those of the snake and fish while her song flowed from her like some Hawaiian lava flow of love and loss, loneliness and near despair.

At the last, the native Japanese magma spirit glimpsed the shape of the spirit who had been shrouding from his influence the tender human who he was going to claim as his abode within the world of the humans. Long dark hair plaited into twin braids held golden hawk's feathers, while the skin of a male deer clothed the Spirit's body. As BlowingWind's song and dance came to an end to carry her prayer to what she had termed "Great Spirit" the two Guides locked eyes over her collapsing form. The human child fell into an exhausted sleep for her body to rest, and her soul to receive more instruction from her Apache ancestors.

The two males stood staring into each other's inner Fire for an untold span of time, each gauging the other's intentions toward the Spiritual Woman who had taken on flesh for this life. The ancient pine trees bowed closer to the ground in the wind that carried this foreign visitor, anxious to know what would happen next. Finally, the departed human must have found the things he was looking for, smiling at the dragon spirit that had called to himself a corporeal human shape.

"Take care of my daughter. Through you, the blood of my Clan will be spiritually replenished."

Surprised to hear such arrogant seeming words from the mouth of a mere human spirit, Ryu was about to utter a retort. However, he fell silent as the child's father came forward and placed in the dragon-man's hands a stringed instrument brought from across the seas.

"Stay with her, though she will try to push you away for a long time. Be sure that she receives this again when she returns."

The wind rose abruptly to shroud the deceased's departure, driving dry needles from the forest floor into the nature spirit's eyes. When it died down again, the human spirit was gone.

Ryu inspected the object within his hands, noticing the contrast of the dark and light woods and the supple curves that the traditional instruments of his own people did not possess. Shaking his head at the trouble he found himself bearing for one lone human woman, when he could easily take any that he desired by force, he allowed a more natural form to house his being.

Ancient courtly silks and flesh dissolved as bone and sinew stretched to become covered by scale and lithe muscle. Black and red could dimly be seen in the moonless light as he wrapped about the little human to preserve her warmth. The price to be extracted for such a liberty was most likely going to be a bit painful when she returned to her body, but he would rather it be so than to see her fall ill. In one large claw he still carefully cradled the guitar, fascinated by the warmth that seemed to exude from it the closer it came to the human's presence. Darkly burning eyes turned at last from the gift to the woman-child, then to once again regard the alluring being that he had claimed as his own.

Through the night he watched, brooding over every rise and fall of the chest as the Divine Wind filled and emptied her lungs. The blood of the human child sang sweetly to him of familiar liquid flows of rock deep below the ground, and for a time the dragon contentedly guarded this newfound treasure.

As all things must though, with morning it came to an end. Clouded skies once more opened upon the physical world and the child hid within the woman once more.

"You perverted scaly Coyote! Remove your coils from me this instant, or I will stuff my medicine pouch with the whiskers from your beard and nose!"

FINDING A FRIEND

FRIGID water reflected the blue of a high summer sky, while the pines danced alongside the shores of Medicine Lake. Blue eyes reflected the lake back to itself, and a little red-headed girl released a lonely sigh to ghost over said lake on the back of the wind.

The girl, BlowingWind, and her mother had moved camp today, Mother being ill at ease to stay long where she had sighted any type of dragon. Hence, they had hauled everything until Mother was sure they were out of its territory. Why her mom could see dragons, but not the Spirit Animals who had once helped her father, she could never figure out, but at any rate it had severely limited her amount of friends before. Thanks to their recent move away from the reservation her father had grown up on, now she had to start all over again.

She had actually been hoping to at least attract a Raven while Mother slept. BlowingWind sang the Raven Song that Father had taught her before he walked the Blue Road home to Creator, but nothing came to keep her company, save for the mosquitoes that bred in sluggish and shallow bays. Fed up, the seven-year-old girl abandoned the lake where she had seen the water dragon, in favor of a run through the forest before Mother woke up from her nap. The wind went with her, and its spirit beckoned her through forest paths that her father had once talked with others about following. Her loneliness grew as she thought about her father, one of the very few people who had understood her.

"He promised he would teach me. Who will teach me the stories now? How can I be like Daddy now?"

Pine needles crushed under her drumming feet to release their sharp scent. Her little voice lifted itself to sing of her sorrows.

"Alone, Alone, Alone.
A wolf cries alone,

A wolf cub hunts
And her pack is gone.

Alone, Alone, Alone.
A fledgling waits in the nest.
Hunter has taken them West
The Ancients have moved on.

Alone, Alone, Alone.
Snake is far from home.
Plucked up by Eagle
But one bite leaves her alone."

Exhausted, the tired child tripped on a stone, spilling down onto Mother Earth and still caught between two worlds. Mud-dark eyes had watched her, shyly hiding in the water and then following behind as she had run away from her camp. Centuries now he had watched humans and their ways, but he had been too shy to purposefully attempt to contact one. This one was as lonely as he was though, and it was hard for him to think of anyone being that lonely. There was a special light inside the girl, and with proper cultivation, it could benefit not only her, but also his lake, and the world at large.

His long, snake-like body contracted, shortening and losing his coils until his body was that of a human's. Black scales hissed and faded away, red plumes which had been his mane and hoary whiskers following them. In their place, midnight waters flowed down past his shoulders to become plaited hair, and water-drowned logs lent their browns to his skin. Satisfied with his disguise, the lake-boy stepped out of the shadows to answer her calls.

"The Forest is a dangerous place. Hikers get lost here, and the Furry People are not tame."

BlowingWind looked at him a moment from the loamy ground, then got up to brush the dirt from her clothes. To her eyes, the boy seemed only about nine years old.

"Father always told me that if I showed respect to my four-legged brothers that I would remain unharmed. A shaman would know such things."

"Then what about rattlesnakes? They grow very big here, and if one were to bite you, what would you do without an adult? I should help you back to your camp."

His comment did get her to look around. Rattlesnakes were big in Arizona too, but she had never had any problem with them. She had often wandered by herself at home so being alone did not bother her. However, she had realized now that she was lost, for the first time that she could ever remember. Tears came to her easily now, because of her recent loss, and so to her embarrassment and his horror, BlowingWind sank down onto a rock bawling. She hid her reddening and crumpling face behind her hands.

The boy's eyes softened, and he reached out toward her with one hand, refraining from touching her as his quiet voice soothed the air. "Don't cry. I didn't mean to make you cry."

"I'm scared. I want to go home. I want to go back with Grandma and Grandpa, and Cousin RedFeather back on the Reservation in Arizona. I miss Daddy's songs, and RedFeather's stories, and my friends. Now I'm lost in the woods with some boy, and I don't even know your name!"

The boy sat down on the rock, carefully reaching out to touch the girl's shoulder. When she didn't pull away, he scooted a little closer and put his arm around her.

"There, there, it'll be alright. I can't do anything about getting you back to Arizona, but I can tell you my name. I'll even be your friend if you want."

BlowingWind wiped her nose with the back of her sleeve, missing the boy's unboylike wince at the gesture and the odd sharpness of his teeth he had been unable to hide in his smile.

"Really? You'll be my friend?"

"Of course. My name is Obsidian. What's yours?"

"That's a nice name. Mine's BlowingWind. Are you Native too?"

Obsidian nodded his head, and looking around his spied a pine cone. Opening it, he prized out the nuts while making his reply.

"I'm from the Shasta Tribe you might say. I have been in the area my whole life. Are you hungry? I've learned these are good for eating."

BlowingWind accepted a few of the seeds from her new friend, thanking him before tasting them. Once clearing off the papery wings, they were actually quite tasty, and reminded her of the piñion nuts her father used to bring her from his treks. The tiny seeds made her feel stronger, and it was only then that she realized it had been a while since her last meal at breakfast.

"There now, much better, huh? I'll help you find your camp. Your mom's probably worried about you. I know mine does when I'm away from home too long."

Obsidian stood up, drawing the human child with him as he then led her through the forest back to the lake. BlowingWind followed easily, no longer feeling quite as lonely as before. Before long, he had brought her back to the edge of her camp. Miraculously, her mother was still asleep, and the portable clock on the picnic table said that she had been gone for only an hour. BlowingWind went over to the cooler and pulled out two cans of soda, one of which she gave to Obsidian. Hers she popped open, but Obsidian only eyed his dubiously.

"Thanks for helping me Obsidian. That soda is to pay you back. Don't you like soda?"

Obsidian looked back up at her. Although he shook his head he was smiling at her kindness.

"I can only drink natural things. This has too many chemicals in it. Thank you though. I need to get going now."

"Ok. Will I see you again? I like having a friend again."

"I'm sure you will. Where is your home, maybe I can visit you someday? If not, you can visit me, I can be easy to find around the lake, well, to the right people anyway."

"Mom got a house for us near McCloud. When school starts, we won't go camping again until next summer."

Obsidian nodded. McCloud was well within his traveling range, and he knew the spirits at the base of Mt. Shasta well. Although he looked like a child to this human for her ease, the dragon intended for her to achieve great things one day. As she had said, her father was a Shaman. He would see that she became one as well.

"Oh, well, I wouldn't worry about that too much. Time is tricky up in these mountains. Besides, we're friends now, friends have a way of finding each other BlowingWind."

Having said that, Obsidian gave BlowingWind a quick hug before dashing off along the shore and out of sight around a bend. She felt a little lonely again now that the boy was gone, but she would see him again. Her hand reached up to fiddle with the snail shell necklace that she had found beside her pillow that morning, and only then did she realize the boy had been wearing one just like it.

"The Creator must have heard my songs last night, and so he and the lake spirit found me a friend. At least I didn't run into Coyote, sneaky old Coyote always gets me into trouble."

Having finished her soda, BlowingWind stowed the can where Mother had taught her to, so that Bear would not pay a visit, and then she went to lay down and napped with Mother. As she slept, she dreamed about her father, who told her how proud he was of her. In her sleep, her new necklace glowed, and somewhere in the depths of Medicine Lake, a black and red dragon entertained some spirits who had been Helpers to her father.

GLOSSARY AND NAMES

THERE are several non-English words and concepts in this story, and this will continue through the rest of the series. To save the reader from having to look for each word's definition, and as a tool for any teacher wishing to use this book in their class, I am including this glossary. I am also including the various deities and spirits that are from the mythologies. Spirits that are purely my own invention will not be listed here, although the translations of their names will be.

Ai – Japanese word for Love.

Aikido – A type of martial art.

Akaname – Filth Licker or Red Licker, some accounts say that this youkai either eats the mold and algae that forms in a bathroom, or causes it (especially in the old fashioned wooden Japanese washrooms).

Aokigahara Jukai – Sea of Trees around Fujisan.

Ainu – Original aboriginal inhabitants of what is now Hokkaido and northern Japan. They are mentioned in the Kojiki as the Onigumo (spider people).

Adios mi amiga – Literally translated it is "Go with God my friend." Adios is a common Spanish language farewell.

Amaterasu – This translates as Heavenly Shining One. A descendant of Izanagi (there are differing versions of the tale, some stating that she is from both Izanami and Izanagi), she rules the day, sun and growth, her brother Tsukiyomi the night and rest, and her brother Susanoo the tides and winds...or sea plain.

Amatsu kami – Heavenly kami.

Aniki – Elder brother.

Ara – Dark or shadow.

Araburu kamitachi – Rough or malevolent kami.

Aramitama – Rough aspect of a person or kami.

Arashi-gami – Storm kami.

Arigato gozaimasu – One polite way to say thank you in Japanese.

Ba'ts'osé – Apache word/name for Coyote.

Brigit – Celtic goddess (later a saint) associated with fire, wells, and creativity.

Chi – Energy. In Japanese it is spelled Qi, but Chi was chosen as the most familiar to readers at the time of the original writing.

Coyotero – Apache for Coyote.

Daitoku – One term for Shinto priest. There are several ranks of priest, all with different terms.

Draigain – Irish Gaelic for dragon.

Geas – Irish word for curse.

Geta – Toothed wooden sandals intended to keep feet dry in muddy conditions. There are several types.

Goshinboku – Sacred tree.

Hai – Yes.

Hakama – Divided skirt pants that were once usually worn by those of the samurai, priestly, or noble classes. These were originally developed for warfare to make riding horseback easier.

Haori – A particular type of over robe or jacket, seen most in the samurai class.

Haruko – Spring child.

Hime-sama – Japanese princess.

Hinoki – Japanese pine.

Hitogami – Human kami, living kami.

Honto ne – 'Really?' in Japanese.

Inugami – Dog Youkai.

Inu-gami-mochi – Sorcerer controlling an inugami.

Izanagi-no-Mikoto – August Male Kami. Part of the Divine pair, he was of the seventh generation of original kami. With his sister-wife and the Celestial Spear they formed the islands of Japan in the old interpretation of the legends. In the modern interpretation they formed the land of the planet earth, which is viewed as a shinging jewel.

Izanami-no-Mikoto – August Female Kami. See above.

Ji-san – Grandfather.

Jinkiniki – Hungry ghost. These are of Buddhist origin.

Jin – Also known as genie. One of the Arabic words meaning spirit...which can be considered a devil or a nature spirit depending on the researcher.

Kami – Japanese word for god or spirit. Living beings may also be kami, as can natural features.

Kami-dana – Spirit shelf. This is the home shrine where prayers are offered.

Kamikushi – Land of the Kami. Kamikushi overlaps the physical and intermingles.

Kanji – One of several 'lettering' systems in Japan, these originally came from China. Other systems are hiragana, katakana and romaji, both of which are more commonly used.

Kannushi – Another word for Shinto priest.

Kazekami – Divine Wind.

Kimono – Traditional Japanese mode of dress, resembling a robe. The less formal version is the yukata, which is unlines, whereas the kimono is usually lined.

Kinickkinick – One of many Native American words for sacred tobacco.

Kitsune – Japanese fox spirit. Most commonly these are classed as youkai, and there are two main varieties, those that are 'wild' and those that serve Oinari. Every hundred years the kitsune will grow another tail, and a nine-tailed kitsune is called kyuubi.

Kitsune-gami-mochi – Sorcerer controlling a kitsune.

Koibito – Little fish person, but this is a term of endearment.

Konohanasakuya-hime – Goddess of Mt. Fuji, and a goddess of beauty. She was offered to a Japanese Emperor in the Kami Age along with her sister, the long lived stone princess. When her sister was turned away, the Emperor unwittingly turned away the gift of long life in favor of short-lived beauty. If both sisters had been kept as wives, the tale goes that the imperial line would have been able to retain both gifts form Okami.

Kunitsu kami – Earthly kami.

Leanbh – Irish Gaelic for love or child. An endearment.

Maeve – Maeve is a battle goddess in Irish mythology. She is also one of BlowingWind's ancestors.

Magatama – Curved stone beads that look clawlike. These are favored by kami, and Amaterasu once had many strands from which she produced children in a contest with her brother Susanoo.

Manga – Japanese comics. These are read in the opposite direction as Western comic books.

Matsuri – Japanese festival. Worship. Celebration.

Miko – Shinto priestess, she is also considered a female shaman of sorts by some researchers and Shinto practitioners. Originally the Miko were possessed by the Kami and acted as mouthpiece. Healing and divination are also abilities once (and still) attributed to them, although they are most often seen as assistants at shrines now. In the modern era female priests are now beginning to be given credence again.

Misogi – Japanese ritual water bathing meditation for spiritual purification and focus. This is used by both Shinto and Buddhist practitioners, as well as many martial arts students, particularly Aikido.

Mitama – Soul piece.

Namaste – Used by Buddhists and others as both greeting and farewell, this translates to "Peace" in Sanskrit and Hindi.

Naorai – The sharing of food offerings with Okami, facilitating mutual exchange and cooperation between Ningen and Okami.

Nigimitama – Gentle aspect of a person or kami.

Nii-san – Polite version of younger brother.

Ningen – Japanese for human.

Ninigi – A descendant of Amaterasu from the Kami Age, he is also the first recorded emperor in the Kojiki. He is also known as Sumemiko.

Nirei nihakushu ippai – Particular method of respectfully praying at a shrine. This is done by bowing twice, clap twice, and bow again, followed often by a clap of thanks. In Shinto the clap is thought to call cami, in Okinawan Shinto however is is thought to signal Okami that the prayer is ended and to signal thanks.

Ohayo – Hello, good day.

Omamori – Protective amulets that come from shrines. They must be returned to the shrine every year and burned for the paper and cloth variety. A metal variety does not need to be burnt, only recharged.

O-miki – Consecrated sake (rice wine or rice beer).

Onegai – Japanese for please.

Oni – One type of Japanese demon. These have their roots in Buddhism.

Onigiri – Rice ball delicacy.

Onmyouji – Japanese word for Taoist elemental master/wizard.

Onna – Japanese for woman.

Onsen – Japanese bath house. This is a place to clean and relax.

Otou-sama – A respectful form of father in Japanese.

Otousan – Another respectful way to say father in Japanese.

Queso – Spanish for cheese. There is a character in the book intentionally given the surname of cheese.

Reidou – Rei is a Japanese word for sacred. Dou was simply a word that sounded good with it. Depending on which Kanji is used, Dou can be copper (material that went into Eight Span Mirror of Amaterasu), change, or magnificent.

Ryu – Earth dragon in Japanese. Tatsu would be the word for Celestial dragon.

Saisen boko – Shinto offering box.

Sakura – Cherry.

San-san-kudo - Japanese wedding cereomony involving three exchanges of sake from one cup.

Sarutahiko – He is the leader of the Kunitsu Kami (earth kami) and is responsible for showing the proper path for kami and man alike. He is also known to some as Dosojin.

Sayonara – Good bye in Japanese.

Sengoku Jidai – Warring States period.

Sensei – Teacher. This is also used for doctors at times.

Seppuku – Ritual suicide performed by members of the samurai class if they had been dishonored or dishonored their lords.

Shide – Sacred folded rice paper. Originally these were strips of folded cloth and originate in the story of luring Amaterasu back out from the Celestial cave. These later were changed to paper so as to preserve cloth for longer lived used.

Shikon – Four souls. In Shinto and Buddhist thought, there are four parts of a spirit that together form the soul. These disperse to different locations on death. Smaller parts can shard off under stressful circumstances.

Shimenawa – Sacred rope, usually having shide. These are used as a marker to denote sacred ground, and can also be used for spiritual protection.

Shin – Wisdom.

Shinsen – Food offering.

Shintai – Another Japanese word for a temporary body for kami.

Shoji – Traditional sliding door in Japanese construction.

Shoujo – Romantic manga, usually dealing with young women.

Su madre – 'Your mother' in Spanish.

Suigami – Water god or Water spirit. These can be either a kami or a youkai, and there are several types of suigami.

Susanowo – Also spelled Susanoo. The translation I see most often is Swift Impetuous Male Deity.

Sutra – Buddhist scriptures.

Taiko – Japanese drumming. It is offered to Okami, but it also served as a way to send messages over a distance and is a form of entertainment. Tsubaki Shrine (both in Japan and in America) offers Taiko drumming to Okami regularly.

Take – Pronounced Tah-kay, this means mountain in Japanese.

Tama – Japanese for jewel.

Tamashii – Another word for soul shards.

Tanuki – Japanese 'raccoon-dog.' The plight of the tanuki in the modern world is covered by Hayao Miyazaki in his anime Pompoko.

Tengu – A Japanese crow spirit. There are two main types. The Karasu Tengu looks most like a crow. The Dai Tengu is dressed as a Yamabushi and is distinguishable by his red face and very long nose. Some sources attribute them as offspring of Sarutahiko. Other sources credit them as offspring of Susanoo. Perhaps both accounts are true.

Tenyo – Buddhist Celestial being or goddess.

Torii- Sacred gateway in the Japanese language, often seen in front of shrines. This is phonetically similar to torri, which is bird. This is no coincidence, as the birds often perch on the gateways in the morning to sing. It is thought by some that the original torii were simply paired trees, connected by a sacred rope.

Tsunami – This is a wave of water triggered by an earthquake or other similar seismic event. Those alive in 2011 will most easily remember the Mar 11 tsunami and the Fukushima disaster. Another example is the 2001 tsunami in Indonesia and surrounding countries.

Uzume – Uzume-no-mikoto accompanied the heavenly grandchild (Ninigi) to the Earth plane from the Celestial plane. She eventually wedded Sarutahiko. She is the kami of marriage, entertainers, dance, and joy among many other things.

Yamabushi – Buddhist mountain priests.

Yaoyorozu no kami – Myriad of kami.

Yomi – Japanese underworld. This is where kami tend to go when they die. It is a place that the living avoid.

Yorishiro – Temporary body or shrine. A spear, rock, or mirror can be a yorishiro. A miko would be a living yorishiro.

Youkai – Also spelled Yokai, this word most closely translates to demon within the English language. Not all Youkai are evil, and not all Kami are benevolent. The line between Kami and Youkai is a blurred one, and is subjective on the beliefs of the researcher or believer.

Yura – Hair.

UPCOMING BOOKS

DRAGON SHAMAN 3:
THE FORGE AND THE WELL

DELVING further into the O'Drake family as the curse and its eventual end plays through, the focus follows more of Marie and Marcella's history. A reunion of Marie with her wayward daughter BlowingWind draws closer, as does young Jewel's place in the complicated tapestry. From Ireland to the jungles of the Yucatan, BlowingWind will have to leave Japan whether she is ready or not. Ryu really has his work cut out for him, but what is a lonely dragon kami to do... other than attempt to figure out how to restore the brightness that once was...

Estimated release: late 2014 or 2015.

SELKIES' SKINS

SELKIES' Skins is a serial tale that will be available as an ebook once finished. Kirsty Makay, part Human, part Selkie - and all Witch - navigates the course of growing up with the secret of what she is, and having to eart her own seal skin. What she desires most is to be an outstanding potioneer and harness the sea's riches for the health of three species, as well as to lead a life with her boyfriend once they graduate.

Her mother, though she has already walked the same road, has other matters to see to, having fully embraced who and what she is. Having fully given herself to the sea, a calling that Kirsty distrusts and sees as dangerous, their paths are not as different as the young Kirsty might think.

And two goddesses are going to make sure that she learns this lesson.

Estimated release: Unknown, though the writing process can be "watched" and influenced by googling the title.

www.ingramcontent.com/pod-product-compliance
Lightning Source LLC
Chambersburg PA
CBHW011520240626
47154CB00009B/2900